APACHE ATTACK

The first Barlow knew of the Apaches' presence was the impact of a body hurled at him from atop a boulder as he was guiding his horse through a narrow, serpentine passage between huge rocks. The impact carried him off the coyote dun, and he landed on his left side, with the weight of the broncho on top of him and the wind knocked out of him. Though he was dazed, and wheezing desperately to get air back into lungs that no longer seemed able to function, Barlow found the strength to throw a backhanded blow that connected solidly with his attacker's jaw. The broncho's head snapped back, and he slumped backward. Barlow scrambled to his feet and clawed for the pistol holstered at his side. His attacker was getting up, recovering quickly from the blow. Barlow figured he was Chokonen, and he didn't want to shoot the broncho unless he had to. So he leveled the pistol at the Apache but did not fire. In that instant he heard the distinctive sound of a carbine's lever action behind him. He threw a quick glance over his shoulder, and saw the second broncho then. This one was standing atop another boulder, the carbine up to his shoulder now, and aimed rock-steady at a spot between Barlow's shoulder blades.

I'm a dead man, thought Barlow.

APACHE STORM

Jason Manning

A SIGNET BOOK

SIGNET
Published by New American Library, a division of
Penguin Group (USA) Inc., 375 Hudson Street,
New York, New York 10014, USA
Penguin Group (Canada), 10 Alcorn Avenue, Toronto,
Ontario M4V 3B2, Canada (a division of Pearson Penguin Canada Inc.)
Penguin Books Ltd., 80 Strand, London WC2R 0RL, England
Penguin Ireland, 25 St. Stephen's Green, Dublin 2,
Ireland (a division of Penguin Books Ltd.)
Penguin Group (Australia), 250 Camberwell Road, Camberwell, Victoria 3124,
Australia (a division of Pearson Australia Group Pty. Ltd.)
Penguin Books India Pvt. Ltd., 11 Community Centre, Panchsheel Park,
New Delhi - 110 017, India
Penguin Group (NZ), Cnr Airborne and Rosedale Roads, Albany,
Auckland 1310, New Zealand (a division of Pearson New Zealand Ltd.)
Penguin Books (South Africa) (Pty.) Ltd., 24 Sturdee Avenue,
Rosebank, Johannesburg 2196, South Africa

Penguin Books Ltd., Registered Offices:
80 Strand, London WC2R 0RL, England

First published by Signet, an imprint of New American Library,
a division of Penguin Group (USA) Inc.

First Printing, November 2004
10 9 8 7 6 5 4 3 2 1

Prologue

Kiannatah was only twelve years old when his band of Bedonkohe Apaches left their rancheria in the mountains to visit the village of the Nakai-Ye. But the fact that he was young did not mean that he failed to understand the significance of the event. For as long as he could remember, the Nakai-Ye—the Mexicans—had been the mortal enemy of the Chi-hinne, or The People, as the Apaches called themselves. It was the Nakai-Ye who had given his people the name of Apache, which meant "enemy" in their tongue. The Chi-hinne had adopted the name and were proud to be known as such. The hatred on both sides ran deep, and Kiannatah had never heard of anyone who knew when or where or why it had started. The Chi-hinne and the Nakai-Ye had always warred against one another. It was simply a fact of life. Many had died violently as a result of this age-old animosity. But, as Ulzana had once told Kiannatah, to die violently was not something an Apache feared. Life was brutal. Why expect anything more from death? Besides, there was honor in dying while on the warpath, trying to kill the Nakai-Ye.

Seldom did either side in this conflict attempt to make a distinction between man and woman, old or young, when it came to killing. As Ulzana had explained it, you killed the Nakai-Ye children because if you let them live they would grow up and one day start killing Chi-hinne. And you killed Nakai-Ye women so that they would not produce more Apache-killing offspring. The Nakai-Ye lived and fought by the same philosophy, although sometimes, Ulzana had told him, the Nakai-Ye were known to take young Apaches prisoner, to turn them into slaves. These slaves would work on the haciendas of the rancheros, or be sold to brothels in the cities. They were seldom recovered by the Apaches, and it was assumed that they did not survive for long. But then, as Ulzana gravely pointed out, if you were made a slave by the Nakai-Ye, why would you want to live long?

Kiannatah looked up to Ulzana, and took everything that the older youth told him to heart. Ulzana would soon be old enough to go on a raid against the Nakai-Ye. It was all he could talk about. His father, Dakoheh, was one of the band's greatest fighters, and Ulzana's dream was to emulate his father. Like his father he hated the Nakai-Ye, even though he'd seldom even seen one. The Nakai-Ye were not generally so foolish that they would venture into the Cima Silkq, the rugged mountains that they called the Sierra Madre, because it was "Apache country." The Chi-hinne had lived there since before remembering. They knew well its deep, twisting canyons and high, treacherous peaks. This was where Kiannatah had lived all his life, where he had been born, and it was the only home he had ever known. He felt out of place here on the flatlands. Out of place and exposed to danger, like a week-old wolf cub venturing out of its birth den for the first time. Even now, as he and the rest of the band neared the Nakai-Ye village that was their destination, a long day's journey from the Cima Silkq, Kiannatah could look over his shoulder and see the mountains, blue in the distance. When he did this he felt a twinge of homesickness—chin-da-see-lee. But he also felt comforted, knowing that his home, his sanctuary, was within sight.

He envied Ulzana, who had been among those who'd stayed behind. Not everyone in the band had consented to come on this journey. There were some who opposed Cosito's decision to make peace with the Nakai-Ye. Even though Cosito was chief, that didn't mean he could compel the members of the band to follow him. It was the same way on a raid; those who accompanied the leader of a raid did so because they wanted to, because they trusted in the skill of the leader, and were convinced he would succeed, and they would come away with horses or cattle stolen from the Nakai-Ye, or at least have the opportunity to kill the enemy, so that the women of the band would sing their praises around the victory fire upon their return, and they would be honored for as long as they lived, and even in the next world.

Ulzana's father, Dakoheh, had been one of the most vocal critics of Cosito's plan. The Nakai-Ye, he said, could not be trusted. So they had sent a half-breed into the Cima Silkq with word that the governor himself wanted to negotiate a peace between his people and the Chi-hinne. The governor had even sent gifts— two pack mules laden with cheap trinkets, and a gold-inlaid fowling piece made in England for Cosito. A very handsome weapon indeed, Dakoheh acknowledged. But just like the promises of the Nakai-Ye, the fowling piece was practically worthless to an Apache. And even if the Nakai-Ye jefe was sincere in his desire for peace, even if he was willing to acknowledge, implicitly, that he could not afford to field enough soldiers to adequately defend the villages of his people that were located within striking distance of the Chihinne rancherias in the Cima Silkq, why would a Chihinne be interested in peace in the first place?

There could never be, warned Dakoheh, a true and lasting peace with the Nakai-Ye, because the Apache had the blood of too many Nakai-Ye on their hands, just as the Nakai-Ye had slain too many of The People down through the generations. Why seek peace, when the Chi-hinne were safe in their mountain stronghold, free to strike virtually at will against their enemies, only to seek the safety of the Cima Silkq once more when the killing was done, and the columns of Federales and Irregulars came chasing after them.

But Cosito had listened intently to the words of the half-breed envoy, who told him that, as far as the leaders of the Nakai-Ye were concerned, the only alternative to peace was the mounting of a full-scale invasion of the mountains, with the intention of wiping out the Chi-hinne once and for all, regardless of the cost in both lives and treasure. It would be cheaper in the long run to do this than to try to protect the Nakai-Ye people forever from the Apache scourge. Cosito listened, and believed. In his heart he was sick of war. He had lost two sons in the fight against the Nakai-Ye, and he had often dreamed of the day when he would no longer have to listen to the wailing of the wives and mothers when a raiding party returned with their dead. It wasn't that Cosito feared death, or the

Nakai-Ye. No one questioned his courage. But in recent years he had begun to reevaluate the traditional Chi-hinne approach to "others"—a category that included anyone who was not born Chi-hinne. That approach had always been to wage war. The Chi-hinne had fought the Comanches, the Navajo, the Spaniards, the Mexicans, and recently even the Americans. From the Chi-hinne point of view, this was their land and always had been, and anyone else who tried to live on it or even pass through it without their permission was indah—an enemy.

Little wonder, then, that the Chi-hinne were feared and distrusted by their neighbors. Little wonder that the Nakai-Ye called them, also, los barbaros.

Cosito had done his share of Apache violence. Now, though, he was thinking there had to be a better way. The numbers of his people were dwindling. If things continued on their present course, soon the Chi-hinne would be no more. Filled with hatred and the heshke—the killing rage—the young broncos did not worry about such things. But Cosito was graying and, as older men do, had begun to contemplate his legacy, and the future of his people after he was gone. In battle the Apache usually won. An Apache would not ordinarily engage an enemy unless he knew in advance that the odds were on his side. So they won the battles. But they were losing the war. There had never been many of The People. These days, though, there were so very few. Cosito had sired three sons. Two were dead, killed in battle at the hands of the Nakai-Ye. His other son had given him two grandchildren. They were the one source of unadulterated delight in Cosito's world. If the other two sons had lived, how many grandchildren might they have produced for him? And so The People grew fewer and fewer in number with every passing year. Cosito hated the Nakai-Ye as fiercely as anyone else in his band. But he was willing to listen to the proposal for peace. He would stop seeking vengeance for his two dead sons, and begin seeking a way to ensure that his third son and the third son's family survived. It was, after all, the duty of a Bedonkohe jefe to put aside personal considerations and do what was best for the band.

And so Cosito had sent the half-breed back with word that he accepted the governor's invitation to meet at the village of Dolorosa, a day's journey east of the Cima Silkq. The governor had given his word that the Apaches would be free to come and go unhampered. Cosito did not necessarily trust the governor's word, but he accepted the risks. So had thirty-nine other Bedonkohe—eighteen men, twelve women, and nine children. Though he would have preferred that the woman and children had stayed behind in safety, Co- sito knew their presence was beneficial. It would serve to allay the fears of the Nakai-Ye, who knew from experience that the Apache never brought his women and children with him on a rampage. The men who accompanied Cosito—including Kiannatah's father— did so of their own free will, fully cognizant of the chance they were taking. Some had left their families behind. Kiannatah's father had wanted to do that. But Kiannatah's mother had insisted on coming along. Later, when he reflected on the events that transpired at Dolorosa, Kiannatah wondered if perhaps his mother had had some sort of premonition. Had real- ized that this might be the end of her time with the man she loved, and for that reason had resolved to spend every moment by his side.

As for Kiannatah, his father explained what was going on to him. He did not keep anything from his son. Besides, Kiannatah had demonstrated an understanding of the realities of life that was very mature for a boy his age. Kiannatah's father did not think it right for an Apache to try to shelter his children from the truth about the world. He would have told Kiannatah's sister, too, except she was too young to understand. Still an infant, she traveled in a tsoch—a carrying cradle strapped to the back of Kiannatah's mother.

Thus, when the band of Bedonkohe Apaches reached a high spot from which they could see the village called Dolorosa, Kiannatah could look upon the place and realize the grave dangers, for himself and for his loved ones, that might lurk there. He was also aware of a vague, undefined sense that, whatever did transpire in the hours to come, it would be of no small importance. That his life, if he lived, would be forever changed.

There was no visible sign of danger. All seemed peaceful in Dolorosa. From his vantage point, Kiannatah could see the small adobe structures in the shade of tall, old elms that grew along a stream—the same stream that supplied water for irrigation ditches that nurtured the dusty fields of maize and beans that would ordinarily have been tended by the people of Dolorosa. But there was no one in the fields today. Kiannatah noticed something else was missing. He could neither see nor hear any dogs. Every Apache knew that the Nakai-Ye villagers depended on their dogs to warn them of the approach of los barbaros. Kiannatah had heard that, on one occasion at least, the people of a village had gotten their hands on the corpse of an Apache bronco, which they had tied, in turn, to the leg of each dog in the village. Try as they might, the dogs could not rid themselves of this unwelcome burden, and after only a few hours of dragging the corpse around, they could be relied upon to set up a howl loud enough to wake the dead if they ever again caught the scent of an Apache. But today there did not seem to be any dogs in Dolorosa. Kiannatah wondered if perhaps the Nakai-Ye had taken their dogs away so that they would not make the Apaches feel unwelcome.

In spite of the dangers he knew existed, and the palpable anxiety of the adults in the group, Kiannatah found himself nearly overcome by curiosity. He wanted most of all to find out how the youths of Dolorosa, the boys and girls his age, lived. What kind of games did they play, what kind of clothes did they wear, what kind of food did they eat? Kiannatah had never seen a Nakai-Ye, adult or child, up close. The Apache raiders of his band did not bring prisoners back alive. Two years ago, the report of a group of gold hunters, Nakai-Ye and Americans both, in the Cima Silkq, had reached the Bedonkohe rancheria. Cosito and his broncos had ridden out to kill the interlopers. None of the gold hunters had survived. Their corpses had been left to the buzzards and coyotes. Kiannatah had wanted to go and see them, if only to find out what the indah looked like. But his father, learning of his scheme, had forbidden him to go near the place.

Two men on horseback appeared, leaving the village to cross the creek and ride toward them. Cosito and two other men went forward to meet them. Kiannatah recognized one of the horsemen as the half-breed who had delivered the governor's message to the rancheria. He did not know much about the half-breed, except that the man was not entirely trusted by either the Apache or the Nakai-Ye. He was not wholly accepted in either world. He did not even dress according to the style of one people or the other, but rather had adopted the clothing of both—a short Mexican chaqueta over an Apache himper and leggings. But it was the other man who interested Kiannatah most of all. He was Nakai-Ye, and the sun shone on the silver of his big-roweled spurs, and on the gold in the band encircling his sombrero, and on the conchos sewn onto his trousers. His face was broad and swarthy, adorned with a sweeping corsair's mustache, and his eyes were as fierce as a panther's. He let the half-breed do most of the talking, but he clearly understood the Apache tongue; most of the time, he scanned the group of Bedonkohe with a gaze that contained neither friendship nor animosity. It was a cold, clinical gaze.

When the discussion was concluded, Cosito returned to his group, spoke to a few of the men, and then led the way forward into Dolorosa. As he entered the village of the Nakai-Ye with his people, Kiannatah found his curiosity growing while his apprehension lessened. The people were there, in their homes, and some of them stood in their windows or doorways to watch the Apaches pass. They were frightened of their guests, and maintained a wary silence, but none made a threatening move or gesture. Kiannatah saw a few children clinging to the legs of their parents or peering over the windowsills. Some were about his age. They did not, he thought, look so different from himself and the other Bedonkohe children.

They reached the zocalo—the square, at the center

of the village—and found a welcoming party that consisted of the governor and his small entourage, as well
as the alcalde of Dolorosa and some of the elders of
the village. There were no soldiers, and Kiannatah saw
no weapons of any kind. This did not escape the notice of the men in his group, and the tension in them
seemed to fade considerably. The governor seemed
delighted to see them. He greeted the Apaches like
long-lost friends, and escorted them to tables set in
the shade of big trees. At his command, the alcalde
called for food, and young women of the village
brought forth bowls filled with frijoles and platters
stacked high with tortillas. Kiannatah was hungry, but
he did not eat until he received a nod of permission
from his mother. Then he filled his belly with the
Nakai-Ye food. Several men of the village were building a large fire, and before long, there were several
goats being cooked on spits. Using the half-breed as
interpreter, the governor carried on a conversation
with Cosito—a largely one-sided conversation, with
the Nakai-Ye jefe doing most of the talking. He was
the only Nakai-Ye who had anything to do with the
Apaches, however. The people of Dolorosa did not
venture too close. Instead they watched from afar, still
wary, still silent. Except for Cosito, whose attention
was focused on the words of the governor, the rest of
the Bedonkohe didn't have much to do except eat and
watch the people of Dolorosa watch them.

The cabrito wasn't ready to eat until sundown, and
when it was served, the governor called for tizwin.
This was served in earthen jugs, and was eagerly consumed by the Apache men. The governor had an apparently never-ending supply, and before long, the
broncos were drunk. Kiannatah was surprised to see

that even his own father was inebriated. When the men tried to walk, they stumbled about, and some fell down, laughing like fools. It occurred to Kiannatah that they were lucky to be among Nakai-Ye who meant them no harm. If there had been a fight, the men would not have been able to defend themselves, or their families. But Kiannatah's belly was full, and the hour was growing late. He sat on the ground at his mother's feet while she nursed his baby sister, and before long he was nodding off to sleep.

For that reason he did not see the governor nod at the Nakai-Ye with the silver spurs, the one who had ridden out with the half-breed to meet the Bedonkohe. This man turned, put two fingers in his mouth, and whistled—a loud, shrill sound. Then he whistled again. The sound jarred Kiannatah awake, just in time for him to see the shadows of men moving just beyond the reach of the firelight, men wearing sombreros, and carrying pistols, rifles and machetes. The firelight reflected off the blades of the big cane knives, and off the glittering eyes of the men who approached the tables from all directions—moving, thought Kiannatah, like wolves stalking their prey. His eyes widened. Some of the Bedonkohe men had passed out from too much tizwin; the rest were too drunk to even realize what was going on. Kiannatah opened his mouth to speak a warning to his mother. But he didn't have to. One of the other Bedonkohe women shouted an alarm. The Nakai-Ye men rushed forward in a crashing din of gunfire. Half of the Apache men were killed outright. The rest, their minds made sluggish by too much tizwin, were slow in bringing their weapons to bear. Kiannatah saw Cosito rise—only to be thrown backward by the impact of the point-blank shot fired

by the governor himself, who brandished a pistol from
beneath his coat.

Kiannatah's mother shouted at him to run. But Kiannatah was too afraid. As one of the Nakai-Ye
leaped upon the table, Kiannatah scrambled underneath it. The Nakai-Ye lashed out at Kiannatah's
mother with his cane knife, but she was too quick,
and escaped harm. Kiannatah's love for his mother
overcame his fear, and he rose up, putting his shoulders against the bottom of the table, and lifting for all
he was worth. The weight of the Nakai-Ye prevented
him from completely overturning the table, yet he was
able to rock it enough to throw the man off balance.
He fell, and only then saw Kiannatah. With a snarl he
was about to rise when Kiannatah's mother came up
behind him and cut his throat from ear to ear. Kiannatah had thrown up an arm to defend himself—now he
felt the hot spray of Nakai-Ye blood on the arm.

"Kiannatah!" It was his mother who spoke, sternly.
"Kiannatah, ugashe!"

Run. He gathered himself up to do just that, but
before he could go his mother took a bullet. Frozen
in horror, he watched her fall. Shot in the side, she
gasped for air and tried to crawl. But another Nakai-
Ye pounced on her, driving the butt of a rifle into her
skull. Then the man smashed the skull of Kiannatah's
baby sister in the same manner. All of this Kiannatah
saw, and as he watched, the blood ran cold in his
veins. Suddenly, the table that sheltered him was overturned, and two men locked in mortal combat stumbled over him. The impact of their bodies knocked
the wind out of Kiannatah. He tried to crawl away,
half-blinded by the sting of dust and powder smoke.
His hand came to rest on something cold and hard. It

was a knife. He picked it up and kept scurrying. But he didn't get far. Someone grabbed him by the back of his himper and pulled him straight up off the ground.

"¿Dónde va usted, pequeño lobo?" The man grinned, baring yellow teeth. It was the one who wore the silver spurs. The one who had signaled for the other Nakai-Ye men to begin the killing.

Kiannatah lashed out with the knife, cutting deep into the man's face. With a yowl of pain the Nakai-Ye dropped him. Kiannatah landed on his feet and started running. Another Nakai-Ye man spotted him and fired a pistol at him from a range of no more than a dozen yards. But the bullet screamed past Kiannatah's skull and slammed into an adobe wall. Kiannatah cleared the adobe wall with the agility of a deer and found himself among the houses of the villagers. Sensing that to hesitate might be fatal, he kept running, and didn't look back until he had plunged into a field of maize that provided him with momentary cover. Only then did he pause to catch his breath. He was trembling violently, splattered with the blood of the Nakai-Ye, the knife clutched tightly in his hand. Someone—probably the man who had shot at him— was giving chase. But in the darkness the Nakai-Ye blundered off in the wrong direction in the maize, cursing, and before long Kiannatah could no longer hear him. He could, however, hear sporadic gunfire, the shouting of men, the screams of a woman. He shut his eyes tightly against the image of his mother and baby sister being killed. A single tear escaped to wend its way down his cheek. He had not seen his father during the attack, but assumed him to be dead. There was only one thing for him to do now. Only one place for him to go.

He moved deeper into the maize, then, with the unerring sense of direction inculcated in all Apaches, turned west, according to the stars. Crossing the creek, he found himself on the wide-open malpais, and though there was no moon, and so insufficient light for him to see the mountains, he knew they were there. He could feel them. Kiannatah began to run, a ground-eating lope that he could maintain—and would maintain—all night. Now and then he looked over his shoulder, thinking that the Nakai-Ye might come after him. If they did, he would kill them. For the rest of his life he would kill any Nakai-Ye he saw. Men, women and children. It didn't matter. They had betrayed his people's trust. And they had killed his family.

One thing an Apache never did was forgive or forget a wrong done him.

Chapter 1

"That boy, he be ridin' like the devil hisself is after him," said Jeremiah, standing at the window of Joshua Barlow's room.

Joshua was giving himself a critical survey in the full-length mirror that stood in a corner of his room. The high black riding boots on his feet had been polished to a high sheen. His yellow doeskin trousers and dark blue frock coat fit him well. At age twenty-four he was in prime physical condition, tall, lean, broad of shoulder, narrow in the hips, and fresh off four years at the military academy at West Point, where he had excelled in the more athletic pursuits: drill, horsemanship, and swordsmanship. Not that he had done too poorly with the academic portion of his studies, either. He'd finished with a ranking of eighth in a class of thirty-eight, and he was content with that. Even though his father wasn't. The elder Barlow, being a typical father, expected more. But then the elder Barlow, mused Joshua, even in retirement was far more dedicated to the military life than the younger. Though cognizant of the high honor bestowed upon him by an appointment to the academy,

Joshua had known from the start that he would be an ambivalent soldier. Still, he had enjoyed his four years at West Point, and was proud of his lieutenant's commission, and didn't really know of anything else he would rather have done. So why not make his father happy and follow in his footsteps?

"What boy is that?" asked Joshua, uninterested.

"That boy what works for the postmaster," replied Jeremiah.

Joshua joined the lanky young slave at the window, looked down to see the boy in question checking a hard-run, lathered plug at the front of the big house. Then he saw his father appear, depending heavily on the staghorn cane to negotiate the veranda steps. Timothy Barlow had suffered a nasty spill from a horse three winters ago, and the leg had not been properly set. Now he was bothered by arthritis, and at times it became particularly severe in that leg, so he had to use a cane to walk. It was not something Barlow liked to do. He was not the sort of man to age gracefully. He didn't like to acknowledge his physical shortcomings. Joshua felt sorry for him. His father was not the easiest man to know, or to live with, but Joshua loved him without reservation, and understood him completely. Joshua wasn't quite sure why. His father had often been away during his childhood, on one mission or another that always seemed to be of the utmost importance to the future of the republic. In fact, Joshua had sometimes resented the United States— or, more precisely, his father's powerful commitment to its preservation—as his chief rival for his father's attention. And when finally Timothy Barlow had retired from active service and was destined to be at home more often, Joshua was grown, and on his way to West Point. Still, there was a connection between them. Difficult to define, but impossible to deny.

"Must be important news," said Joshua.

Jeremiah looked at him, and Joshua knew what he was thinking even before he spoke. "You reckon it's the war, finally come, Joshua?"

It was at Joshua's insistence that Jeremiah—that all the slaves who worked the plantation—called him by his first name, without the customary addition of "Master." And that was just the sort of attitude that set the Barlows apart from the rest of the north Georgia gentry and that had prevented his father, and himself, from ever being fully accepted. Timothy Barlow, being Northern-born, probably never would have been, considering the times. But Joshua had been born right here. He was Southern by birth. And yet nearly every white person in the area treated him as though he were a Northerner just like his father, which was to say, a foreigner, and an unwelcome one, at that. It had something to do with Timothy Barlow's role in putting down the nullifiers in Charleston, South Carolina, thirty years ago. And now trouble was brewing in Charleston again.

"Maybe," said Joshua, trying to sound casual. "But I've got more important things to worry about. Like getting up to Beulah on time."

Jeremiah grinned. "Yassuh. Dat's right. A gennelman cain't be worryin' about a little thing like war when he's gwine riding with Miss Jennie Randolph."

Joshua grinned back. "Exactly. Now how do I look?"

"If I do say so myself, you look like a prince."

"You'd say that even if it weren't true."

"Why, yassuh, I sure would."

Joshua laughed, then glanced out the window again, and stopped laughing. "Where the blazes is Blue with my horse?"

"I'll go see what's holdin' him up."

Joshua nodded, and as Jeremiah left the room, he lingered at the window, looking down at his father. Timothy Barlow was engrossed in the newspaper clutched in his hands—so engrossed that, for a moment, he forgot the newspaper boy. The latter sat his winded horse, though, until Barlow glanced up at him. A moment later the boy was urging his weary mount back up the lane toward the road, a silver coin clenched between his teeth since he needed both hands free for the reins. Slowly, then, his attention once more focused on the newspaper, Timothy Barlow turned and went inside, moving out of Joshua's line of sight.

Joshua sighed, and hesitated. No doubt the news was about war, or the coming of war—that was just about the only topic covered these days, in print or conversation. A few months ago, representatives from the states of South Carolina, Georgia, Alabama, Florida, Mississippi, Louisiana, and Texas had met in Montgomery, Alabama, in a three-day convention that ended with all seven of the states formally seceding from the Union and creating a new nation, the Confederate States of America. Jefferson Davis of Mississippi had been selected president, and Georgia's own Alexander Stephens—who, not long before, had spoken out with passionate eloquence in favor of the Union—was named vice president. And all because a man named Abraham Lincoln had been made president of the United States last November.

Of course it wasn't just because of Lincoln, but

rather because of what Lincoln represented, that the Deep South had decided it could no longer be a part of the republic. Even though Lincoln had clearly stated he had no intention of meddling with the institution of slavery where it already existed, the Southern secessionists weren't buying it. They knew that Lincoln's Republican Party stood squarely against the expansion of slavery into the western territories. They also knew that, if slavery wasn't introduced into at least some of those territories, then before long the antislavery faction in the United States Congress would hold sway in the Senate, as they already did in the House of Representatives. And once that happened, the institution of slavery was doomed. And with it the economy of the South, not to mention an entire way of life. To preserve that economy and that way of life, the men who'd met in Montgomery this past February had exercised what they called "states rights"—and parted company with the North.

Eager to establish its sovereignty, the new Confederate States of America had insisted that the United States of America give up all its military outposts in the South. Some had been given up by their commanders without a fight. But the new president had refused to accede to the South's demands. One fort in particular was a thorn in the side of the Confederacy—Fort Sumter, in Charleston harbor. Ringing the harbor with batteries of guns aimed at the fort, the Confederates had given the Union commander, Major Robert Anderson, a choice. He could surrender the fort and leave, with his troops, without hindrance. Or he could stay and face the certainty of defeat—and, quite possibly, death. Major Anderson had chosen the latter course.

Standing at the window of his room, Joshua had a

hunch that, if the news was of war, then it was bound to have begun at Charleston. That seemed appropriate. Charleston had long been a hotbed of nullifiers and secessionists. Joshua suspected that was why President Lincoln was so adamant about holding on to Fort Sumter at all costs. No other circumstance could be as intolerable to the Confederacy than to have federal troops positioned in the middle of Charleston harbor.

Glancing down, Joshua saw that Jeremiah was in front of the house now, holding the reins of his horse and looking up at the window. Joshua raised a hand to acknowledge Jeremiah's presence, then steeled himself and left the room. Proceeding quietly down the stairs into the broad main hallway, he noticed that the doors to the parlor were open. He assumed his father was in there, hopefully so engrossed in the newspaper that he wouldn't notice his son slipping out of the house.

But he'd taken only a half dozen steps toward the door before his father's booming voice froze him in his tracks.

"Joshua? That you? Come in here a moment, would you?"

With a sigh, Joshua altered course and sauntered into the parlor like a young man without a care in the world, making sure that none of the annoyance he felt showed on his face.

His father was sitting in a chair over by the cold fireplace, looking more stern than usual.

"There's something here you should see," said Barlow, holding out the newspaper.

Joshua didn't take it. He could read the headline clearly enough. It was emblazoned across the front page:

WAR! FORT SUMTER FALLEN!

"It was bound to happen," said Barlow grimly. "Lincoln made it so that it had to happen."

"The president has said repeatedly that he didn't want war, Father."

"That's what he said. But what politicians say and what they really mean are often two entirely different things. But I didn't say he wanted it. I said he made it happen in a certain way. I think he knew it was inevitable. He wanted to make sure that the Confederates fired the first shot."

"Why would he do that?"

"In hopes that the other states that have talked about secession would feel the stirrings of patriotism and rally to the Stars and Stripes. It explains how he went about it, right here." Barlow tapped the newspaper. "It says the president informed Governor Pickens of South Carolina that he intended to reprovision Fort Sumter. Pickens immediately ordered General Beauregard to force the evacuation of the fort. Lincoln is no fool. He must have known he was forcing the issue."

"Yes, sir, he must have," said Joshua, thinking about the horse waiting on him outside, and of how Jennie Randolph would make him pay for being late for their ride together. "But I wouldn't be too concerned, Father. There will be a fight or two, and then some concessions made on both sides, and before you know it, the crisis will have passed."

"No," snapped Barlow, disturbed by his son's casual attitude. Too agitated to remain in the chair, he got up, wincing at the pain in the joints of his bad leg, and hobbled a few steps to the fireplace, gripping the mantel

for support. "No, it won't be settled that easily. This
trouble has been a long time coming. Thirty years, at
least. And many will die before it is resolved. No matter
what the cost, though, the Union must be preserved!"

"And if you were able, you would be right in the
thick of the fight," said Rose Barlow as she entered
the parlor.

Joshua half-turned, relieved, thinking that with his
mother's entrance his father might be sufficiently dis-
tracted that he could make good his escape. Rose
smiled at her son, gave him a peck on the cheek in
passing, and proceeded across the handsomely ap-
pointed room to her husband.

"Yes, I would be," said Barlow bluntly. "And thank
God Abraham Lincoln resides in the White House.
Some of his predecessors would have let the South go
its own way without lifting a finger to stop it. But not
Lincoln. He'll fight to save the Union. He knows, as
I do, that two sovereign Americas, hostile to one an-
other, cannot survive in today's world."

"Of course, dear," said Rose sublimely. She turned
to Joshua. "I noticed Jeremiah outside, with a horse.
Are you going riding?"

"Yes, with Jennie Randolph."

"Oh, how delightful. Well, then, you had better run
along, hadn't you?"

"Yes," said Joshua gratefully. "Thank you, Mother."
He glanced at his scowling father. "We'll talk more
about what's happened this evening?"

Barlow nodded curtly, and watched Joshua make a
quick exit. A moment later he heard the clatter of
hooves as his son rode away down the lane. He shook
his head morosely.

"This hardly seems an appropriate time to go courting," he said.

"As I recall," said Rose, with a sly smile, "when we fell in love it was hardly an appropriate time for either one of us."

Barlow had to laugh. She was right. He had been in Georgia at the behest of President Andrew Jackson to check into the problems between the whites and the Cherokees when he'd met Rose, and he'd found that the whites were causing more of the trouble than the Indians were. He'd met her again in Charleston during the nullification crisis, when he had entered the city disguised as a sailor, and ended up defending the federal arsenal against a secessionist mob led by Rose's own brother. She had risked her life to save his. And even though his had become one of the notorious names in the South—especially after he had killed Rose's brother—she had stuck by him. They'd had the odds stacked against them from the start. And yet here they were, still standing tall, despite the fact that he was still persona non grata in most circles.

"I don't see how it will ever work out for him," said Barlow. "Edmund Randolph is a devout secessionist. He has yet to speak a civil word to me. I'm surprised he even lets his daughter associate with my son."

"As I recall, my father strongly advised me not to have anything to do with you," said Rose.

"So you think this Jennie Randolph is so in love with our son that she's willing to defy her father?"

Rose crossed the room to the window, where he stood. "Would that be so bad?" she asked softly.

"No, of course not. Except that I shudder to think

what they would have to endure to be together. Especially now . . . now that there's war."

She gazed at him a moment, trying to read him. She knew her husband as a man who did not always say what was on his mind. Timothy Barlow was a very private man who kept his innermost thoughts and fears private, sometimes even from her. He did this, she knew, because he thought it would spare her, despite the fact that she had told him countless times that she didn't want to be spared, that she wanted to share everything with him, the bad as well as the good.

"Are you concerned about the role Joshua may decide to play in this war?"

"You're asking me if I'm worried that he might fight for the Confederacy?" Barlow shook his head. "No, by God, I'm not. He would never take up arms against the Union. Never."

Rose nodded, suppressing a gentle smile. It sounded to her as though her husband was trying to convince himself.

"What concerns me," she said softly, "is that he is placed in harm's way, regardless of the uniform he wears."

"Surely you wouldn't countenance his fighting with the secessionists."

"I would not condone it, no. But I also know that he is a Barlow. He has our blood in his veins. And that means when he makes up his mind to do something, he'll do it, regardless of what we or anyone else wants."

Barlow was scowling, gazing out the window still, even though Joshua had long since passed out of sight. "Then perhaps it's just as well that he's apparently indifferent to the entire business."

"He's not indifferent. He just has other things on his mind."

"Jennie Randolph." Barlow shook his head. It didn't seem right to him that his son would while away his time daydreaming about a young woman when his whole world was about to burn down around his ears.

"But, indifferent or not, he is a recent graduate of the military academy," said Rose. "That means he will be called upon to fight. And I want you to do me a favor, Timothy."

"Of course. Anything." Barlow peered at her, brows furrowed, wondering what she was about to say. Rose rarely asked him for anything. When she did it meant a great deal to her.

"I want you to use whatever influence you may wield with the United States Army to have our son posted somewhere well away from this war."

Barlow stared at her. "You're kidding me."

Rose shook her head. "I know how much I'm asking of you. You would never dream of using your influence for personal considerations. So do this for me. The worst thing about this war, whether it lasts a month or a year, or ten years, are all the mothers and wives who will have to grieve before it is over. I thank God that you are not able to serve, even while I know it may anger you that I think that way. I do not want to be one of those grieving mothers, Timothy. If it is within your power to spare me that, I wish you would."

Barlow was silent a moment. She knew what she was asking of him, how difficult it would be for him to swallow his pride and beg for special consideration from the War Department. But she was right—he knew the people who could arrange things so that

Joshua was posted well away from the bloody battle-
fields that he had envisioned long before those Confederate batteries had opened up on the federal
garrison at Fort Sumter.

"He'll hate me for it," he said, with a sigh of
resignation.

She touched his face. "But I will love you for it."

"But you already love me," he said, trying to lighten
the mood.

She laughed softly, whirled away, as spry and lovely
a coquette as she had been thirty years ago. "And you
love me. Which is why I know you'll save our son."

Barlow nodded. "I'll go into town today, and send
a telegram to Washington."

At least, he thought, a distant posting would put
Joshua far removed from the temptation presented by
Edmund Randolph's daughter.

Chapter 2

Kiannatah lay still as death among the boulders on the steep slope above a narrow canyon in the Sierra de Sahuaripa Mountains. He wore a white himper, deerskin leggings, and n'deh b'ken, Apache moccasins. The color of his attire helped him blend into his environment of pale yellow limestone rocks and white sand. His black hair was coated with clay, to redden it. The sun, at its zenith, blazed in a summer sky bled of all its color. The heat was oppressive, but Kiannatah did not pay it any attention. He had perfected the technique known as enthlay-sit-daou—to abide without moving. This concept had a variety of meanings, all of them related. It meant he could endure pain without flinching. It also meant he could be calm and courageous in the face of events, no matter how unexpected they might be. It meant he would not display anger, fear, or grief. In short, he was unmoved, both by physical privation and emotional turmoil. It was necessary when on the warpath, and particularly when lying in wait for the Nakai-Ye, to adopt this technique, because to do so would truly make one invisible to one's enemies. One could stand in plain view of an indah, and if one had perfected enthlay-sit-daou, one would not be seen. Kiannatah had perfected the technique. Though only sixteen years of age, he had impressed Goyathlay and the other Bedonkohe wild ones with his abilities. Not just to hide in plain sight, but also with his enthusiasm for killing Mexicans. He was as ruthless as any one of the other self-proclaimed Netdahe, the Avowed Killers—the Apaches who had sworn upon the blood of their lost loved ones never to make peace with the Nakai-Ye.

Kiannatah knew that two dozen other Netdahe lay among the rocks on both sides of the canyon. But he did not bother looking for them. He would not be able to see them. Neither would the Mexicans who rode with the pack train that, according to Goyathlay, would pass through this narrow defile sometime today. The mule train carried silver from a mine somewhere in these mountains. But the Apaches were not interested in silver. They wanted the mules, and the deaths of the Nakai-Ye, not to mention the weapons their intended victims carried. The silver shipment would be heavily guarded. But that had not dissuaded Goyathlay. The Netdahe would have the element of surprise. And besides, their enemy were Nakai-Ye and, therefore, inferior to the Apache in the arts of war, and certainly no match for two dozen Netdahe.

Kiannatah had been lying in the same position among the rocks since midmorning. He had not eaten anything, or drunk any water. A small stone lay upon his tongue. By rolling his tongue and causing the stone to slide deeper down his throat, Kiannatah could make his mouth water. He was not perspiring despite the heat, nor was he dehydrating. He did not dwell on what was to come, but rather whiled away the time thinking about his leader, Goyathlay, the one the Mexicans had nicknamed Geronimo.

Goyathlay—the One Who Yawns—had been born forty summers ago, at the headwaters of the Gila River, not far from the site of the old Fort Tulerosa. His father, a Chiricahua Apache, had married a Bedonkohe woman, and joined her band, which was led by Mangas Colorado. When he was but seventeen, Goyathlay had been accepted into the council of warriors. A year later he married Alope, the daughter of the warrior Noposo. She bore him three children. Goyathlay's Bedonkohe band had stopped near the Nakai-Ye village of Kaskiyeh. It was known that the people of Kaskiyeh traded with the Apache. Unlike many of their kind, they preferred to profit from a business relationship with the Indians rather than to participate in the seemingly unending conflict between Apache and Mexican. For several days the Apache band remained in the vicinity; each day the men would go into Kaskiyeh to trade. One day they returned to their camp to find that Mexican soldiers had passed through, killing many of the women and children. Among the dead were Goyathlay's beautiful Alope and their children. Mangas Colorado knew that his handful of warriors were no match for a large force of Mexican federales, and so he led what was left of his band northward. Goyathlay went with Mangas Colorado, but his heart burned with a desire for revenge. It was a desire he would never be able to quench, no matter how much blood he spilled.

A year later, three groups of Apache warriors entered Mexico. One, the Bedonkohe, was led by Mangas Colorado. Another, the Chokonen, was led by

Cochise. The third, the Nedhni, was led by Whoa. Geronimo served as scout for all three bands. They en-
camped near the town of Arispe, and when a detail
of Mexican soldiers wandered too close, the Apaches
captured the horsemen. The soldiers were tortured
and killed. More soldiers came in search of the missing
detail. They too were captured and killed. Then the
entire garrison of Arispe ventured forth—two companies of infantry and two companies of cavalry. Mangas
Colorado allowed Goyathlay to direct the battle, since
he had lost his entire family at Kaskiyeh. The fighting
lasted most of the day. When it was over, hundreds
of Mexican troops lay dead. Goyathlay had proven
himself an able tactician.

The Battle of Arispe satisfied most of the Apache
warriors. They had avenged Kaskiyeh, and a half
dozen other massacres engineered by the Nakai-Ye.
But Goyathlay was not satisfied. Time and again he
would persuade fellow warriors to follow him into
Mexico to kill Nakai-Ye. Sometimes only two or three
would go with him. Sometimes dozens would go. It
was on one of the occasions when Goyathlay was
finding it difficult to interest other warriors in a raid
that he recruited a more-than-willing Kiannatah. The
third warrior's name was Ahkochne. Others warned
Goyathlay that a raiding party numbering only three
was just asking for trouble. But Goyathlay wasn't worried. Neither was Kiannatah. Like Goyathlay, the
man he looked up to, the one he wanted to emulate,
Kiannatah was consumed by the hesh-ke, the killing
craze. The image of his mother and infant sister being
murdered by the Nakai-Ye would not release him.
Though they never spoke of such things, he felt sure
that Goyathlay was haunted by similar memories.

What did they care if they died, as long as they died killing the Nakai-Ye? As Ulzana had once told Kiannatah, such an end was to be sought by a true Apache broncho.

But the others were right—they did run into trouble. They were surrounded by a company of Mexican irregulars. The Nakai-Ye seemed to come out of nowhere. It was the first time Kiannatah had ever seen Goyathlay caught by surprise. It was rumored that Goyathlay had special powers. People said he could see into the future. But if that was so, his special powers failed him on this occasion. The three Apaches fought like wildcats, but the odds against them were too great, and the Mexican irregulars refused to give up, even after ten of them had been killed or wounded. Then Ahkochne fell, shot through the heart. A moment later Goyathlay was struck by a bullet, right below the eye. When he fell, Kiannatah thought him dead. But he was not going to leave his hero's body on the field of battle, to be mutilated by the Nakai-Ye. Darkness was falling, and Kiannatah had already spotted a possible way out of the trap. A twisting arroyo filled with deadwood from a long-ago flash flood was within reach. Carrying Goyathlay's limp body over his shoulders, Kiannatah slipped into the arroyo and hid in the deadfall. The Mexican irregulars searched frantically for their prey, but Kiannatah knew how to move without leaving sign, and the Nakai-Ye had to settle for mutilating and scalping one Apache corpse instead of three. Later that night, the Mexicans rode away. One did not linger in an area where one knew an Apache was lurking.

Kiannatah remained in his place of concealment until a few hours before dawn. During that time he discovered that Goyathlay was not dead. The Nakai-Ye had taken their ponies, and they were a long way from home. But none of this deterred Kiannatah. He was determined to return to the Bedonkohe che-wa-ki with his leader, or he would not return at all. And so he carried the wounded Goyathlay, walking without stopping all the next day and into the night. Only then did he lie down to sleep for a couple of hours. Then he was on his feet, with Goyathlay on his back, guided by an unerring sense of direction across the desert. On the second day he reached his destination. The Bedonkohe were amazed that Goyathlay was still alive, considering the severity of his wound. They were even more amazed by Kiannatah's feat. From that time on, Kiannatah was treated with the respect reserved for warriors who have proven their valor many times in battle. His youthfulness no longer made a difference. And when he was back on the warpath after a long recuperation, Goyathlay always went to Kiannatah before he started recruiting for a raid.

Now, as he lay in the rocks above the narrow canyon, Kiannatah was the veteran of a dozen raids into Mexico. He had killed seven Nakai-Ye. And each time he had experienced a savage exultation. There was not the slightest remorse in his heart. He had wondered if killing the enemies of his people would in any way slake his thirst for revenge. But it did not. There were many Apaches—even some among his own Bedonkohe, who spoke of the futility of continuing to war against the Mexicans. The Nakai-Ye were many, the Apaches few. They could not kill all the Nakai-Ye. Kiannatah did not concern himself with such thoughts. He scoffed at those who spoke of trying to live in

peace. They reminded him of Cosito, who had paid
for such foolish thoughts with his life—and with the
lives of many of his people, including Kiannatah's entire family. It did not matter to Kiannatah if, in the
end, this perpetual state of war with the Mexicans led
to the extinction of the Chi-hinne. They were doomed
anyway, whether they fought or not. So it was better
to fight. That way, when they were no more, they
would at least be remembered with respect by their
enemies.

The first thing he heard was the clatter of loose
stones beneath shod hooves. The slightest sound was
magnified as it echoed off the steep slopes hemming
the canyon in. A few moments later the pack train
came into view. Through eyes narrowed into slits
against the glare of the sun, Kiannatah began counting. There were fourteen mules, twenty-two men.
Each mule was being led by a man on foot. The rest
of the men were mounted on horses. They were armed
to the teeth, and very watchful. These men weren't
fools. They knew the canyon was a perfect place for
an ambush, and because they were escorting a king's
ransom in silver, they were expecting trouble.

None of that concerned Kiannatah. He didn't care
that the men down below were watchful, well-armed,
and expecting trouble. They were Nakai-Ye—that was
all that mattered to him.

For the first time in hours, he moved. His hand
rested on the Sharps carbine that lay beside him. Now
his finger touched the barrel, hot from the sun. He
had taken the carbine from a dead Mexican soldier a
year ago. He had become proficient with the weapon.
And he was eager to use it again today. But he had
to wait. Goyathlay would fire the first shot. That

would be the signal for the rest of the Apaches to spring the trap. And if Goyathlay did not fire, there would be no ambush. He was the jefe on this raid, and everything was up to him. No one dared question his authority. And Kiannatah trusted the older Bedon-kohe's warpath wisdom.

So he waited, and waited some more, and the pack train made its way through the hot canyon, passing Kiannatah's position. He watched it pass with slitted, unblinking eyes. Then a single shot. One of the mounted Nakai-Ye toppled backward off his horse. Kiannatah exploded into action, his body springing off the ground like a tightly wound spring suddenly released. The carbine came to his shoulder. He drew a quick bead, and fired. So did a dozen other Apaches almost simultaneously. Deafening gun thunder bounced off the canyon walls. Down below, the Mexicans scrambled for cover. Several of them fell, shot dead. Others limped or staggered or crawled to find shelter from the withering fire from the rocky slopes. As soon as he fired, Kiannatah moved. He knew that the Nakai-Ye had a propensity for firing at the puffs of powdersmoke from the barrels of their enemies' guns. But an Apache seldom fired twice from the same location.

With the agility of a mountain goat, Kiannatah bounded twenty yards through the rocks, at an angle along and down the slope. Several bullets ricocheted off stone near at hand—more than one of the Mexicans was firing at him. But he moved too quickly, too erratically. Abruptly he stopped, brought the carbine up, picked a target, and fired again. His second victim went down. The canyon bottom was a scene of mass confusion. Some of the Mexicans were determined to

stand and fight. Others were fleeing. Some of the
pack mules were scattering. A few, completely un-
nerved, were bucking and spinning. Some of his fellow bronchos were bringing down the mules.
Kiannatah didn't bother with that. He had come to
kill Mexicans, not mules. Again he began to move,
still angling down the slope, this time in the direction
opposite the one he had taken before. Again bullets
singed the air around him. But the Nakai-Ye could
not hit him. Disdainful of their attempts to do so,
Kiannatah once again came to an abrupt halt,
brought up the carbine, and squeezed off a shot. As
he had done twice before, he hit his mark, and another Nakai-Ye fell.

Some of the other bronchos were following his lead.
An Apache did not normally expose him needlessly
to the enemy. It was customary to remain unseen until
most, if not all, of the enemies were dead. It was a
saying among the Nakai-Ye that you did not see an
Apache until he was killing you. But Kiannatah was
too impatient to do things the customary way.
Bounding from rock to boulder to ledge, he was
clearly eager to reach the bottom of the canyon and
close with the enemy. And after his third shot, he
accomplished that goal in a matter of seconds. A Mexican came out from cover, a pistola in hand; running
toward Kiannatah, he aimed the pistol with a snarl of
triumph on his face. Before Kiannatah could bring the
carbine to bear, the Nakai-Ye pulled the trigger. The
pistol misfired. With a laugh, Kiannatah shot the man
in the chest. The impact of the bullet at such close
range picked the Mexican up off his feet and slammed
him backward. Whirling, Kiannatah saw that another
of the Nakai-Ye was trying to escape aboard one of

the silver-laden mules. Kiannatah got off a snap shot
and killed the mule instantly with a bullet through the
beast's brain. It went down headfirst, and the Mexican
went flying. He started crawling, then passed out.
Crouching in the canyon bottom, Kiannatah searched
for his next target. But, as quickly as it had begun,
the shooting stopped. A few of the Mexicans,
wounded, were still moving. The rest were dead. Kiannatah was disappointed. He had taken only four lives
this day. Or perhaps five. He turned his attention back
to the man who had been thrown by the dying mule.
Moving closer, he saw that the Mexican was still
breathing. Either he was out cold, or feigning uncon-
sciousness. Kiannatah knelt beside the man, gazed at
him a moment—and drove the blade of his knife
through the Mexican's left hand. The Mexican rolled
over, screaming in agony, a scream cut short as, with
a quick and accurate stroke, Kiannatah cut his throat.

Sitting on his haunches, his face impassive, Kiannatah watched the Nakai-Ye die, choking on his own
blood, his body convulsing as he tried in vain to draw
air into his lungs.

As horrible as his death was, Kiannatah's last victim
got off easy compared to the fate that lay in store for
the other Mexican wounded. Both of these unfortu-
nates were staked out in the canyon bottom. The geni-
talia of one was cut off, and he was allowed to bleed
to death, screaming until he could make no further
sound. The eyelids of the other man were removed,
and his head bound to stakes with rawhide thongs so
that he could not move it. He, too, screamed, as the
blazing sun blinded him. Some of the bronchos, Kiannatah among them, stood or sat nearby and watched

his suffering with clinical detachment. Finally the man was disemboweled.

Goyathlay took no part in this recreation, nor did he intervene. He did not care that the Nakai-Ye wounded suffered. They had caused much suffering among his people. Nor was he at all interested in taking prisoners, especially wounded ones who would only slow him down. Besides, he understood the motivation behind torture. Outsiders were convinced that Apaches tortured their victims simply because they were brutes. This wasn't the case. The longer an enemy prisoner could withstand torture, the stronger his spirit, and therefore, the greater the honor conferred upon the warrior or warriors who killed him. And there was a very practical reason for allowing the bronchos their sport, one that did not escape someone like Goyathlay, who always considered the effects of his actions upon others. Finding the mutilated remains of their own kind only magnified the dread of Apaches exhibited by the Nakai-Ye. And there was great advantage in being feared.

The killing done, the raiders collected several of the mules, those that had not strayed too far from the scene of battle. They cut away the packs containing the silver, which they would leave behind. Mules, though, were considered a real treat—Goyathlay and his followers would slaughter one tonight when they made camp. But that would be many hours from now, and many miles from the canyon. Goyathlay wanted to get out of Mexico as quickly as possible. His repeated raids had so alarmed the governments of the northern states that the border country was crawling with patrols, both federale and irregular. These patrols would not cross into the United States, however. Once north of the border, the Apaches would be safe.

Or so Goyathlay thought. He could not know that all of that was about to change, and that soon the Apache would have to deal with another enemy: the United States Army.

Chapter 3

Joshua Barlow woke to the sound of reveille, and for an instant thought himself back at West Point and facing another long day of mental and physical strain. Then he realized where he was—just about as far from the military academy, perched on a high plateau above the placid, beautiful Hudson River in New York, as a person in this army could get. Fort Union, an army outpost in the middle of the New Mexico Territory. Which was just another way of saying, as far as he was concerned, in the middle of nowhere.

The drummer and fifer were making their circuit of the garrison, which brought them along officers' row and from there to the enlisted men's barracks. The drummer was tapping out a quick step on a maple drum, the same sort of drum that the army had been using since the days of the Continentals under George Washington. Barlow sat up and looked around. His three roommates were also stirring, with the usual chorus of muttered curses and groans and the coughing to clear night gather from the throat.

"Look on the bright side, gentlemen," said John Hammond. "At least it's not a bugle. At least the colonel has seen fit to provide this post with an honest-to-God band so we don't have to wake up to a goddamned bugle."

"I don't think that's why he did it," replied Frederick Trotter, who, like the other three in the small room, was a lieutenant assigned to the Second Cavalry Regiment. Of the four, he was senior, in terms of both age and tenure with the regiment. "He did it because he thinks he deserves an honest-to-God band, and it has nothing to do with the sensitivity of our eardrums at five thirty in the morning."

Barlow got to his feet, struck a sulfur match, and lighted a lantern, keeping it turned low so that their eyes could adjust more easily, yet it provided enough illumination so that he could mix his morning tonic: a cocktail of whiskey, water, bitters, and sugar.

"I'll have one of those," said Hammond.

"Make it three."

Barlow glanced at the fourth man in the room. "And yourself, Charlie?"

Charles Summerhayes was still stretched out on his narrow bunk. He shook his head, but didn't say anything. He had arrived at Fort Union at the same time as Barlow—two weeks ago. But where Barlow had been readily accepted by the garrison's officers, Summerhayes remained aloof from the others. He seldom spoke. He didn't play cards. He didn't curse. He didn't drink. That was more than enough to brand him as something of an odd duck in the eyes of his peers. Barlow's theory was that Summerhayes was suffering from a bad case of homesickness, and was willing to give him the benefit of the doubt, expecting that he would snap out of it, in time, and become more sociable. As for himself, Barlow had learned to excel in card playing and drinking and the other social skills expected of an officer in the army at the military academy. It hadn't been all book learning and drilling. There had been other things, equally as important, to learn. And Barlow had learned them well. He knew how to adapt to any situation. Even Fort Union. Which was why the other officers had readily accepted him.

After downing his eye-opener, Hammond went to the room's single window and glanced out at the parade ground. The first tinge of daylight was shading the sky to the east. He could just barely make out the figures of the enlisted men as they tumbled out of the barracks lined up across from officers' row. This was the first roll call of the day. There would be another at sundown. With a sardonic curl at the corner of his mouth, Hammond watched the soldiers stumbling about, trying to line up in the correct order.

"Well, gents," he said, "I suppose we have before us another day of pointless drill."

"It isn't pointless," said Trotter. "Drill is never pointless."

Hammond glanced across at Trotter, then looked at Barlow. That sardonic curl was still there, and Hammond shook his head. Barlow knew what he was thinking. Hammond was one of those fellows who liked to act the ne'er-do-well. He was quick to find the humor or the irony in any situation, and it was normal for him to make light of others as well as himself. Trotter was altogether a different sort, a humorless man and almost as by the book as Colonel Hartwell Lyman himself.

"It is with those men," said Hammond, meaning the

troops gathering on the parade ground. "You know why they're here and not back east in the war. Because they're not fit to serve in the army. So they've been sent to us. The thieves, the cutthroats, the slackers, and the deserters. If there was any half-decent place in this godforsaken country for them to run to, half of 'em would be gone by sunset."

Trotter shrugged as he donned his tunic, checking to make sure the steward who served all the junior officers had polished every last brass button to his satisfaction. "Perhaps so. But they're still in the army, and it's our job to whip them into shape. We have to make them good soldiers."

Hammond groaned, but said nothing more on the subject. He knew instinctively when to stop kidding around, knew just how far he could go with Trotter before giving offense. Knowing too that an offended Trotter might even let it slip to the colonel that there was a malcontent in the officers' mess. And Colonel Lyman was every bit as humorless as Lieutenant Trotter.

Barlow was dressed first, and headed for the day. He noted that Summerhayes was still in his longjohns, sitting on the edge of his bunk, listless and gazing at the floor between his bare feet, looking every bit like a man completely uninterested in life.

"Better get to it, Charles," said Barlow. "You know how the colonel feels about stragglers."

Summerhayes looked up at him with an uncomprehending expression on his face, then nodded. Barlow left it at that and went outside, buckling on his sword. He was joined a moment later by Trotter, and then by Hammond. He looked to his left, at the section of the barracks reserved for married officers. Several of the wives were gathered in front of one of the adobe structures to watch the roll call and chat among themselves. Seeing them made Barlow think about Jennie, and he felt a pang of regret—or was it self-pity? He knew that the principal reason for his presence here on the frontier was his mother's concern for his welfare. But he had sometimes wondered if his father would have so readily agreed to do her bidding were it not for a desire to remove his son from the vicinity of Jennie Randolph.

Not that Barlow harbored any ill will toward his father or mother. He didn't blame them for what they'd done. And while he sometimes deemed it necessary to pretend that he was upset by the fact that his famous father had pulled strings to have him assigned to Fort Union so that he was missing the war that waged in the East, he was, in truth, ambivalent on that score. Even though the war, six months old now, had already gone on longer than he'd anticipated, he was still convinced that the Union would prevail in a fairly short time, and the Confederate states would be brought back into the fold, and things would be pretty much as they had been before, without even the issue of slavery resolved. He couldn't envision any other result. And he wasn't alone in that. Who could imagine that the sections would fight for a year, or two, or more, and that tens of thousands would perish in battle after battle? Even more to the point, who could envision the republic surviving such a bloody convulsion?

It wasn't that Barlow feared going into battle. In fact, he looked forward to his first action. His baptism of fire. What soldier didn't want to put that behind him? He just didn't feel, as a few did, that he ought to be back east, involved in the struggle between North and South, in order to do his part to save the Republic from extinction. His father was one of those who held firmly to the belief that this war to put down the Southern rebellion was the defining moment in the nation's history. Joshua Barlow didn't see it as that. But he recognized the irony in the decision by his father to arrange to have him sent out west; Timothy Barlow, who on more than one occasion had demonstrated a willingness to sacrifice himself for the Republic, had left himself open to charges that he didn't care enough about the Republic to sacrifice his only son's life for its preservation. That was the price the elder Barlow would have to pay for acceding to his wife's wishes.

As for Jennie, there were times when Joshua missed her company. What man wouldn't? But he was wise enough to realize that this didn't necessarily mean that he was in love with her. Not that he was completely confident in his knowledge of what love meant. It wasn't that he couldn't live without her, because he could. It was more along the lines of he wished he didn't have to. A large part of his infatuation with her—if, indeed, that was the most accurate description for his feelings where she was concerned—had to do with her position in their little piece of the world, as the most desirable belle in all of northern Georgia, and his own, as the not-quite-accepted son of the notorious Yankee officer who stood for everything that most people in Georgia despised. It had been good for his ego that a woman like Jennie Randolph had been willing to risk the anger of her father and the scorn of her friends and acquaintances to associate with him. Of course he'd always suspected that she'd done so merely for the shock value, and not because she was really in love with him. He had written her two letters since his arrival at Fort Union a month ago, but had not received any in return. That didn't necessarily mean she had gotten over him— mail service to a frontier outpost was notoriously slow and unreliable. She'd certainly seemed devastated when he'd told her he was going away. Then too Southern belles like Jennie were very talented actresses.

With a sigh, Barlow tore his attention away from the ladies. There wasn't much point in feeling sorry for himself. Or in longing for a little female companionship. All the young women at Fort Union—with the exception of Captain Reynolds' nineteen-year-old daughter—were taken. The captain's daughter was a plain and doughty creature, as different from Jennie Randolph as night was from day, and Barlow had no interest in her. There were some unattached women in the tent town located in a ravine about a half mile west of the outpost, but they were all working girls, and Barlow made a point of staying away from them. They, like all the other denizens of the tent town, were there for one reason—to relieve the officers and enlisted men of the Fort Union garrison of their hard-earned pay.

"Heads up," murmured Hammond. "Here comes the colonel."

Barlow turned his head to look in the direction of the fort's headquarters building, which also served as the commanding officer's quarters. Colonel Hartwell Lyman, as usual, cut a fine figure in his nicely tailored and impeccably groomed uniform. He was a tall, slender, handsome man, with a luxurious mustache and

sideburns. His hair was mahogany brown, save for the
silver at his temples. He walked with long, purposeful
strides, impatiently tapping a leg with a riding crop.
Hammond had called him a martinet on one occasion.
From Barlow's point of view, Lyman wasn't any different from the instructors at the military academy; he
was accustomed to aggressive, enthusiastic, by-the-
book officers. That was the only kind he had ever
known.

Reaching them, the colonel gave them all a sweeping once-over, followed by a curt nod. Lyman expected his officers to set a good example for the
men in all things, not least their appearance. Then
his gaze moved past Barlow, Hammond, and Trotter, and it hardened into something akin to cold
steel. Barlow knew what had drawn his attention—
and his ire—without turning to look. It had to be
Summerhayes, coming out of the barracks. Seething,
and whipping even more vigorously at his leg with
the riding crop, Lyman waited until Summerhayes,
still buttoning his tunic, had joined his messmates
before speaking.

"So glad you saw fit to join us, Lieutenant," said
Lyman, his words dripping with sarcasm.

"Yes, sir." Summerhayes didn't know what else to
say.

Lyman turned to his second-in-command, Major
Henry Addicks. "I trust you will take care of this matter, Major."

"Yes, sir." Addicks glowered at Summerhayes.

Lyman turned back to the lieutenants. "Mr. Trotter,
Mr. Barlow, I will see both of you after roll call."

"Yes, sir," said Barlow, echoing Trotter—and wondering what lay behind the summons. He could only

hope it was an assignment of some sort that would take him away from Fort Union, and break the monotonous drudgery of outpost life.

"Carry on, then," said Lyman, and walked away.

Major Addicks lingered long enough to jab a finger into Summerhayes's chest. "And I'll see you after roll call, mister."

Once the major was out of earshot, Hammond glanced with ill-concealed contempt at Summerhayes, and shook his head. "What's wrong with you, Summerhayes? You're making us all look bad. If you don't want to be here, why don't you resign your commission and be on your way?"

"You wouldn't understand," said Summerhayes.

"Probably not," said Hammond, with disgust, and walked away.

"I'm sorry," said Summerhayes, directing this at Barlow. "If I am making you look bad, I'm sorry."

"Don't worry about us," replied Barlow, surprised. It was, as far as he knew, the first time Summerhayes had addressed him so directly. "Just take care of yourself."

He moved on to his command, Troop E, and stood by while the sergeant called the roll. Joshua tried to pay attention, but he was preoccupied with speculating about the reason for his summons before Colonel Lyman. As soon as the roll call was completed, he rejoined Trotter and together they made for the post headquarters. Barlow wanted to ask Trotter his opinion of what was about to transpire. After all, Trotter had been there the longest of any of them, and he knew the colonel better than most. But Joshua didn't want to come across as a wet-behind-the-ears shavetail. So he kept his mouth shut, and tried to adopt the slightly bored demeanor of a veteran cavalryman who couldn't be fazed by anything. The drum and fife were sounding stable call, and the troopers were on their way to care for their horses. Colonel Lyman believed a good cavalryman always took care of his horse before taking care of himself. Barlow wasn't sure that he agreed. It seemed more logical to him that a man would take better care of his horse on a full stomach, rather than having to spend a hour or more with brush and currycomb, resenting the fact that the animal was breakfasting on the oats in his feed bag while he himself had to suffer pangs of hunger.

They were escorted into the colonel's office immediately, and found Lyman in the company of a civilian who was introduced as Jonathan Grenville.

"Mr. Grenville," said Lyman, "is here to negotiate a treaty with the Apaches. This agreement will result in the Indians being placed on reservations. The two of you will accompany him, with your respective troops, of course."

"Yes, sir," said Trotter. "So I take it we can expect some trouble."

Barlow had been thinking the same thing. Two troops of cavalry were a considerable show of force, especially at treaty negotiations.

"Quite right," replied Lyman. "These are Apaches we're talking about, after all."

"Of course we all hope to conduct this matter peaceably," said Grenville. "I think you gentlemen should know that I have negotiated similar treaties with a number of other tribes. I have as much experience at this sort of thing as anyone else in the Indian Bureau."

Barlow looked the man over. Grenville was tall, on the slender side except for a protruding belly. He had a thick goatee and heavy jowls, and he wore a travel-worn suit of brown tweed.

"Still," said Lyman, "we should keep in mind that the Apaches have never been defeated by an enemy, so they may have some difficulty understanding why they should give up most of their land and take up farming on a reservation."

Barlow's attention turned to Lyman. He had already learned that the colonel had a fairly low opinion of civilians in general. Clearly, he was not impressed by Grenville, nor was he optimistic about the Indian agent's chances of success.

"The government is willing to be generous with respect to the annuities we will provide the Apaches if they sign the treaty," said Grenville. "I have high hopes that this will entice them to agree to our terms."

"If I may speak freely, sir," said Trotter.

"Go ahead, Lieutenant. Mr. Grenville, Lieutenant Trotter knows as much about the Apaches as anyone else on this post."

"Then I will be grateful for his counsel," replied Grenville diplomatically.

"Some of the bands will probably go along," said Trotter. "But others probably won't. And then we can't forget the teiltcohes."

"The what?" asked Grenville.

"The troublemakers. Like Geronimo and his bunch. They've been conducting raids across the border in Mexico for several years now. They'll never agree to lay down their arms and live out their lives on a reservation."

"I agree," said Lyman. "But we'll deal with Geron-

imo and the others like him in good time. For now,
the main thing is to prevent the troublemakers from
scotching Mr. Grenville's efforts to get the rest of the
Apaches to accept the government's terms. Since none
of us can possibly know what to expect from the
Apaches, I'm afraid I cannot give you more specific
orders, Lieutenant. But I am counting on your knowledge of the Indians, and the common sense which you
have heretofore demonstrated."

"Yes, sir," said Trotter. "But Lieutenant Barlow has
no experience with the Apaches, sir."

Barlow was stunned. He hadn't expected Trotter to
protest his presence on the mission. They certainly
weren't friends, but they were messmates, and that
alone, in Barlow's book, bought him at least some
consideration, not to mention loyalty, from Trotter.

"All the more reason for him to go with you, Lieutenant," replied Lyman, "so that he can learn."

"Yes, sir," said Trotter, without enthusiasm.

"You will leave tomorrow. That is all."

Outside, Trotter glanced at Barlow. "No offense,
Barlow," he said. "But when you're dealing with the
Apaches you really don't have the time to tutor the
inexperienced."

"Well, Lieutenant," said Barlow coolly, "I'll try not
to be too much of a burden."

Trotter nodded, and walked away. As Barlow
watched him go, two words came immediately to his
mind: pompous ass. But he knew there was more to
it than that. Trotter didn't want to share any glory
that might be derived from participation in what
would be—if it succeeded—an historic accord between
the Apaches and the United States. Frederick Trotter
wanted to be known as the officer who presided over

a peaceful negotiation, and it had to rankle that now he would have to share that honor with a fellow officer—one he considered to be, at best, an indifferent soldier.

Chapter 4

The Chokonen *che-wa-ki,* located high in the Mogollon Mountains, was not what Barlow had expected. The cowahs didn't look like much—cone-shaped huts made of adobe and thatch and hides. The inhabitants of the village were the first "wild" Apaches Barlow had laid eyes on; previously he had seen only the *reducidos,* the tame ones, the ones who lingered in the vicinity of army posts seeking the protection of the Pinda Lickoyi, not to mention the wherewithal to eke out a living. Many of the *reducidos* were half-breeds and outcasts. Barlow had expected the wild Apache to stand in striking contrast to the wretched tame ones. But the dwellers of these cowahs didn't look like much to him. Their clothing consisted of faded calico or deerskin dresses for the women, a loincloth or a loincloth and cotton himper for the men. The himper was a long shirt reaching almost to the knees and belted at the waist. Most of the Chokonen went barefoot—some of the bronchos wore the high-desert moccasins called n'deh b'ken that laced up to the knee in order to protect the wearer from scorpions and rattlesnakes and cactus spines. None of the Apaches Barlow could see wore any sort of beadwork on their clothing, or any paint to decorate their bodies. Some had applied clay to their hair, turning it stiff and reddish in color. Barlow's first impression was that they lived in a sort of primitive squalor. And what he found most hard to believe was all the tales he'd heard at the fort about the prowess of the Apache warrior, and how formidable The People, as they liked to call themselves, could be. These people, decided Barlow, didn't look like anything to write home about. He was aware, though, that looks could be deceiving. And as he rode closer to the village with his troop, accompanied by Lieutenant Trotter and his troop, along with the Indian agent, Grenville, Barlow didn't even for a moment let down his guard.

In Trotter's troop was a sergeant named Farrow, who spoke the Apache tongue fluently, as he had lived for years among the Chi-hinne, and had taken an Apache wife. When they reached a creek that ran along the western edge of the Chokonen village, Trotter called a halt. He told Barlow that he intended to ride on into the che-wa-ki, accompanied by Farrow. Barlow would wait here, with the command, and with Grenville, until Trotter had ascertained that the Apaches intended to be good hosts.

Watching Trotter and the sergeant ride across the shallows of the creek and into the village, where several hundred Apaches onlookers—men, women, and children—had congregated, Barlow was unaware of Sergeant Eckhart's presence at his side until the grizzled noncom spoke up.

"Ain't that a grand sight, sir?" drawled Eckhart. "It's just like Lieutenant Trotter to ride in like that, bold as brass."

"He's a very brave man," said Barlow.

"Brave? Oh, well, yes, sir, Lieutenant, I guess you could call it that."

"What would you call it, Sergeant?"

Eckhart smiled. "Let's just say I've seen a lot of commissioned officers come and go, sir. Some of 'em, like Lieutenant Trotter, seem to care more about fame and glory than they care for their own lives. I don't need to spell out why a lot of the enlisted men don't relish serving under the command of such officers. All too often out here, those officers wind up getting themselves killed—and sometimes they get a lot of their men killed in the process."

Barlow nodded. He considered himself quite fortunate to have Eckhart for his sergeant. The man had the respect of the cavalrymen of Troop E, and for that reason he was able to keep them in line. He was stern, but fair, and—best of all, from Barlow's perspective—he was experienced. Eckhart had spent his entire life—or at least since he was sixteen years of age—in the army, and much of that time had been in service on the frontier. The sergeant had his flaws. One of them was a propensity for speaking his mind about anything and everything—including his superior officers. Occasionally the sergeant flirted with insubordination. But Barlow didn't mind, and had encouraged Eckhart to speak freely in his presence.

"Sergeant," he said, "go down the line and remind the men that they are to remain calm and are to keep their hands away from their weapons unless and until they are fired upon."

"Yes, sir."

Barlow continued to watch Trotter and Farrow, who were now being enveloped by the Chokonen crowd;

for a few anxious moments he lost sight of them completely. But then they emerged from the crowd, coming back across the creek to rejoin the column. Trotter addressed the government man.

"Mr. Grenville, Cochise says he is eager to begin the negotiations."

"Excellent, Lieutenant, excellent. Thank you."

"Lieutenant Barlow, Sergeant Farrow and myself will accompany Mr. Grenville into the village. You will be in command of the detachment until I return. You are to make camp over there"—he pointed to open ground nearby—"and await our return. Under no circumstances are you to take action against the Apaches unless it is clear that Mr. Grenville, Sergeant Farrow, and myself have met with foul play. Is that clear?"

Barlow said that it was. He had hoped to bear witness to the treaty negotiations, since that would have provided him with ample opportunity to get a closer look at the Apaches, but evidently this was not to be. Of course this way Trotter could honestly say that he was the only commissioned officer present at the signing of such an important document, if indeed the negotiations proceeded that far.

Barlow had his doubts on that score. The terms Grenville would present to Cochise called for the Chokonen to limit their movements to a certain area around the Mogollon Mountains. In return, the United States would pledge itself to provide the Chokonen with an annuity—an annual payment of merchandise. There was another pledge, as well: The United States would recognize Chokonen sovereignty over the Mogollons forever.

Having been raised on stories about the poor treatment received by the Five Civilized Tribes—the Cherokee, the Choctaw, the Chickasaw, the Creek, and the Seminole—Barlow had a skeptical view of his country's ability to keep its end of such bargains. His father had been involved in the removal of the Cherokees, the same people who had fought so loyally beside him in the First Seminole War. In exchange for their aid in quelling the Seminoles, the Cherokees had been robbed of their lands and moved westward, into the Indian Territories, because gold had been discovered on the land. Barlow expected that the same thing would happen to the Chokonen, assuming Cochise signed the peace treaty. It might not be gold, but sooner or later Barlow's own kind would find a reason to justify taking the rest of Apacheria. So this peace treaty that Mr. Grenville was so committed to making a reality was more or less just a means by which one would delay the inevitable. And it would allow people like Mr. Grenville to say that they had done everything they could do to bring peace to the land.

Lieutenant Trotter and Sergeant Farrow accompanied Grenville back to the Chokonen village. Barlow led the two troops of cavalrymen to the open ground Trotter had indicated. This plateau of land, just south of a rocky ridge, and due west of the che-wa-ki was as good a place as any to make a night camp. It was at a slightly higher elevation than the village; Barlow figured that he would be able to keep a watchful eye on events within the che-wa-ki by using a pair of binoculars. And while the plateau itself was virtually devoid of timber, there was a thick stand of wind-twisted and cold-stunted cedars to the north, right along the rimrock. Best of all, it provided no cover for any per-

son or group of persons who might desire to attack
the camp, regardless of the direction whence they
came. There was a clear field of fire at every point of
the compass.

The cavalrymen had been in their saddles for the
better part of the day, and they were more than ready
to settle down by a nice warm fire and rest sore mus-
cles and fill empty barrels with beans and biscuits.
Eckhart picked three men as a wood-gathering crew;
their job was to hike up to the stand of trees and
return with as much kindling as they could carry. At
the same time, they would make sure the trees did
not conceal potential enemies.

Barlow remained in the saddle, taking the field
glasses out of their hard case and scanning the Chokonen village. He could not see Lieutenant Trotter or
Farrow or Grenville. The cowahs were built so
closely together they blocked his view of the center
of the village. But he could see plenty of Apaches,
and just by watching them for a moment Barlow became convinced that nothing was terribly amiss
there.

The rifle shot made him jump. It was followed by
two more shots in rapid succession. He wheeled his
horse around. The troopers in the camp were running
this way and that, snatching up their weapons and
looking for the enemy. But, as far as Barlow could
tell, they were not under attack. He was bewildered—
but only for a moment. Another shot rang out, and
this time he saw the puff of powder smoke from the
trees up on the rimrock. And then he saw the woodcutting crew. One of the troopers was lying facedown,
and Barlow knew somehow that he was dead. A second man was crawling, obviously seriously wounded.

The other two were also on the ground, seeking cover. In the crew of four, two of the men carried carbines, while the other two carried axes. In that way they could take turns chopping wood and standing guard. The two with the rifles were returning fire now, but they didn't have anything to shoot at. Whoever it was up in the cedars, they were using the cover to good advantage.

Another flurry of rifle fire—and Barlow calculated that there was more than one shootist in the trees, and probably more than two. They had the woodcutters pinned down. There was no cover for them, and no one in the camp seemed inclined to rush out to their aid. Barlow didn't blame the other soldiers for hesitating—it would be tantamount to suicide to run out there into the open. But something had to be done—it was just a matter of time before the three survivors of the woodcutting crew were picked off by the sharpshooters in the woods.

Barlow pulled the carbine from its saddle scabbard, which rested snugly under his right leg, and raked his spurs across the flanks of the horse under him. The mount leaped forward. He dimly heard Sergeant Eckhart howling at the cavalrymen in camp to cover their lieutenant. Charging up the slope toward the spot where the three troopers were pinned down, Barlow stayed low in the saddle. He heard a crack, then another—loud enough to make him wince. He knew the bullets were passing far too close for comfort. Reaching the woodcutting crew, he checked the horse, brought carbine to shoulder, and began to fire at the woods. "Get going!" he shouted at the men. The two uninjured men helped their comrade. Barlow fired seven rounds—all that the carbine would hold. Only then did he throw a quick glance back at the camp. The three woodcutters were just then reaching their comrades. Good enough. Barlow turned his horse and again dug spurs. Just as the horse leaped the bullet struck it, entering right below the jawbone and carving a path of destruction through the brain. The animal died instantly. Barlow tried to hurl himself clear. He fell, rolled, came up a bit unsteadily, and drew his pistol. A bullet cut a groove in the front of his tunic. Aiming at the puff of smoke, he squeezed the trigger. The cavalrymen in the camp, seeing their commanding officer go down, increased their rate of fire. A squad of three troopers, led by Eckhart, ran out to collect Barlow, who assured him that he was unhurt. With a nonchalance that he did not feel, and that he realized probably made him look ridiculous under the circumstances, he walked into the camp on his own volition.

"Are you hit, sir?" asked Eckhart, checking him over, as solicitous as a mother hen.

"Not a scratch," said Barlow, feeling a bit giddy.

"That was the damnedest thing I ever saw," admitted the sergeant. "You riding out like that. Are you trying to get yourself killed, sir? 'Cause, if so, that's an excellent way to go about it."

Barlow looked at Eckhart and at the gaunt, dirty faces of the half dozen or so cavalrymen who had gathered round him to see how he was doing—and he realized that his little stunt had won them all over. He had been worried about when, and even if, the men of Troop E would accept him, but that hadn't even crossed his mind a few minutes ago, when he'd made up his mind to cover the withdrawal of the woodcutters. But the men certainly saw him in a different light, of a sudden. Here was an officer, they thought, who cared as much or more for the welfare of the men under his command as he cared for his own well-being.

"What are you men gawking at?" he asked crossly, because all of this attention was making him feel uncomfortably self-conscious.

"Go on with yourselves, you ugly vultures!" roared Eckhart. "Are you sure you're all right, then, Lieutenant?"

"Get your hands off me," said Barlow gruffly, and stood up, looking in the direction of the Chokonen village.

"There seems to be a big commotion over there," said Eckhart. "And you should be keeping your head down, sir."

His order had been to ride to the rescue of Trotter, Farrow and Grenville if trouble erupted. But he hesitated to send troops into the che-wa-ki. What if this attack had surprised the Apaches as much as anyone else? If they saw a detachment of horse soldiers galloping into their village, they might perceive it as an attack, and open fire. Barlow shook his head, frustrated. He needed more information before he could make a well-reasoned decision with respect to Trotter and the others.

"We've got to clear those trees," he told Eckhart. "I want ten men on horseback ready to follow me. We're going to circle wide to the rim and flank the enemy's position. We'll come in from the side, and when we do, you'll cease fire from here. I'd rather not be killed by my own men, thank you."

"Let me lead the flankers, sir."

"Damn it, Sergeant. Stop second-guessing me."

"Yes, sir."

"Get me a horse."

"Use mine, sir."

Barlow mounted up, and a moment later was leading ten cavalrymen in a sweeping flanking movement to the west. Beyond rifle range from the cedars, he swung round to the rim, and returned to the trees. On Barlow's approach, Eckhart silenced the troopers' guns. Only then did Barlow realize that the men in the trees were no longer shooting. He had a hunch they were gone.

Reaching the trees, he sent five men around to the other side of the bosque and, dismounted, led the other five into the brush. They moved in a line abreast from west to east through the trees, always keeping the man to left and to right in sight. The trooper immediately to Barlow's right was the first to find any sign of the attackers—a pile of spent shells. A few minutes later, another cavalryman found the place where three horses had been tethered. They were shod horses, which meant it was unlikely that the attackers had been Apaches. But why had three men fired on an army camp? What had they hoped to gain? Barlow knew only one thing for certain—the three men, whoever they were, had hightailed it out of the cedars as soon as they'd seen him lead the flanking detachment west.

Barlow emerged from the woods to find himself confronted by Lieutenant Trotter, on horseback, and accompanied by Sergeant Farrow.

"What the hell is going on?" asked Trotter. He was seething with anger. "What was all the shooting about?"

"Three men hidden in these trees," said Barlow.

"They opened fire on my men. We returned fire. They got away."

"They got away," rasped Trotter. "Who were they?"

Barlow shook his head. "I haven't got a clue."

"Were they Apaches?"

"No. White men."

"Are you sure, Lieutenant?"

"Pretty sure."

"Well, the Chokonen are gone too," said Trotter, disgusted. "Soon as the shooting started, they just faded off into the brasada. Every man, woman, and child. Vanished. I've never figured out how they manage it."

"They call it enthlay-sit-daou, sir," remarked Sergeant Farrow. "The closest I can come to by way of a translation into English is 'to become one with your surroundings.' It's mostly just a frame of mind. If you believe that you are invisible to your enemies, then you will become invisible."

"What nonsense," said Trotter, impatiently. "The fact is, they're gone, and I doubt they'll be back anytime soon."

"Not while we're still in these mountains," said Farrow. "They seemed to think it was some kind of mischief on our part—maybe an ambush gone bad."

"That's pure speculation on your part, Sergeant, and I'll thank you not to repeat it to anyone else," snapped Trotter.

Barlow suppressed a smile. Trotter's main concern was how this debacle would reflect on him. Trotter's mind was already feverishly at work, trying to devise a plausible explanation that would exonerate him, Barlow supposed.

"Sounds like Cochise and his people were as surprised as we were," said Barlow. "So who were the three men who started the trouble? Who would profit from sabotaging the treaty negotiations?"

"The Rebels, that's who," said Farrow. "In fact, I've heard rumors ever since the war started that there was Confederate agents all over this neck of the woods."

Barlow nodded. That made sense to him. "Let me go after them," he said to Trotter. "It's my fault that they got away. I think I'd have a fair chance of catching them."

"Yes, it *was* your fault," said Trotter, seizing on that idea as a potentially useful contribution to the story he was manufacturing. "But your request is denied. We're returning to Fort Union. I will not divide my command with an untold number of hostiles in the vicinity."

"Hostiles? You mean the Apaches?"

"If the sergeant is right, and they think we botched some sort of ambush, then they might decide to stop running and turn right around and attack us."

Barlow shrugged. He wasn't going to press the issue.

"I saw what you did, Lieutenant," said Farrow. "Riding out like that to cover those men that were pinned down out in the open. It was something to see, wasn't it, sir?" This last was directed at Trotter.

"I don't know what you're talking about," said Trotter brusquely. "Collect your men, Lieutenant. I want to start back at once."

He rode away. Farrow grinned and shook his head.

"If I was a betting man, I'd bet everything I owned that what you did back there won't get into Lieutenant Trotter's report. He doesn't like to be upstaged, you understand."

"Keep your opinions to yourself, Sergeant," said Barlow, and walked away.

Chapter 5

Less than a month after the events that aborted the peace negotiations with the Chokonen, Colonel Lyman called Barlow into his office.

"John Ward owns a ranch a couple of days north of here, Lieutenant," said Lyman, indicating the general location of the ranch on the territorial map that hung on the wall behind his desk. "He's a good man. Pulled up stakes and moved here from Texas, lock, stock, and barrel, when that state seceded from the Union. He runs between one and two thousand head of cattle on the range east of the Mogollons. We eat his beef, by the way. Ward has a contract to provide this outpost and several others with beef."

"Yes, sir." Barlow was puzzled. What did all this have to do with him?

"It seems John—Mr. Ward—is having some Indian problems. For the past fortnight someone has been killing his cattle. He's not sure how many, but at least twenty, so far. They're usually butchered on the spot, and the sign seen around the carcasses is clearly Indian, or so Ward's men say. And his men are all vaqueros who've spent a lifetime in Apache country. So they would know."

"Yes, sir. Probably just a band of outcasts. The cattle are obviously being killed for food. Winter's coming on. Game is getting hard to come by."

"It doesn't matter why they are being killed, Lieutenant," said Lyman curtly. "They are the property of John Ward, and I am responding to his request that the United States Army assist in protecting that property."

"Why can't his own men take care of the problem, sir?"

"They have a ranch to run. If Ward sends his men out to patrol the borders of his ranch, searching for the culprits, who will gather the cattle on their winter range? This time of year, he must move his stock down out of the foothills. If they are left in the high country, and the winter is hard, he could lose hundreds of head. I don't know why I am bothering to explain all of this to you, Lieutenant. All you need are your orders. Here they are."

Lyman handed a piece of paper across the table to Barlow, who read the orders once, and then again. He could not shake the feeling that he wasn't being told everything he needed to know. This was about more than just a few head of cattle lost to human scavengers. Lyman had better things to do with his soldiers than send them off to patrol a cattleman's range. Apache renegades had begun attacking the Butterfield stagecoaches that ran a route a day and a half to the south of Fort Union. Both Hammond and Summerhayes were out there now, trying to protect over a thousand miles of stage line, dozens of way stations, and hundreds of company livestock—not to mention the lives of the Butterfield employees and patrons.

But Barlow sensed that he would get no further information from the colonel, so he said, "Yes, sir," gave a salute, and took his leave.

It was Trotter who filled in the blanks. That night, after supper, they spent some time on the porch of their quarters, with Trotter firing up his pipe. One of Barlow's troopers, Flanaghan, had broken out his bagpipes, and was playing a spirited tune, and the sound of the pipes came lilting across the darkened parade ground, broken up occasionally by wind gusting forcefully out of the north, a wind that carried with it the smell of snow. Trotter asked Barlow about his visit to post headquarters, and when Barlow told him about the business with Ward's cattle, Trotter muttered a curse.

"That should be my assignment," he rasped. "The colonel is still making me pay for what happened at the Chokonen village."

"Why should it be yours?"

"A couple of reasons. For one, John Ward is an Indian hater. Back in Texas, the Comanches killed his wife and oldest son. And when he came out here, he apparently ran afoul of Cochise. Some of the Apaches were helping themselves to Ward's cattle. So he killed a few of them. Cochise answered back by burning down Ward's place. It could have been worse. I suspect the Apaches could have wiped the Wards out. But Cochise just wanted to drive them away. You see, just about all of the graze that Ward claims for his own is on Chokonen land. The truth of the matter is that most of the land belongs to the United States. Federal land. Ward laid claim only to the land surrounding the water sources. That way, only his cattle can survive on the land, because he controls the water.

"At any rate, Ward hates Cochise with a passion. I'm sure the feeling is mutual. So whenever anything happens to a single head of his cattle, Ward's first impulse is to blame Cochise and his people. You're probably wondering why Ward isn't handling this little problem by himself. He has nearly sixty men who ride for him."

"The colonel said it was because they were busy moving the cattle to winter range."

Trotter smirked. "More likely Ward intended to handle it himself. He would like nothing better than to have a war with the Chokonen. Give him an excuse to kill every last one of them. I suppose that would be the next best thing to killing all of the Comanches—the ones who had murdered his wife and son—if killing all the Comanches was actually possible."

"You're saying the colonel talked him into letting the army handle this."

Trotter nodded. "That would be my guess. The colonel isn't afraid of war, but he recognizes that his job right now is to keep the peace. Peaceful frontiers is what the Union needs right now, while it tries to deal with the Southern rebellion. So Colonel Lyman wants to forestall a war between Cochise and his friend Ward."

"Now it's beginning to make sense. But you said there were a *couple* of reasons why you should be the one to have this assignment."

Trotter frowned. "That's personal." He looked at Barlow, debated whether to speak of it, then shrugged. "Ward has a daughter. Kathleen. I'm . . . rather fond of her, you might say. And I have reason to believe she feels likewise about me."

"I see." Barlow suppressed a smile. "Well, if I see her, I will be sure to give her your regards."

"You'll do better than that. I will write a letter to-night, and rely on you to deliver it to her. Can I have your word on that? Between gentlemen?"

"Sure," said Barlow. He doubted Trotter would have done the same, had their situations been reversed. But he saw no harm in delivering a letter; to do so would not be an inconvenience.

Troop E left Fort Union at daybreak the next morning. On the second day out, they arrived at the Ward ranch.

The rambling, two-story house looked somewhat out of place in the middle of the desert, where wood was scarce and the building material of choice—and necessity—was adobe. There were numerous outbuildings, including several bunkhouses, a smokehouse, a stable and barn, and several corrals and breaking pens. The place was bustling with activity. But everyone stopped what they were doing to watch the arrival of the soldiers. One person seemed particularly interested: a boy of about nine or ten years of age, with round cheeks and bright, inquisitive blue eyes and a shock of unruly yellow hair. He ran straight up to the column and, spotting Barlow, snapped off a salute.

"I'm Linus Ward," he announced. "Are you a general?"

Barlow had to laugh. "Not hardly. Just a lowly lieutenant."

"I bet you'll be a general someday. You just wait and see. That's what I'm going to be. A general."

Barlow extended his arm. "Hop on back," he sug-

gested. He didn't want the boy to be trampled by the
column of cavalrymen following along behind.

Eyes wide with excitement, Linus grabbed his arm
with both hands and allowed Barlow to swing him up
and astride the back of the saddle. In that way they
continued on to the main house, where a slender but
broad-shouldered man with graying hair stood watching. Barlow assumed this had to be John Ward. And
the young lady who stood behind and a little to one
side of him had to be Kathleen. Like her brother, she
had hair the color of cornsilk, and it gleamed in the
afternoon sun. The wind whipped her dress against
the willowy but shapely figure of a girl just now bud-
ding into womanhood. Barlow thought she was very
pretty, with delicate features set off by a stubborn jaw
and bold blue eyes.

Reaching the big house, Barlow swung the boy
down to the ground and then dismounted. Ward
stepped up to shake his hand.

"I'm John Ward," he said. "Thank you for coming,
Lieutenant. I suspect you will want to bivouac for the
night somewhere nearby. I'll make sure that your men
and horses are well fed. In the morning, when you set
out to catch the Apache vermin who are killing my
cattle, I will send along a man who can serve as
your guide."

"I appreciate the offer, sir, but I don't need a
guide."

"This man knows every inch of the country. He
knows the Apaches too. He's a half-breed. But I don't
hold that against him."

"No, thanks." The last thing Barlow thought he
needed was one of Ward's spies riding with him.

Ward shrugged. "If there's anything you do need, just let me know."

He started to turn away. There was no more to be said to Barlow, who was, after all, merely another hired hand there to do a job. That, at least, was the attitude Ward conveyed.

"I do have one question, Mr. Ward."

"Yes?"

"We'll catch the men who've been killing your cows. But what if it turns out not to be Cochise's people?"

Ward's eyes narrowed into flinty slits of gray as cold and hard as gun metal. "What makes you think it won't be?"

"Because Cochise wants peace, for one thing."

Ward scoffed. "An Apache wanting peace is like a fish wanting to live out of water. You know right off that there's something very wrong."

"I was present at the Chokonen village in the Mogollons when Cochise was prepared to sign the treaty."

"Was he now? Tell me, Lieutenant, did he sign that treaty?"

"Well, no. There was some trouble—"

"Trouble. There will *always* be some trouble around here as long as the Apaches are allowed to run loose."

He turned and went inside the big house, followed by several of his vaqueros. Linus was running up and down the column of horse soldiers lined up behind Barlow, while his sister lingered on the porch of the big house, watching Barlow with a soft smile. Barlow remembered the letter that Trotter had written. He walked up to the steps of the porch and, removing a leather gauntlet from his hand, reached under his tunic to produce the letter. It was dusty and stained with his sweat.

"This is for you, Miss Ward," he said. "Excuse its condition."

"For me?" She sounded delighted. But when she saw Trotter's name on the front of the envelope, she had to force the smile to remain on her full, soft lips. "Oh, yes. Lieutenant Trotter. How sweet of him to think of me. So tell me, Lieutenant . . . ?"

"Barlow. Joshua Barlow."

"Kathleen Ward. Tell me, Lieutenant Barlow—does Lieutenant Trotter speak of me often in your presence?"

"Well, we share the same quarters. It's difficult, under those circumstances, to keep a secret. But he managed to keep his acquaintance with you a secret until very recently. Now that I've met you, I can understand why."

"Oh," she said, breathlessly, "what a gallant thing to say, Lieutenant Barlow. Are you from the South?"

"Yes, I was born in Georgia."

"And yet you wear Union blue?"

"I am not a secessionist."

"Well, neither am I. I like to take a morning ride. Would you care to join me tomorrow?"

Barlow was startled. "Your father lets you take morning rides when, apparently, there are hostile Indians about?"

"I won't lie and say that he likes the idea. But he knows better than to try to stop me. Besides, I can take care of myself. I don't ask you to accompany me because I need protection. I just like to take any opportunity to have an intelligent conversation with someone. Such opportunities, around here, are . . . infrequent."

Barlow was intrigued—and had to remind himself that even while she acted quite mature, and she had an animal magnetism that was impossible to deny, Kathleen Ward was still barely more than a child. Trotter had told him that she was only sixteen. Of course, in the South, and especially on the frontier, where lives were generally short and one had to live fast if one wanted to experience much at all of life, sixteen years old was marrying age. Back in Georgia, Jennie Randolph had been nineteen, and some members of her family warned her of impending spinsterhood if she did not soon wed. Clearly, Kathleen Ward thought she was a woman, and whether the pressure was biological or otherwise really didn't matter. As far as Barlow was concerned, she was as dangerous as a dozen Apache bronchos. Maybe more dangerous.

"I'm afraid I can't, miss," he said, trying to sound genuinely regretful. "But I'll have my duties to attend to tomorrow."

"Then hurry up and kill those old Indians or whoever," she said, pouting, "and then when you come back you will ride with me."

She turned and went inside, and Barlow watched her toss Trotter's letter, unopened, to an elderly Mexican woman, probably a housemaid.

Having seen the whole thing, Eckhart, still mounted, urged his horse a little closer to where Barlow stood.

"It appears that Lieutenant Trotter is out and you're in, sir."

"You find that amusing, Sergeant?"

"Um, no, sir," lied Eckhart.

Barlow didn't find it amusing, and he wished that tomorrow morning was already here.

Barlow made sure that E Troop was in the saddle and on the move before first light, because he wanted

to put the Ward ranch house far behind him before
Kathleen awoke from a sleep filled with what Barlow
feared were dreams of him. The men had gone only
a few miles when a trooper in the rear sent word up to
the front of the column that they were being followed.
Barlow felt a stab of panic. Could it be Kathleen?
Had she pursued him? If so, he could only imagine
what the troopers would think. No doubt she would
cause a scene in front of his entire command of the
sort that he'd never be allowed to live down.

Brandishing his field glasses, he checked the lone
rider. At this distance all he could make out was that
the horseman was a man; he wore a bent stovepipe
hat and a plain brown pancho—and he wasn't actually
a horseman at all, since he was sitting astride a lanky
mule. Barlow handed the field glasses to Eckhart.

"What the hell is that, Sergeant?"

Eckhart took a long look. "Damned if I know, sir.
But he doesn't seem to be in a hurry to catch up with
us. So I guess he's not a messenger. And he's sure not
a wild Apache." He returned the field glasses to Barlow. "Want me to take a couple of men and find out
what he's up to?"

"No. Maybe it's just coincidence. Maybe he's just
traveling in the same direction that we are."

"Maybe," said Eckhart, with the dubious tone of
one who had long ago stopped believing in coin-
cidences.

They continued on, and the lone rider stayed behind
them. By midafternoon his presence was beginning to
wear on the nerves of E Troop's cavalrymen. Barlow
was about to change his mind—and send Eckhart back
to learn the man's business—when they happened
upon fresh tracks.

Sergeant Eckhart called up Yancey and Horton—
the two men who, by unanimous consent of all members of E Troop, were the best trackers in the bunch.
Barlow had learned that Eckhart himself was possessed of a certain skill in that regard. The three of
them took a long look at the tracks, then conferred
for a moment before Eckhart returned to Barlow to
give his report.

"They're definitely Indians," he said. "About fifteen
of them."

"Apache? Chokonen?"

Eckhart shrugged, squinting off to the west, against
the setting sun, in the direction of the not too distant
Mogollons. "Might be. They're headed into Chokonen country."

"But we don't know if they're the ones killing
Ward's cattle."

"No, sir." Eckhart could have said more—such as
it was likely, though, that this was the bunch they were
looking for. These were all bronchos, no women and
children among them, so they were out here for a
reason—either hunting or raiding or some other broncho enterprise. He didn't have to say all this because
he knew his lieutenant was a smart man who wasn't
given to deluding himself.

"How far ahead of us, do you think?" asked
Barlow.

"No more than a couple of hours, sir."

"Then we'll follow them. But first we have unfinished business to tend to. Sergeant, come with me,
please."

Eckhart mounted up, and accompanied Barlow.
They made for the lone rider, who had been shadowing them all day. When the man realized they were

coming, he stopped his mule and simply waited. Drawing closer, Barlow could see that the man was old—his face deeply creased by the years. He looked Indian, but he wore the clothes of the white man, and the stovepipe hat was the most congruous item of apparel. Across the saddle in front of him was a .50 caliber Remington Rollingblock rifle—a long gun preferred by buffalo hunters, or so Barlow was given to understand, because they were extremely accurate and had a lot of stopping power over distance.

"I just want to know two things," said Barlow. "Who are you? And why are you following us?"

"They call me Short Britches. I am following you because John Ward told me to."

"Why does he want you to follow us?"

"To make sure you look in the right place for the ones who have been killing his stock."

"You're the one he mentioned yesterday. The one he said he wanted to send along with us."

Short Britches nodded. "You wouldn't have any tobacco on you, would you?"

"No," said Barlow. "Now why don't you go back to Mr. Ward and tell him we appreciate the offer, but we'll handle this?"

"John Ward said you would try to send me back. He said I was not to come back even if you tried to send me. He said I was to keep an eye on you, just to make sure you found the ones who are killing his cattle."

"You're a scout, then," said Eckhart.

Short Britches nodded. "It is what I do. What John Ward pays me to do. I ride all over the place, keeping my eyes open. That way I always know what's going on."

"Really," said Barlow. "And how long have you known about this cattle-killing business."

"From the very beginning."

"Then you must know who's doing it."

"Apaches."

"You know where to find them?"

Short Britches gestured toward the mountains. "They hide in the mountains of the Mogollon."

"You know so much," said Eckhart suspiciously, "then how come you can't stop them from killing all these cattle."

"I told the padrone that I could take twenty men into the mountains and probably kill the Apaches who are killing his cattle. But I also told him that only about half his men would come back alive. Maybe less. I also told him that I could track them down by myself, and probably kill two or three, maybe even four or five, with this Big Fifty." He patted the buffalo gun. "But then they would kill me. So the padrone made up his mind to bring in the army."

Barlow glanced at Eckhart. "I guess he doesn't care if half of us get killed," he said dryly.

"Guess not," said the sergeant. "And frankly, I don't much care if we ever find the ones who have been killing the cattle. But then I guess that's what this feller is really doing here. He's spying on us. So he can go back and tell his padrone if we're doing our job or not."

"I will ride with you," said Short Britches. "I can help you find the ones you seek."

"Like I told your boss, I don't need your help," said Barlow. "Thanks just the same. You can go back and tell Ward that I have my orders and I'll carry them out, which means I'll get the men who've been killing his stock."

"I cannot go back until the job is done," said Short Britches.

"Suit yourself," said Barlow. His first impression of the old scout was a negative one. Short Britches didn't strike him as a man who could be trusted very far. "But you're not riding with us. So just stay out of sight. You make my men nervous."

Short Britches didn't appear to be offended. He merely shrugged, and his expression didn't change one bit. "Well," he said, "I hope you find them in a hurry. Because I am out of tobacco, and I need to go pay a visit to the trader on Pronghorn Creek and buy some more."

Chapter 6

They followed the tracks, and when the day came to a close, they found themselves deep within the foothills of the Mogollon Mountains. Barlow figured that by this time the Apaches were probably aware that they were being followed. They would be on the alert—after all, they were killing the cattle of the Pinda Lickoyi. They were on a raid, and expected to be pursued. One or two bronchos, Eckhart said, would be left behind to watch for any sign of pursuit, and when they saw something they would rush back to the main group with the news. And even though Barlow traveled with two men on point and two on each flank, it was unlikely that any of them would see the Apache scouts. The question wasn't really whether they could follow the Apaches without being seen. The real question was what the Apaches would do about it. Would they try to outrun their pursuers? Would they split up into smaller groups and try to elude the yellowleg soldiers that way? Or would they turn and fight? If the latter was their choice, Eckhart reminded his lieutenant that their most likely tactic was ambush.

Barlow doubled the guard on the night camp. Eckhart assured him that, in his experience, which was considerable, Indians did not like to fight at night. They reckoned, said the sergeant, that if they died their spirits might be lost in the darkness. Unable to find their way to the happy hunting ground, they would be doomed to wander forever in limbo. Barlow didn't think he should put much faith in that particular frontier absolute. He doubted that Apaches were quite so predictable as all that.

The night passed without incident, or so Barlow thought as he hunkered down next to a morning cook fire and took his first sip of coffee, "crank" made the army way, which was strong enough to float a horseshoe. He didn't get a second sip. Eckhart came running up to him. The noncom looked alarmed. And Barlow knew Eckhart well enough to know that when the sergeant looked alarmed there was ample reason for everyone else to worry.

"What is it, Sergeant?"

Eckhart glanced at the three cavalrymen who were also hunkered down around the fire, and Barlow understood that the sergeant did not care to convey his news in front of the rank and file, which meant the news had to be very bad indeed. Barlow turned and walked far enough to be out of earshot of the troopers, who, of course, were watching him and the sergeant, well aware that the only reason they weren't going to be allowed to overhear what was about to be said was because it meant an ill wind was blowing their way.

"One of the night sentries is missing, Lieutenant," said Eckhart.

Barlow stared at him. "What do you mean, missing?"

"It's Hanrady, sir. He was at his post at four o'clock—I saw him when I made my rounds. Two hours later he was gone."

"Yes, I understand that he's gone. But gone where?"

"I fetched Yancey over to take a look around. He found sign. Footprints. Two or more Indians. Apaches, according to Yancey, who can tell such things by the way their moccasins are sewn."

Barlow was stunned. A pair of Apaches had snuck up on one of his sentries, caught the man completely by surprise, overpowered him without making a sound, and then dragged him off into the darkness, with no one the wiser. He could scarcely believe it.

"But why?" he wondered aloud. "Why would they go to the trouble of kidnapping one of our guards."

Eckhart shrugged. "To show they can do it, maybe. To unnerve the men."

"Will it?"

Suddenly, Barlow had visions of mass desertions by the men under his command. That sort of thing would put an end to his career just about as effectively as anything else he could imagine.

"I doubt it," said Eckhart. "These are good men, sir, for the most part. More than half have seen action before, and as for the green recruits, well, they've got plenty of backbone too."

"There are a couple of other possibilities," said Barlow, grimly, "as to why they took one of our men, that is."

Eckhart nodded. "Yes, sir. I believe I know what

you're thinking, Lieutenant. They could try to draw us off from the main bunch by getting us to chase after the ones who took Hanrady."

"Or they could use him for bait."

"So what you want to do, Lieutenant?"

"We stick to their sign. But I want Yancey and Horton and a half dozen of the most experienced men to ride ahead. If the Apaches are aiming to set a trap, then they'll have a chance of seeing it before it's sprung."

"Yes, sir. Permission to lead the detail, sir."

Barlow hesitated. It was a dangerous duty, and he was loath to lose Eckhart, but, on the other hand, the detail's chances of survival would be considerably enhanced with the sergeant leading them.

"All right," he said. Fishing a timepiece out of his tunic, he said, "I've got a few minutes to six."

Eckhart produced an old stemwinder. "I've a few minutes past."

"We'll set them both to six, straight up. At the top of and the bottom of each hour I want you to fire two shots. If you don't hear two answering shots, come back. It'll mean you've gotten too far ahead. If I don't hear two shots from you, I'll bring the rest of the troop in a hurry. It's not like we have to worry any more about the Apaches finding out we're here. Looks like they already know."

"I reckon they knew a long time ago," said Eckhart.

"Good luck, Sergeant. Stay above snakes. That's an order."

The noncom grinned. "I'll do my best, Lieutenant."

They had proceeded only a few miles when Barlow heard gunfire from somewhere up ahead. Not just one or two shots, but a flurry—and he knew that Eckhart's patrol was in trouble. He led the rest of E Troop forward at double-quick time, aware that he might be leading his men into an ambush, but equally as aware that he had no alternative. Every institution had its own code of conduct, its rules of behavior. The United States cavalry was no exception. And one of those rules was that you rode to the sound of the guns because it meant that your comrades were engaged with the enemy, and possibly in great peril. The rule wasn't written down in any book, but that didn't make it any less of an ironclad imperative.

The path they took, a dry riverbed confined by steep, rocky slopes, took them deeper and deeper into the foothills. It twisted this way and that, so they could seldom see more than a stone's throw ahead or behind them. Coming around one of the bends, they spotted two riderless cavalry mounts galloping toward them. Barlow shouted an order over his shoulder, instructing someone to catch the horses, and then spurred his own mount to greater exertion. Now there was no question in his mind. Eckhart and his detail had walked straight into trouble. But the gunfire continued—that meant there was still hope. They were still alive.

Coming around another bend, Barlow found himself confronted by a reasonably straight and narrow canyon about three hundred yards in length. At the far end the dry riverbed twisted abruptly to the right. In the middle of the canyon floor lay two dead troopers and one dead cavalry mount. A couple more cavalry horses were standing riderless. Barlow spotted Eckhart crouched behind a rock not far from where the dead cavalrymen lay. The sergeant was shouting at

him, but Barlow couldn't make out the noncom's
words above the din of battle. Unseen men—Apache
bronchos, no doubt—were shooting down from the
canyon slopes, hidden behind the rocks on both sides.
They had Eckhart and his men pinned down in the
scant cover along the canyon bottom. And now,
thought Barlow, as he heard the loud crackling of bullets passing close by his head, the Apaches had his
whole command caught in a deadly cross fire. He
looked behind him, to see several saddles already
emptied. The rest of the troopers were trying to return fire from horseback—a response Barlow considered to be an exercise in futility. He had a choice—
he could lead his men back out of the canyon now,
or he could get them off their horses and behind the
rocks with Eckhart and what was left of the detail.
Once again, though, he realized it wasn't really much
of a choice. He couldn't abandon the sergeant and
his men.

"Dismount!" he roared. "Every third man holds
horses! The rest find cover and fire at will!"

E Troop responded. This was where the drill paid
off—all those hours of mind-numbing repetition on
the Fort Union parade ground that the soldiers (and
the officers) had groused about. The cavalrymen
grabbed their carbines and pistols and ammunition
pouches and ran for cover, while every third man took
charge of his horse and two others. Dismounting, Barlow ordered the horse handlers to take the mounts
back around the bend; he wasn't sure if the Apaches
were doing so on purpose, but they had already
brought down two of the animals. If they wanted to
ensure that their intended victims could not escape

the trap that had been set, then killing the horses made perfect sense.

Bullets kicking up dust around his feet, Barlow ran for Eckhart's position. He wedged himself into a space between two slabs of rock that was barely large enough to accommodate Eckhart by himself.

"Damn it, Lieutenant," said Eckhart, "you should have turned right around and hightailed it out of here."

"Is that what you would have done, Sergeant, in my place?" Barlow fired at a puff of gunsmoke on the northern slope of the canyon, while Eckhart cut loose with his carbine on a target on the southern slope.

"Damn right, sir."

"For a sergeant in the United States cavalry, you're a poor liar."

"Thank you, sir. Damn!"

They both hunkered down as a hail of bullets ricocheted off the rocks that sheltered them.

"Still say there're fifteen of them, Sergeant?" They had followed the tracks of fifteen unshod horses, but the men they'd been following could have been joined by others.

"Maybe a few less than fifteen now, sir," replied Eckhart with grim satisfaction.

"At least we've got them outnumbered," said Barlow dryly.

"Yes, sir. But not for long."

Barlow took a quick look around. Up and down the canyon, his troopers were returning fire, but several more had already fallen. The Apaches didn't need superior numbers—they had all the other advantages stacked in their favor.

"What the hell happened here, Sergeant?"

Eckhart nodded. He knew what Barlow was really asking. How had he allowed himself to be caught in this predicament? The canyon was a prime ambush site, and a man of his considerable experience should have known that—and should have avoided it.

"Hanrady," said Eckhart grimly. "He's still alive. Kind of." He glanced bleakly at Barlow. "They got him staked out at the far end of the canyon. Horton was riding point. He saw Hanrady first, called back to us, and I ordered him not to advance. But he did anyway. In his defense, Lieutenant, I'll just say that he and Hanrady have been friends for a long time."

Barlow nodded. He didn't need Eckhart to tell him the rest. Horton had gone in to save Hanrady, and Eckhart and the rest of the patrol had come in turn to save Horton. And now he had brought the entire troop into the ambush to save those who had come before. To have criticized Eckhart, under the circumstances, would have been the height of hypocrisy.

He had to hand it to the Apaches. They were smart. Diabolically clever. They'd not only found a way to negate his superior numbers, but had a better than fair chance now of wiping out his entire command.

Looking again at his men, scattered along the canyon bottom, some dead, some dying, the rest bravely standing their ground and fighting ferociously, Barlow made up his mind that, somehow, he would get them out of the trap that he'd led them into.

He scanned the slopes. He hadn't yet seen a single Apache. All he'd seen of this enemy was tracks. The tracks made by fifteen horses. So he had to assume that there were at least fifteen of them up there in those rocks, some on the northern slope, some on the southern. If there were *only* fifteen, and they were equally divided . . .

"Sergeant," he said, "we're going to attack the enemy on . . . this side." He gestured at the northern slope.

"Say what?"

"You heard me. I'll lead. You make sure the men follow."

"Lieutenant . . ."

Barlow wasn't listening. He didn't need to hear the sergeant's mother-hen routine. Extricating himself from between the slabs of rock, he stood up and shouted at the top of his lungs, hoping at least some of his men would hear him over the din of battle. Then he turned and began climbing the northern slope, hoping that those who hadn't heard him would see him. Eckhart was right behind him, his stentorian voice rising above the gunfire. Barlow looked back once—and was relieved to see that the troopers still standing were swarming up the northern slope both to the left and to the right of him. Confronted by this rising tide of bluecoat soldiers, several of the Apaches broke cover. One rose up from the rocks almost directly in front of Barlow, who fired his pistol at point-blank range, even as the broncho triggered his carbine. Barlow watched the Apache fall—then checked himself in disbelief. He was unharmed. He picked up the dead broncho's carbine and kept climbing. A bullet slammed into the carbine's stock, shattering it and knocking the weapon from his grasp. He felt a pain in his thigh, and stumbled. Eckhart was there immediately, searching for the wound.

"Help me up, damn it," said Barlow through clenched teeth. His men were charging up the slope, exposing themselves to the fire of both the Apaches on the slope above them and those positioned on the southern slope—and they were doing it because he'd told them to, because he was leading the way. He feared that if he fell, they would falter, and all would be lost. Ignoring the pain in his leg, he hooked his left arm around Eckhart's shoulders. The sergeant shifted his pistol from right hand to left, and hooked his right arm around Barlow's waist. In that way they continued, slowly, clumsily, up through the rocks, both continuing to fire as the bronchos, darting from boulder to boulder, slowly withdrew in the face of the cavalry onslaught.

Then Eckhart was hit, high in the shoulder, and the impact of the bullet spun him around, knocking them both off balance. In the same instant Barlow glimpsed a broncho rising up from the rocks to his right, not ten feet away, but instinctively he had tried to grab Eckhart and prevent the sergeant from falling, and the sergeant's weight was turning him away from the broncho, and he couldn't bring his pistol to bear in time. He heard a boom, akin to the report of a cannon, and quite distinct from the crack of pistol or carbine. Something picked the Apache up off his feet and hurled him a dozen feet downslope. His lifeless body bounced off a rock and slid out of Barlow's view. Barlow looked up at the rimrock above him and saw the silhouette of a man that was immediately recognizable thanks to the bent stovepipe hat.

It was Short Britches. He was on the move, running along the rim from east to west. He stopped suddenly, raised the .50 caliber Rollingblock to shoulder, and fired. The Apaches on the slope, aware that an enemy was behind them, were showing themselves now, some firing at Short Britches, others moving laterally along the slope, trying to escape the cross fire. Thus exposed, they began to fall prey to the old scout's buffalo gun and the carbines of the cavalrymen.

Sensing that the tide was beginning to turn, Barlow shouted at his men to concentrate their fire on the southern slope. After a few moments of intense firing, the Apaches across the canyon began to fade away. And just like that, it was over, and Barlow could indulge in a moment of amazement. But only for a moment—then he was kneeling at Eckhart's side, checking the wound in the sergeant's shoulder. The bullet had passed clean through. Eckhart insisted that he was fine, and struggled to his feet to prove it. Barlow sat down on a rock and checked his thigh. The wound had been caused by a large splinter of wood from the carbine's shattered stock. He gripped the end of the splinter firmly between thumb and forefinger, grit his teeth, and gave the splinter a sharp tug. A gasp escaped him as the splinter came free. He tossed it aside in disgust, and sat there for a while, watching his men as they scoured the slopes for dead or dying Apaches. The troopers in charge of the horses reappeared in the canyon bottom. Eckhart made his way to the bottom of the canyon. And Short Britches came down from the rimrock, approaching Barlow, who only became aware of the old scout when the latter's shadow passed over him. Short Britches took a look at Barlow's blood-soaked trouser leg; setting the Big Fifty down, he removed his neckerchief and used it to bind the wound and stop the bleeding.

"These Apaches," he said as he worked, "they aren't Chokonen. They're Mescalero."

Barlow stared at him. "Are you sure?"

Short Britches just glanced at him, and said nothing. *A stupid question,* thought Barlow. *Of course he's sure.*

"They were done killing John Ward's cattle," continued Short Britches. "They had all the meat they could carry, and were heading home. Winter is coming. And it will be a long, hard winter. Their women and children will go hungry."

"Sorry," said Barlow. "They might have gotten away with it, except they took one of my men. They staked him out, down there, and used him as bait."

"Yes, I know," said the old scout. "And they tortured him. That's the Apache way. White men say it is because the Apache is cruel. But the Apache tests the courage of his enemy, and he honors the man who is brave."

"Is that before or after they kill him."

Short Britches stood and picked up his Big Fifty. "There is no saving the man who was taken. He will die before the sun sets. Someone should go down there now, and kill him, so that he suffers no more. I will do it for you."

"No," rasped Barlow. He was grateful to the old scout—the appearance of Short Britches on the rimrock had turned the tables on the Apaches. But the man had the smell of death strong upon him; he was a cold-blooded killer, and Barlow didn't want him anywhere near Hanrady. "No, that's one of my men down there. I'm responsible for him."

Short Britches gave him a long, speculative look, and Barlow knew why; the old scout doubted that he had the stomach to do what needed to be done.

Without another word, Barlow got to his feet and made his way down the slope to the canyon bottom. Eckhart and two other men had already ventured to the end of the canyon, where Hanrady was located. Now they were coming back, and as Barlow watched them, he saw that one of the men was violently sick, doubling over several times to vomit. As Barlow drew near, Eckhart looked up at him, and it surprised Barlow to see the sergeant so visibly shaken; he hadn't imagined that anything could rattle the grizzled veteran. But he'd been wrong. Ashen-faced, Eckhart looked at Barlow and shook his head.

"I wouldn't go any closer, Lieutenant," he advised.

"Well, is he alive or not?"

"I'm . . . I'm not sure."

That angered Barlow. "So what do you suggest, Sergeant? Should we just leave him for the buzzards?"

He didn't wait for an answer, but walked on.

Hanrady had been stripped naked and spreadeagled on the hot sand of the canyon floor, wrists and ankles lashed with rawhide thongs to stakes driven into the ground. Deep gashes had been cut into his thighs from knee to groin. Much of the skin had been peeled away from his chest and along the rib cage. His face was a bloody mess, so mutilated that Barlow would not have been able to identify the body if he hadn't already known who it was. Barlow pulled up twenty paces away, horrified by what he beheld, and thinking— hoping—that Hanrady was dead. But that wasn't the case. A leg twitched, then the head moved, and the mouth opened, and the trooper made an incoherent sound. His tongue had been cut out. Barlow's stomach did a slow roll. Bile rose in his throat. His hand trembling, he raised his pistol and fired. And fired once more, just to be sure. Only then did he give in to the powerful urge to throw up. He puked until there was nothing left in his stomach to expel. Then

came the dry heaves. Finally, he wiped his mouth with
the sleeve of his tunic, turned his back on what had
once been a human being named Hanrady, and
headed back up the canyon.

Chapter 7

When Goyathlay arrived at the Chokonen village in the Mogollon Mountains, he was accompanied by a handful of bronchos. Among them was Kiannatah. They were all Bedonkohe, and they were heavily armed. The Chokonen people were wary. Why had these men appeared among them? Had Mangas Colorado, the leader of the Bedonkohe, sent them? Many of the Chokonen knew Goyathlay by reputation. He was Netdahe—an Avowed Killer—a man who had for years made war upon the Nakai-Ye, seeking revenge for the murder of his family. He was a ruthless and cunning warrior, and it was said that he was possessed of strong medicine, that he had visions of what the future held in store, not only for himself, but for all The People, and that he even had the power to stop the wind, and had once even stopped the sun in its path across the sky. It had to be assumed that the men who rode with him were also Avowed Killers. They certainly looked the part. But as to their purpose for coming to the Chokonen che-wa-ki, Goyathlay made it clear that he would provide the answer only to Cochise.

Cochise welcomed Goyathlay into his cowah. They had been comrades-in-arms, had fought together in Mexico, and while Cochise did not think of Goyathlay as a friend and, in fact, was leery of the man, he was as curious as anyone else to know the intentions of the Netdahe.

When Goyathlay sat down across the fire that provided the cowah with warmth against the chill carried by the winter winds that howled around the rugged Mogollon peaks, the bronchos who rode with him sat arrayed behind him. With Cochise sat Nana and Nachita. The wife and daughter of the Chokonen jefe provided the men with meat and bread and tiswin. Kiannatah was struck by the beauty of the daughter of Cochise. There was something about the way she moved that mesmerized him, a kind of sublimity so alien to the realities of the life he led that he wondered if he might be dreaming. Shyly aware of his inordinate attention, she smiled slightly as she placed the food and drink before him. It was the smile most of all that pierced the hard shell around Kiannatah's fierce heart.

He had never seriously contemplated attempting to lead a normal life—to find a woman and to sire children. When loneliness stalked him, as it stalked everyone at one time or another, he would bring the terrible, bloody visions of the massacre at Dolorosa to mind, and this would suffice to remind him that he had been spared the fate that had befallen the rest of his family because his life was meant to be devoted to a special mission. He had been forged by the events at Dolorosa into an avenger for all the wrongs done to The People. A warrior on such a crusade had no time for a normal life. A wife and children would be distractions. Worse, they might become liabilities. He lived to kill, and lived too with the knowledge that because he was an Avowed Killer, his life would be short and brutal. The hatred that seared his heart, hatred for the Nakai-Ye in particular, dispelled the loneliness whenever it stalked him.

But now, in the presence of Oulay, daughter of Cochise (though he did not, at the time, know her name), mustering up the old horrors could not shield him from her allure. The loneliness, stymied for so many years, welled up in him so overwhelmingly that he felt his eyes burn with tears. Kiannatah could not believe what was happening to him. He had not wept since that night after the massacre, when he hid, in the darkness, all alone with the knowledge that those he loved lay dead, slaughtered by the Nakai-Ye. He turned his face away from the other men in the cowah, for fear that they might see the emotion etched upon it. Then he chanced to look up at Oulay. She now sat in the back of the cowah, at the edge of the firelight, her duties performed. But she was watching him, and *she* could see that he was deeply moved, and she looked puzzled, even somewhat alarmed, for an Apache broncho—especially a Netdahe warrior—was not expected to show emotion, and she didn't know what to make of Kiannatah now.

Having partaken of the food and the tiswin provided by his host, Goyathlay was speaking to Cochise.

"We have been with Mangas Colorado this past moon," explained Goyathlay, "and while we were there, we heard that Cochise was talking peace with the White Eyes. I have come to find out for myself whether this is true and, if it is, to beg Cochise to reconsider."

"Does Mangas know you have come?" asked
Cochise.

"No. I have come here on my own. But I can tell
you that Mangas, who considers you his good friend,
could not believe, at first, that the news was true. He
himself told me that Cochise would never sign a treaty
paper if it meant giving up one foot of Apache land
to the Pinda Lickoyi. We reminisced, Mangas and I,
about the days when the three of us warred against
the Nakai-Ye, and we both remembered Cochise as
the greatest and most ruthless of warriors. A man who
showed no mercy to the enemies of the Chi-hinne.
That Cochise, we decided, would never sign such a
paper."

"I did not sign a treaty paper," said Cochise coldly.

"I am relieved," said Goyathlay, smiling. "And I
know Mangas will be too."

"But I may still sign one," continued Cochise. "I
was willing to talk to the Pinda Lickoyi, but the
yellow-leg soldiers were attacked, and since we did
not know why, or by whom, I led my people away
from this place, up onto the Rim. But if the Pinda
Lickoyi again ask to talk with me, I will listen to what
they have to say. There is no harm in that."

"If the Chokonen agree to a treaty of peace with
the White Eyes, then they will expect all the other
bands to do the same. And when they refuse, the
White Eyes will see that as an act of war."

It was Cochise who was smiling now—a humorless
smile. "Isn't that what you want? No. If you truly
believed what you've just said, Goyathlay, you would
not be here, asking me not to sign a treaty paper.
What you fear is that if I do agree to live in peace
with the Pinda Lickoyi, then perhaps Mangas and oth-

ers will decide to do the same. Then what would the Netdahe do? The day would come when Mangas would turn them away, and they would be outcasts among their own kind."

Goyathlay was silent for a moment, and the Net-dahe bronchos who sat cross-legged behind him watched him intently, because Cochise had, in effect, called him a liar, and they weren't sure how their leader would react. Goyathlay, though, was a man of tremendous self-control, and he revealed not a trace of anger in voice or expression.

"Cochise was once a great warrior," he said, solemnly. "Even now he must realize that this is the time to strike the White Eyes, when they are few in number. Every day we wait brings more of them into Apacheria. Soon they will be as many as the grains of sand in the desert. When that time comes we will have no hope of defeating them. But if we strike now, they may think the price they would have to pay in blood to take our land away from us was too high. This is especially true at this moment, when they are fighting a great war among themselves."

Cochise shook his head. He had heard this same argument from some Chokonen bronchos—among them Nana, who sat beside him. But his vision was broader than theirs, and truer.

"I have heard what has happened to the Lipan and the Kiowa and the Pawnee when they tried to stand against the White Eyes. Now the few that are left have no home. For every Pinda Lickoyi they killed, ten more came to take his place. The Chi-hinne are few in number to begin with. If many of our young warriors die in a hopeless war, then The People will soon be no more. No. It is better to accept the truth, no matter how bitter it may be, and do whatever is necessary to ensure the survival of our people."

Kiannatah heard all of this. Under ordinary circumstances, he would, by now, have been incensed by what Cochise had said. But he didn't care. His attention was riveted upon Oulay, as he longed for what she represented: serenity, softness, warmth, love—all those things that had been absent from his life. He realized then that he needed her the way a man dying of thirst needs water. She could be his refuge. She was the dream that could banish his nightmares.

But suddenly Goyathlay was on his feet, and Kiannatah knew that the talking was almost over, and that Goyathlay and Cochise would part company as enemies rather than friends—and for the first time he resented Goyathlay, and his relentless pursuit of blood vengeance, because now it was interfering with his dream, and worse still, it might make realizing that dream an impossibility. He even entertained, briefly, the notion of driving the blade of his knife into Goyathlay's heart, after which he could present himself to Cochise as a man who had disposed of the greatest single threat to peace with the Pinda Lickoyi and, perhaps, ingratiate himself upon the leader of the Chokonen to such an extent that Cochise would favor his courtship of his daughter.

Kiannatah squeezed his eyes shut. This was madness. His anger, irrational and blind, swung madly from Goyathlay to Cochise and then to Oulay and finally upon himself. How was it that this nahlin had such power over him that he would even consider slaying his mentor, Goyathlay? What magic did she possess that just the sight of her could make him forget that the purpose of his life was to kill the enemies of the Chi-hinne. Nothing else gave meaning to the terrible loss that he had suffered in Dolorosa. He forced himself to turn his gaze away from Oulay. Forced himself to stand, dutifully, along with the other Netdahe bronchos, behind Goyathlay.

"You think you can buy time for our people by laying down your rifles and giving up our land," Goyathlay told Cochise, with more than a trace of contempt in his voice. "Maybe you are right. But what good is life if it is without honor? If we do as you say, we will shame ourselves, and the White Eyes, seeing that we are without honor, will have no respect for us, and will treat us like dogs."

He started for the cowah entrance, paused, then turned back to Cochise.

"I believe that any Apache who will not fight to keep what is rightfully his *should* be treated like a dog."

Nana shot to his feet. While he agreed with much of what Goyathlay said, he was still Chokonen, and as such was fiercely loyal to Cochise, and he was not one to stand by and allow any person—even the Netdahe leader—to speak to his jefe in that manner. But Cochise touched Nana's arm, and the Chokonen broncho made no move against Goyathlay, but rather stood there, fists clenched, glaring at the Avowed Killers.

Goyathlay led his Netdahe out of Cochise's cowah. Many of the Chokonen had lingered in the vicinity, curious to know why the Avowed Killers had come calling. They could not discern much from the expressions on the faces of Goyathlay and his bronchos, but Cochise, Nana, and Nachita followed them out, and the people knew their leader, and could tell how the

talks had gone by the look on Cochise's face. They
were silent and watchful as the Netdahe mounted up
and, without another word, left the che-wa-ki. Only
Kiannatah looked back, hoping to see Oulay one more
time. But she had not come out of the cowah. Every
step his horse took seemed to increase the unique anguish in his heart—a feeling he had never experienced
before, and he knew that he would not be able to rid
himself of that pain until he had made Oulay his own.

That night, in their camp in the foothills of the Mogollons, Goyathlay told his Netdahe bronchos of his
intentions. They would ride south, and conduct raids
against the Butterfield stage route. The waystations—
and the coaches that traveled between them—would
be easy pickings. They would pursue this course of
action until the United States Army responded by
sending detachments to protect the stage route. After
that, they would seek temporary sanctuary south of
the border, in the Cima Silkq.

Kiannatah listened to Goyathlay's plan, and knew
that it made perfect sense—the stage route was the
most vulnerable target available to them, and Goyathlay wanted to keep the White Eyes stirred up against
the Apaches so they would not *wish* to make peace
with the likes of Cochise. But he didn't like the plan
because it would take him far from the Mogollons,
and even though he was no longer welcome in the
Chokonen village, and could not, therefore, simply
ride in to see Oulay when he wanted to, he nonetheless wanted to remain as close as possible to her. It
wasn't logical. From a practical standpoint, it would
avail him nothing. But the farther away from her he
traveled, the more acute would be the anguish in his
heart. Still, he resolved to ride south with Goyathlay.

He was, after all, Netdahe, and his life's purpose was to fight the enemies of the Chi-hinne. Even when his heart was no longer in it.

Having sent Short Britches back to the Ward ranch with word of the fight in the canyon, and relying on the old scout to inform the cattleman that it had been Mescalero Apaches, not Cochise and his Chokonen, who had been responsible for the slaughtering of his beeves, Barlow took E Troop back to Fort Union. Their losses had been heavy—eight men killed, a dozen wounded. But it could have been worse—much worse. And they had accomplished the mission Colonel Lyman had assigned to them. Short Britches had been certain that the Mescaleros who had survived would go home, and Barlow was quite willing to accept that assessment. He could have delivered the good news to John Ward personally. But he wanted to avoid the rancher—not to mention the rancher's amorous daughter. Ward might well have treated him and his troopers as heroes, but Barlow didn't feel like celebrating, not with eight corpses draped over horses at the end of the E Troop column.

On the day he arrived back at the fort, the first snow of winter fell. The low gray sky and the chill that reached into a man's bones suited his mood. Even a rare "well done" from Colonel Lyman didn't cheer him up. For the first time he had led his men into battle, and even though Lyman's report to the military district headquarters described the conflict as a great victory over the Apaches, Barlow wasn't feeling victorious, particularly on the day that nine men—one of the wounded had died—were buried in the post cemetery.

In the weeks to come, word arrived that Apaches were attacking the stagecoaches of the Butterfield Company. The attacks were made all along the line, in no particular pattern. The military district ordered the commandants of three posts, including Fort Union, to deploy troops to protect three segments of the line. Barlow was relieved when Lyman picked Hammond and Summerhayes to take their troops south and perform this duty.

And then, six weeks after his return to the fort, Barlow was officer of the day when a familiar face showed up at the gate. It was Jonathan Grenville, the Indian agent. He greeted Barlow warmly, and then, pitching his voice low, in a conspiratorial whisper, informed the lieutenant that he was back to try once more to make peace with Cochise.

A short while later, Major Addicks informed Barlow that the colonel wanted to see him.

"You know Mr. Grenville," said Lyman, when Barlow arrived at his office. "Apparently, Washington wants him to make another attempt at negotiating a treaty with the Chokonen. I want you, Lieutenant, and your men to provide escort to the Mogollons for Mr. Grenville. And this time, make sure there are no interruptions in the negotiating process, if you please."

"Yes, sir."

"I will give you Sergeant Farrow. Of the few men here who know the Apache tongue, he is the most fluent."

"Yes, sir. May I ask—is Cochise expecting us?"

Lyman glanced at Grenville, who was sitting in one of the chairs facing the colonel's desk, savoring one of Lyman's cigars. "Yes, he is," said the Indian agent. "In fact, this is his idea."

"You succeeded admirably, Lieutenant, in resolving the problem John Ward was having with the Apaches," said Lyman. "I expect you to succeed in this endeavor as well. Is that clear?"

Barlow said that it was.

Chapter 8

When Barlow arrived at the Chokonen village with Jonathan Grenville, Sergeant Farrow, and E Troop, the first thing he did was to have his men search the woods that had concealed the ambushers on his previous visit. Then he set out pickets, and told Sergeant Eckhart, fully recovered from his wound and back in the saddle, to bivouac the troop in the clearing west of the Apache village. He informed the sergeant that only he, Grenville, and Farrow would enter the Chokonen village. In addition, he instructed Eckhart that no other soldiers were to enter the village unless it was clear that he, Grenville, and Farrow were in mortal danger. The situation didn't suit Eckhart. Like the rest of the E Troop veterans he could sense that tension was running high among the Apaches. Heavily armed bronchos had begun shadowing the column miles away from the village. That wasn't a good sign.

Barlow could sense the danger too. But he was putting his faith in Cochise. The rest of the Chokonen might view the arrival of the yellow-leg soldiers with apprehension and even hostility. He figured that was due to the worsening situation among the Apaches and the whites caused primarily by the troublemakers who were wreaking havoc on the Butterfield stage route. And there was the possibility that the Chokonen had heard of E Troop's clash with the Mescaleros who had been killing John Ward's cattle. Still, Cochise had expressed a desire for negotiations, so Barlow was committed to treating that as an invitation.

When he and Grenville and Sergeant Farrow entered the che-wa-ki, they were greeted immediately by Cochise himself, who personally escorted them to a cowah, which, through Farrow, he announced would be theirs for the duration of their stay. He would return later, at which time they would begin to talk of peace between their peoples. Until then, he bid them partake of the food provided by his daughter, Oulay, and several other nahlins.

With that, Cochise left them. Barlow was impatient. He declined the food offered to him by the Apache maidens. Grenville, on the other hand, seemed resigned to waiting for as long as it took to begin the negotiations. And Farrow seemed quite relaxed, smiling and flirting with the Apache girls, who laughed and shyly averted their eyes.

"You might as well relax, sir," Farrow said. "This could take a while."

"He's right, Lieutenant," concurred Grenville. "I've dealt with a number of Indian tribes, and it almost always starts out this way. Cochise just wants to establish that he's in charge of this business, so he'll keep us waiting for a while. All we can do if we want to accomplish anything here is to play by his rules."

"Fine," said Barlow. Concerned lest Grenville and Farrow think he had succumbed to a bad case of nerves, he sat cross-legged beside the fire that crackled

warmly in the center of the cowah. The Apache maidens had retired to the back of the lodge, but as Barlow
sat down, one of them rose and brought him a bowl
that contained a fragrant paste. He had no idea what
the paste consisted of, but Farrow was downing it with
relish, using his fingers to dip it out of a bowl placed
in front of him, and shoveling it into his mouth. But
Barlow had no appetite, and once more he declined.
The Apache girl silently joined her companions. But
her gaze remained fixed on Barlow. He began to feel
self-conscious under such intense scrutiny. Farrow
chuckled.

"I think that one's taken a shine to you, sir," remarked the noncom.

"What?" Barlow was taken aback.

Farrow nodded. "Yep. It's pretty clear. Apache
women don't play games, the way white women do.
A white woman might pay you no attention at all,
even if she cottons to you. But there's no guesswork
with an Apache woman."

Barlow peered more closely at Oulay, and realized
just how beautiful she was. Her features were far more
aquiline than those of most other Apache women. She
was taller than most, and willowy in bend. Most
intriguing of all her attributes, he thought, were her
eyes. They were wise beyond her years, and it was a
wisdom that allowed her to contemplate the world
around her, with all its troubles and all its ugliness,
with a serenity that usually came to a person only in
the passage of many years. Fascinated, Barlow continued to look at her and suddenly, the tables turned,
Oulay was the one who felt self-conscious.

"That's Cochise's daughter, by the way," said Farrow. "I think he said her name was Oulay."

A short while later, Cochise returned, accompanied by Nana and Nachita. Upon his arrival, Oulay and the other nahlins departed the cowah. Barlow was sorry to see her go.

Cochise opened the discussion by telling them what Barlow already knew—that although only a couple of months had passed since they had last attempted to negotiate a treaty of peace, it would be much more difficult now to convince his people that it was the best course of action. Many of his warriors—Nana among them—thought war was the better option. Cochise placed much of the blame on the Netdahe, the Avowed Killers, led by Goyathlay, the one also known as Geronimo. It was the Netdahe who were attacking the stagecoaches in the south. But Cochise's people did not expect the Pinda Lickoyi to make a distinction between the Netdahe and other Apaches. They expected the whites to blame all of them for the misdeeds of a few. They had decided it was inevitable that sooner or later they would have to fight the White Eyes, and that it would be better to do it sooner, when there were fewer White Eyes.

For his part, of course, Cochise disagreed. This was why he had extended the invitation for Mr. Grenville to return, so they might resume negotiations. But, he reminded them, he could not force his people to accept a peace treaty. He could not dictate to the Chokonen. That was not the Apache way. They would have to agree of their own free will to abide by the terms of the treaty.

Grenville said that he understood, and respected the traditions of the Apache people. He insisted that the White Father in Washington, D.C., desired only peace between the Chi-hinne and his own kind. But, just as

Cochise could not speak for all of his people, or tell
them what to do, neither could the White Father dictate to his fellow Americans. It was inevitable that
more Americans would soon enter Apacheria, and it
was impossible for the White Father or anyone else
to prevent that. But what the White Father *could* do—
and *wished* to do—was secure a treaty with the Chokonen, and then with all the other Apache bands. The
Americans would respect such a treaty, and acknowledge that the United States government had given a
solemn guarantee to the Apaches that they would be
able to keep certain portions of their land for all time,
without fear of encroachment. That way, there would
be plenty of land for Americans to use, and they and
the Apaches could live in peace.

The White Father, continued Grenville, realized that
he was asking Cochise and his people to sacrifice a
great deal. But there was no alternative, apart from
more conflict with the Americans, who believed it was
their destiny and their right to extend their holdings
from the eastern seaboard to the Pacific coast. In exchange for this sacrifice, the White Father promised
to provide the Chokonen with a generous annuity. He
would pledge an annual gift of beads, cloth, cooking
utensils, farm implements, knives, axes, blankets, tobacco, and anything else (within reason) that the Chokonen requested. The Chokonen could remain in
possession of the Mogollon Mountains, in the heart of
the region they had traditionally called their own. And
the White Father further pledged that if the Chokonen
agreed to these terms, the United States Army would
be used, if need be, to make sure that Americans did
not encroach on the Mogollons.

Cochise remarked that the Apache had no use for

farm implements. But if they were to promise to give up much of their land, and to remain in the mountains, they would need food, especially in winter, when in the high country the game became scarce.

Grenville seemed to have anticipated such a request, and quickly assured Cochise that an arrangement could be made for the delivery of a certain number of cattle, every other month or so, or perhaps even on a monthly basis during the winter months. This was only fair, since, if they agreed to the treaty, the Chokonen would no longer be able to range far and wide in search of game.

Cochise told the Indian agent that he would present the White Father's offer to his people. He had asked that the Chokonen prepare for a council meeting that evening. He warned that this might be a lengthy affair, and that Grenville should not expect an answer until the morning.

Until then, continued Cochise, they were welcome to remain in the village, and to use this *cowah* for shelter. They were free to come and go as they pleased, and they would be provided with an evening meal, and anything else they required.

Once Cochise and the others had departed, Grenville turned to Barlow. "I guess that means we can rejoin your soldiers, Lieutenant, if that would make you feel more at ease. But I recommend that we stay right here, to show we have faith in Cochise—and in his people to honor their leader's wishes where we're concerned."

"I agree, sir," said Sergeant Farrow. "And then too there's a little matter of respect. They'll have more respect for us if we stay right here in the midst of them."

Barlow shrugged. If Grenville and Farrow thought that they had to sell him on the idea of remaining in the Chokonen village, they were mistaken. While he hadn't forgotten the risks involved, or that there were some Chokonen who did not want them here, and did not wish to see a treaty of peace successfully negotiated, he had no desire whatsoever to leave. Not, at least, until he'd seen the *nahlin* named Oulay again.

That night, it seemed as though every inhabitant in the Chokonen village attended the council summoned by Cochise. This meeting was held in the center of the che-wa-ki, in front of the jefe's cowah. The council consisted of Cochise and the Chokonen elders, along with several younger men, like Nana, who had distinguished themselves in one way or another. Men who were not on the council would be allowed to speak if Cochise permitted them to do so. The women and children, of course, could not participate. But they were present, because all the Chokonen knew what was at stake.

Barlow and his two companions were not invited. Farrow built a fire out in front of the cowah, as the evening had turned out to be a pleasant one. They whiled away the hours there, and were served the evening meal, as Cochise had promised, by Oulay and the other maidens who had fed them earlier in the day. When they had finished eating, most of the Apache women took their leave. But Oulay lingered, sitting cross-legged at the very edge of the firelight. Barlow found that every time he glanced her way she was gazing at him, and he found this disconcerting.

Noting Barlow's discomfort, Farrow chuckled. "She's interested—that's plain," drawled the sergeant. "Were you an Apache she might just walk right up to you and touch your hand. But you're Pinda Lickoyi, so she's not too sure how to go about it."

"How is it that you know so much about Apache women, Sergeant?" asked Grenville, in a good-natured way.

"I took one as my woman. That was a good many years back. Before I joined the army. Best years of my life."

"Where is she now?" asked the Indian agent.

Farrow's voice was bleak. "She died." That was all he said, and he obviously didn't want to linger on that particular subject. He turned his attention back to Barlow. "Thing about Apache women is this, Lieutenant: You don't have to beat around the bush with them. Just go straight up and tell them what you want. The way she sees it, life is too short, and happiness too hard to come by, to be playing any games."

"It would help if I knew a little of the lingo," said Barlow.

"In this case I doubt you'll need any words," said Grenville. "The language of love is universal, isn't it?"

Barlow nodded. He was nervous about approaching Oulay, but, on the other hand, he didn't want to hang around the fire any longer, because this conversation was intensely embarrassing for him. He figured that if he went up to Oulay and got turned down cold he would die of shame right then and there. And yet he knew he had to take that chance. Because if what Sergeant Farrow said was true, then this was an opportunity he didn't dare pass up.

So he steeled himself, walked over to her, and extended his hand.

Surprised, she looked up at him for a moment—a

moment during which Barlow felt as though his heart had ceased to beat. And then, with a pleased smile, she reached up and slipped her hand into his. She stood, and he turned his back on Farrow and Grenville, not wishing to see their expressions, and walked quickly away, with her by his side.

"Of course," murmured Grenville, watching the couple disappear into the darkness, "this might not be the best of times to court an Apache woman."

Farrow nodded. "Don't have much faith in your peace treaty, eh, Mr. Grenville?"

"Well," said Grenville, picking his words carefully, "we can always hope, can't we? The thing is, we've made many treaties with many different tribes. Yet all too often peace proves to be fleeting. I love my country, Sergeant, as I'm sure you do. But I must admit that we don't have a very admirable history when it comes to our dealings with the native tribes."

"I wouldn't worry too much about those two," said Farrow. "If that's honest-to-God love I've been seeing between the two of them all day today—and I believe it is—they'll be able to handle just about anything that comes their way."

Barlow intended merely to walk a short way with Oulay, keeping to the village. But right away she pulled him between a couple of cowahs and led him down to a creek that ran alongside the che-wa-ki. Across the creek, up on the high, windswept plateau, Barlow could see the fires of E Troop's bivouac. Oulay sat down in the grass at the top of a cutbank, and tugged at his arm; Barlow took the hint and sat down beside her. She was all smiles now, and that made her even more beautiful. And she seemed quite content just to be with him, and never mind the obstacle of language. Over in the cavalry camp, someone was blowing a tune on a harmonica, and Barlow got the impression that Oulay liked the plaintive sound. And way off along the Rim, a coyote yapped a lonesome lament. She gazed for a while at the stars, and he gazed at her profile, knowing that it was a vision that would remain with him forever.

He lost track of time, but eventually she gazed over her shoulder—and he looked to see that the Chokonen were moving among their cowahs. The council was over. Oulay was no longer smiling. It was time for her to go, and she didn't want to. Barlow didn't want this time with her to end, either. With a heavy heart, he stood, and once more extended his hand. She took it, and rose beside him, standing very close to him this time, and with her free hand touched his chest to feel the beating of his heart. Barlow wanted to kiss her, wanted it more than he'd ever wanted anything in his life. Farrow had told him that he should be bold in letting her know what he wanted, and yet he simply couldn't bring himself to take such a liberty. She looked up at him with those big dark eyes that seemed wise far beyond her years, and somehow she seemed to know exactly what he was thinking, and the gentle, understanding smile on her lips seemed to say that it was all right. Or maybe he was just imagining things.

They walked back to the cowah. Farrow and Grenville were nowhere to be seen. In their place stood two bronchos. One of them spoke curtly to Oulay, sending her away. She gave Barlow one last smile—this one tinged with sadness—and then turned to go.

Barlow felt as though his heart was being torn out by its roots. Unable to watch her walk away, he went into the cowah.

Cochise was there, along with Nachita—and Farrow and Grenville too. The Indian agent looked ecstatic.

"They've agreed to the treaty conditions, Lieutenant!" he exclaimed. "They want twenty head of cattle each month, as well as a few rifles and powder. Frankly, I don't think there will be any problem in meeting those requests."

Cochise was watching Barlow as he spoke curtly to Nachita, who translated his words. "Cochise asks one other thing. That this man"—and Nachita pointed at Barlow—"be the one to deliver the cattle."

Grenville looked at Barlow. "Do you see any reason why Colonel Lyman would object to that condition, Lieutenant?"

"No, I don't."

"Then it's settled."

Through Nachita, Cochise said that at first light he would sign the treaty paper. With that, he shook Grenville's hand and departed.

"So what was all that about?" asked Barlow. "Why does he want *me* to deliver the cattle?"

"I reckon it has something to do with his daughter," drawled Farrow, grinning. When Barlow fired a suspicious look at him, the sergeant shrugged innocently. "Well, you didn't expect it to stay a secret, did you, sir? Apaches don't miss much. And they tend to be big gossips. My guess is that Cochise figures you might think you've got a vested interest in keeping this peace now, so he wants you to be in charge of the beef delivery."

"Look on the bright side, Lieutenant," said Grenville. "This means you'll get to visit a lot more often."

Barlow nodded. He wouldn't mind the duty, for that very reason. The one thing he did mind—the thing he knew he would have a lot of trouble with—was the inescapable fact that tomorrow morning he would have to leave the Chokonen che-wa-ki. He would have to part company with Oulay. And even if it was only for a while, even a day away from her would, he suspected, seem like an eternity.

Chapter 9

When he got his first look at the twenty cattle destined for Cochise and his people, Barlow was stunned. John Ward himself, accompanied by a pair of vaqueros, delivered them to Fort Union, and Barlow had never seen a sorrier bunch of animals. It looked as though the rancher had taken great pains to cull the oldest, scrawniest, and sickest beeves from his herd. A couple of the steers were lame, and Barlow wondered how they had managed to survive the journey from the Ward ranch to the fort.

"You couldn't get a decent meal off the whole lot of them," remarked Hammond, standing with Barlow in front of their quarters in Officers' Row, watching the cattle amble by on their way to a holding pen on the other side of the stockade.

As he watched Colonel Lyman greeting Ward like a long-lost brother, Barlow felt his anger rising, quick and hot. He waited until the two men had reached the colonel's quarters before following in their footsteps. Having handed the cattle off to some of the soldiers, Ward's two vaqueros had nothing else to do but sit on the porch of the headquarters building. Major Addicks was talking with them in their native language. All three men turned to look at Barlow as he approached. The vaqueros recognized Barlow, and smiled amiably. But Addicks knew him better—and with one look could see that there was going to be trouble.

"You can't go in there right now, Lieutenant," said the major.

Barlow didn't seem to hear him; he climbed up onto the porch and started for the door.

Addicks swiftly moved into his path. His voice, when he spoke next, was colder. "Maybe you didn't hear me."

"I heard you, sir. I want to see the colonel right away."

"Colonel Lyman is busy."

"And I want to see that son of a bitch Ward too."

The vaqueros weren't smiling anymore. Both were on their feet now, backing away, but not because they were afraid. They were just putting some distance between themselves and Barlow so that neither would be in the other's line of fire. Their hands were resting on the pistols at their sides, perceiving that Barlow posed a threat to their padrone. They weren't quite sure yet how serious the threat was, but they were prepared to deal with it.

"What is this about, Lieutenant?" asked Addicks.

"You know, sir."

"It isn't any of your business. You and I—we just carry out our orders."

Barlow tried to get past him then. Addicks grabbed his arm, and tried to swing Barlow away from the door. But as he spun around Barlow threw a rock-solid fist that connected squarely with the major's jaw.

Addicks went down hard. A heartbeat later Barlow heard the distinctive sound of hammers being cocked as the vaqueros drew their pistols. A heartbeat after that, Sergeant Eckhart arrived. He was accompanied by a pair of cavalrymen from E Troop. And they were all armed.

"Put those pistolas aside, boys, if you want to stay healthy!" warned Eckhart.

The cavalrymen were carrying carbines. They brought the rifles up and took aim, each covering one of the vaqueros.

Eckhart looked to Barlow. "Lieutenant Hammond suggested that I ought to come check on you, sir."

"You're right on time, Sergeant, as usual."

The door behind Barlow opened, and he turned to see Colonel Lyman.

"What's going on here?" His gaze came to rest on Addicks, who was still down. Propped up on an elbow, the major was rubbing his jaw. "What is the meaning of this?" asked Lyman, with a suspicious glance in Barlow's direction. "Did this man strike you, Major?"

"No, sir," said Addicks. "There was a patch of ice—and I fell down."

Barlow glanced at him, surprised. Major Addicks had never, to his knowledge, stuck his neck out for anyone. He had always been the colonel's reliable right-hand, consistently upholding Lyman's edicts, and never voicing his own opinion. And since Lyman did things by the book, that was the way the major did them too. But this wasn't by the book—because, if it had been, Barlow would have been on his way to the guardhouse now, facing the prospect of a court-martial on the charge of striking a superior officer.

Lyman didn't believe it. He turned his attention to

Eckhart, thinking that he might get the truth from another source—then realized that Eckhart wasn't going to tell him anything different. So he gave up, disgusted.

"I think I know what you're doing here," he told Barlow, sarcastically. "Come with me."

He went back inside. Barlow gave Eckhart a nod, and as he followed Lyman, he heard the sergeant ordering the troopers to lower their carbines.

John Ward was sitting in a chair facing the colonel's desk. He was savoring one of Lyman's cigars, and although he had to have heard the commotion outside, he appeared to be without a care in the world. He smiled at Barlow. There was nothing friendly about that smile.

"I'm glad you're here, Lieutenant," said the rancher. "I was just telling Hartwell—Colonel Lyman—what a fine job you did clearing the Apache vermin off my ranch. The colonel was telling me that you've been handpicked by none other than Cochise himself to deliver my cattle to the Chokonen."

"And you'll be leaving first thing in the morning," said Lyman, circling his desk to sit behind it.

"You're not seriously considering delivering those cattle to Cochise," said Barlow.

"Absolutely," replied Lyman. "As per the terms of the treaty Mr. Glenville negotiated with the Indians."

"Those cattle aren't . . . suitable."

Ward chuckled. "Come now, Lieutenant. These are Apaches we're talking about, after all."

"They're human beings. Women and children. And they'll starve to death this winter if they have to depend on cattle in such poor condition as the ones you brought."

"That's not my problem. I agreed to deliver twenty cattle, and I've done that."

"And I've signed a receipt," added Lyman. "In my view, the cattle are acceptable, and you *will* deliver them tomorrow, Lieutenant."

"Why are you doing this, sir? You must know that Cochise will look on this as an insult. And when his people are starving, he will have no choice but to break the terms of the treaty."

"You mean his bucks will start killing my cattle again," said Ward, no longer smiling. "Well, when that happens, I'll start killing Apache bucks."

"Oh, that's helpful," said Barlow caustically. "Then his men will start killing yours, and before you know it, we'll have a war on our hands." He turned back to Lyman. "Or maybe that's what the colonel wants. I'm afraid there won't be much glory to be had in this war, though."

"I don't like your tone, Lieutenant. Who are you to lecture me? You will obey your orders, and deliver those cattle. And if they don't suit Cochise, then that's just too bad, because I don't give a good goddamn."

"Yes, sir," said Barlow coldly. "I know. I'll be lodging a written complaint."

"You do that. Now if there's nothing else . . . ?"

Barlow saluted, glanced once more at John Ward and his taunting smile, and left the room.

Eckhart and the six troopers who accompanied Barlow to the Chokonen village on the Mogollon Rim were nervous as they drew near their destination. So was Barlow, but he tried not to show it. They all knew that Cochise would consider the twenty cattle they were delivering to be an insult. The question was, how

would the Chokonen jefe react? The sergeant told
Barlow that, in his opinion, the Chokonen would send
their scalps back to Fort Union to reflect their displea-
sure. Barlow was hopeful that Cochise would prove
too wise for that, although he suspected that the jefe
would have trouble from some of the younger
bronchos, who in their outrage would want to strike
back.

On the second day out of Fort Union, they arrived
at the Chokonen che-wa-ki. The excitement demonstrated by the crowd of Apaches as they gathered to
observe the arrival of the cattle quickly faded, re-
placed by bewilderment and sullen anger. Some of the
young men hurled insults at the troopers. Barlow had
already issued strict orders that his men were not to
touch their weapons unless they were being physically
attacked. They were sitting on a powder keg, and one
wrong move could result in an explosion.

The Chokonen had prepared a corral of cedar posts
to hold the cattle, and as his men drove the beeves
into this pen Barlow saw Cochise for the first time.
Standing beside him was a furious Nana. Nachita was
there too. Barlow dismounted and approached them.
A pair of young bronchos stepped in his path. He
knew what they wanted. This was a provocation; they
expected him to take offense, to let his pride get the
better of him. But he wouldn't give them the satisfaction. Barlow glanced over his shoulder. As he'd expected, Sergeant Eckhart and the troopers were
watching him—and the bronchos—like hawks, ready
to spring into action. He gestured for them to stay
where they were, and started to walk around the two
men who stood in his way. The broncho nearest him
spat on the ground right in front of him. Barlow felt

a surge of anger—but wouldn't give in to it. He forced a smile, and kept walking. Foremost in his mind at that moment was the fact that Cochise—who had witnessed the whole thing—had not seen fit to call off the bronchos, or to rebuke them. That wasn't a good sign. Though the jefe's craggy features betrayed no emotion, he was clearly furious. As Barlow drew near, Cochise spoke curtly to Nachita, who turned to Barlow with a translation.

"Cochise says he thought you were different from the other Pinda Lickoyi he has met," said Nachita. "He says he thought you truly wanted the peace he had agreed to keep. But if this was so, you would not have brought these cattle."

"I had my orders," replied Barlow. "But tell Cochise that I do not consider these cattle to be part of the bargain he agreed to when he signed the treaty paper."

Nachita relayed his message. Cochise looked puzzled.

"Cochise does not understand what you mean," said Nachita. "If these cattle are not part of the annuity the Pinda Lickoyi promised the Chokonen, then what are they?"

"They are John Ward's effort to start a war," said Barlow. "But Ward won't have his way—unless Cochise lets him."

Listening to Nachita's translation, Cochise fixed his gaze on Barlow. Then he nodded—and for the first time Barlow dared hope that there was a chance to avoid violence.

"Tell him," said Barlow, "that I intend to bring him twenty more cattle—and they will be strong and healthy, and will fill many Chokonen bellies." He glanced at the two bronchos who had tried to provoke him. They stood a short distance away, glaring at him. "All I need is a little time, and for Cochise to keep his young men from letting their pride goad them into doing something that we will all regret."

As he listened to Nachita's translation of Barlow's words, Nana was overcome by fury, and he spoke angrily to Cochise. Barlow didn't need to understand the broncho's words to comprehend their meaning: Nana was advising his jefe not to listen to the yellow-leg soldier. Undoubtedly Nana believed that he was part of a Pinda Lickoyi plan to lull the Chokonen into inaction—until it was too late for them to act. Barlow had no illusions about the danger he and his men were in. One word from Cochise and they would be killed.

But Cochise did not respond to Nana. He acted as though he had not even heard the broncho's tirade. Instead, he spoke to Nachita, who turned to Barlow.

"Cochise says he cannot tell his men what to do and what not to do. He can only hope that they respect him enough to do as he does. And he has decided that there will be time enough to go to war. Today he will keep the peace, so you will have time to prove your words and your heart are true, and to prove also that if war *does* come, it will not be because Cochise and the Chokonen people did not keep their word."

Barlow breathed a sigh of relief, and nodded. He threw a quick look around at the Apache faces that encircled him and his men, hoping to catch a glimpse of Oulay. But she was nowhere to be seen. He wanted to ask Cochise if he could see her, but realized that this was hardly an appropriate time to indulge in such personal preferences—not when so many lives depended on his actions.

There was a commotion on the outskirts of the che-wa-ki. A moment later, a broncho arrived, leading a pony. He spoke excitedly, and for a moment it seemed that Barlow and his men and the cattle were forgotten. Cochise and Nana and several others examined the horse and then conferred briefly among themselves. Nana walked away with the long, quick strides of a man on a mission.

Barlow walked over to Nachita, who stood a little apart from the other Chokonen, watching and listening.

"What's going on?"

"Two of our young men went out hunting this morning," said Nachita. "The horse belonging to one of them has just returned, without its rider. There is blood on the horse, but the horse is not hurt."

It occurred to Barlow that sooner or later someone would suggest the possibility that he and his men might be responsible for whatever had befallen the missing hunter—and even as this thought crossed his mind, he heard a savage cry, and saw a broncho launch himself at one of the troopers, carrying the cavalryman off his mount. The other soldiers flew into action, drawing their carbines. Shouts of alarm rose up from the Chokonen, and Barlow flew into action. The broncho and the trooper grappled for a moment, with the former trying to plunge a knife into the latter's heart. But the trooper had the advantages of size and experience; he wrestled the knife away, threw the broncho off and, in the next instant, was straddling the Chokonen, a heartbeat away from killing the Apache with his own knife. Barlow reached him just in time to grab his wrist and stop the fatal downward thrust. At the same time he shouted at the other troopers to hold their fire.

"Goddamn it, Lieutenant!" rasped the cavalryman with the knife. "The bastard was tryin' to kill me!"

"Get up and stand back."

The trooper resisted. Barlow didn't fault him for it. His men lived in a brutal world where the law of the jungle—kill or be killed—held sway. The broncho had tried to kill the trooper and now he was bound and determined to return the favor, and there were no other options as far as he was concerned—it was as simple as that. He wasn't thinking objectively and under the circumstances Barlow didn't expect him to. But, objectively, if he plunged the knife into the Chokonen, they were all going to die.

Barlow gave the cavalryman a hard shove. Thrown off balance, he nearly fell. Instinctively he started toward his new assailant. Then the habits instilled by years in the army kicked in, and the trooper came to his senses. No matter what, you didn't strike an officer. That was what stopped him—not reason, but instinct.

The broncho had no such habits. Bounding to his feet, he started toward Barlow—the most convenient target, who, best of all, had his back turned. Eckhart triggered his carbine, putting a bullet in the ground directly in front of the broncho. That stopped him cold. A dozen or more bronchos in the crowd began to surge forward, their own instincts bringing them into the fray to help their brother. But Cochise shouted a command that cracked like a whip through the noise, a shout that seemed to bring order out of chaos.

Barlow caught his breath and took a look around and was more than a little surprised that he was still alive. They'd all been teetering on the edge of destruction, yet somehow they had managed to step back from the abyss. He looked at Cochise, who spoke curtly to Nachita. The translator stepped closer to Barlow.

"He says you are to go. Now. Before blood is spilled."

"Whatever happened to your hunters, we had nothing to do with it."

"Cochise knows this. Now you must go, at once."

Again Barlow thought of Oulay. There was absolutely no hope of seeing her, after what had transpired. Cochise was right—the only thing left to do was to take his men out of the Chokonen village.

Trying to ignore the heaviness in his heart, Barlow went to Eckhart, who was holding his horse. He took the reins and climbed into the saddle. The Chokonen were gravely silent as they watched the soldiers leave their village. Once they were clear of the che-wa-ki, Sergeant Eckhart breathed his own sigh of relief.

"I thought for sure we were done for," he confessed, throwing a glance over his shoulder just to confirm that a hundred angry bronchos weren't coming after them. "I don't know how you did it, Lieutenant. But that was pretty slick talking, and it worked. We've still got our skins."

"You'll be in charge of the detail, Sergeant. Take the men back to Fort Union."

"What about you, Lieutenant?"

Barlow looked at him. "It wasn't just slick talk. I intend to get twenty cattle."

"From where?"

"John Ward."

Eckhart looked at him as though he were crazy. "He won't give 'em to you, sir."

"I won't be asking him to *give* them to me. I'm

willing to buy them. And he is, after all, in the business of raising and selling cattle."

"The colonel won't like it."

"No, I don't expect he will."

"If you ask me, he'll lock you in the brig and throw away the key if you do this."

"Maybe so," said Barlow, exasperated. Eckhart wasn't telling him anything he didn't already know. "But damn it, somebody's got to try to set this right. Somebody has to try to talk some sense into Ward. I'd rather not be the one—but I don't see anyone else doing it."

When they reached the foothills, he took his leave of the detail, turning his horse to the east and riding for the Ward ranch.

When they happened upon the two Chokonen hunters, Kiannatah decided that Goyathlay truly had magic.

He did not believe in coincidence, and so there was no other way to explain this fortuitous turn of events. They had come to the Ward ranch to kill cattle, so Ward would blame Cochise, and would, possibly, spill Chokonen blood and start a war. But here, suddenly, were two Chokonen braves who had ventured down out off the high peaks of the Mogollons, where there was so little game in the heart of winter, ventured down into the foothills where their chances of making a kill were much improved. And they did so on the very day that Goyathlay led his Avowed Killers through those very same foothills, since crossing the desert flats was to be avoided whenever possible. When they saw the hunters, Kiannatah immediately used his rifle to kill one, at a range of two hundred yards. The other one turned his horse around and made a run for it, but Kiannatah gave chase, and a few minutes later rejoined his Netdahe brethren with the second Chokonen's corpse draped over his horse. A couple of the other bronchos objected to Kiannatah's actions, and complained loudly to Goyathlay that Kiannatah had doomed them all. They were already hunted by the Nakai-Ye and the Pinda Lickoyi, and now, thanks to Kiannatah, they would be hunted by Cochise and the Chokonen. None of the other bronchos who rode with Goyathlay liked Kiannatah anyway; he kept himself apart from the others, and acted as though it didn't matter to him whether they even existed, as though he had no need for them, and would fare as well, or perhaps better, by himself than in their company. Then too they were afraid of him. None would have admitted this, but it was so, and Kiannatah knew it. They were afraid of him because he killed without hesitation, and without emotion. They were all killers, but Kiannatah was different. He did not betray anger when he killed, nor did he indulge in exultation after the fact. It was as though killing, to him, was as mundane an act as breathing.

Kiannatah listened to their complaints. He did not defend his actions. He looked to Goyathlay for vindication. He expected Goyathlay to understand why he had slain the two Chokonen. And Goyathlay *did* understand. He told the other bronchos that Kiannatah had done well. They would continue on until they found some of Ward's cattle. These they would slaughter, and when they were done they would leave the two Chokonen corpses behind. This would persuade John Ward that it was Cochise's people who killed his cattle. As for Cochise, he would never know that two of his people had been murdered by the Netdahe. He would assume that John Ward's men had done the deed. The gods were smiling on them, continued Goyathlay. This proved that they were doing the right thing in trying to orchestrate a war between the Pinda Lickoyi and the people of Cochise. And when war finally did break out, the other Apaches would no longer treat the Netdahe like outcasts. They would seek the expertise of the Netdahe, for who better than an Avowed Killer to slay the enemies of The People? They would one day be honored by their people, instead of shunned.

Kiannatah listened to this speech with ambivalence. He cared nothing for acclaim, or for acceptance. He did not care if his people thought of him as an outlaw or a hero. All he cared about was escaping the nightmares—nightmares haunted by the ghosts of his family who cried out for vengeance. Every time he killed, the ghosts seemed to grow content. At least for a while. But always they returned to disturb his dreams. If Goyathlay got his wish, and there was war, he would have plenty of chances to kill. It didn't matter that the war would be against the Pinda Lickoyi, who'd had nothing whatsoever to do with the massacre of his family at Dolorosa. All that mattered was the opportunity to do what he did best, what he lived for.

Chapter 10

Barlow wasn't sure what sort of welcome he would get once he arrived at the Ward ranch, but such doubts didn't stop him from riding in as though he belonged there. Several vaqueros were gathered around the corrals over beyond the barn; they were busting broncs. Winter was almost over, with spring roundup just around the corner. The idle months in a cowboy's year were coming to a close, and the busiest time was nearly upon them. Each would need a string of good horses.

They saw him as he rode across the hardpack toward the main house, but his presence didn't stir up any unusual attention. Reaching the house, he was about to dismount when the front door opened and another vaquero emerged. Seeing Barlow, he was startled, and stopped dead in his tracks. Barlow recognized the man as Sanchez, Ward's segundo, or foreman.

"What are you doing here, Lieutenant?"

"I want to see Ward."

Sanchez was nervous. "He-he is a busy man, senor. He cannot see you now."

Barlow stepped down off the coyote dun. "He's going to have to."

He started to pass Sanchez, but the anxious segundo stepped sideways to block his path. "You cannot go in."

"You're making a mistake," said Barlow.

Sanchez looked into his eyes—and saw that this was so. He had considered trying to intimidate the lieutenant. John Ward had picked him to be segundo because he was able to handle the rest of the crew. It was a crew of rough men honed by a dangerous existence in a perilous country, but there wasn't a man in the bunch that dared challenge him. Yet, in a glance, Sanchez could see that it would avail him nothing to try to cow Barlow. The lieutenant was not going to back down, and Sanchez suddenly found himself questioning whether he really wanted to challenge this man.

"Wait here," said Sanchez, his tone one of sweet reason now. "I will tell him you have come."

"Don't be too long about it," advised Barlow. "I'm busy too."

Sanchez nodded, and disappeared inside. Barlow bided his time for several minutes, watching the activity around the distant corrals, until the segundo returned.

"You will wait here, *por favor*," he said. "The padrone will be out to—"

Barlow swept past him before he could finish, and Sanchez reflexively grabbed his arm to restrain him from crossing the threshold. Turning on the segundo, Barlow dropped his hand to the pistol at his side.

"Let go of me," he rasped.

Sanchez let go.

Pausing just inside the doorway, Barlow heard the muted voices of men behind a set of doors to his left. Two long strides brought him to the doors, which he threw open. A man he had never seen before, a pale-haired man in range clothes, rose so quickly from the dining room table that he overturned his chair. He was reaching for his pistol, but Barlow drew down on him before the man could yank the gun clear of holster leather, and he froze.

"Sit down," snapped Barlow, "and keep your hands on the table."

The pale-haired man complied. Only then did Barlow glance at the other three men in the room. One was John Ward. The other two, also clad in nondescript range garb, were strangers.

But Barlow had a pretty fair idea who they were.

"How dare you barge into my house like this!" roared Ward, outraged.

"And how dare you put the entire territory at risk of an Apache war for the sake of making a few dollars."

"I don't know what you're talking about. But I have a feeling Colonel Lyman will be very interested to hear about your behavior."

"It wouldn't surprise him. I'm here about the twenty old, sick cattle you provided for Cochise and his people."

"I'm trying to conclude a business deal here."

Barlow looked at the strangers again. The second man had a large frame, but it was more muscle than flab, and an unkempt black beard concealed most of his features. The third was tall and lean and watchful, and a sardonic half-smile curled the corner of his mouth.

"I'll let you get back to it," said Barlow, "as soon as you conclude your business with me."

"I have no business with you," insisted Ward, still fuming.

"Yes, you do. You're going to give me twenty healthy cattle."

"Am I?" Ward's eyes narrowed. "I'm thinking the colonel doesn't even know you're here. That's it, isn't it, Lieutenant? You're trying to buffalo me on your own stick."

"There are people trying to keep the peace around here, and what you've done puts all their work in jeopardy. The worst part of it is, you know Cochise isn't going to sit still and accept sick cattle as part of the annuity promised his people. In fact, you're counting on him to make trouble. Peace with the Chokonen is the last thing you want."

"I fulfilled my end of the bargain. I agreed to provide the army with twenty cattle four times a year. That's what I did. Now get out of my house before I throw you out."

"I didn't come here expecting you to do the right thing," said Barlow dryly. "So I'll make you a proposition. I'm willing to buy twenty more head of cattle from you."

"No."

"Why not? My money is good. Or is it that you're dealing only in Confederate notes today?"

The color drained from Ward's face. He suddenly looked afraid. But the tall, lean man with the half-smile burst into hearty laughter.

"Mr. Ward," he said, "you should see your expression! It looks to me like the lieutenant has the wrong impression about us." He stood up, and even so simple a movement demonstrated the coiled strength and natural grace of his lanky frame. Offering a hand, he said, "My name is Clay Burnett. It's true. I'm Southern born and bred. I am a Texan, by way of Alabama. But I'm not a Confederate. My associates and I intend to buy a few cattle and start our own enterprise somewhere to the north. And Mr. Ward here has kindly agreed to negotiate that sale."

Barlow nodded. He was sure now that Burnett was the leader of the trio. He was well-educated, well-spoken, and cool under pressure.

Burnett turned to Ward. "It seems to me that the lieutenant has a valid argument, and I am willing to wait until your transaction with him has been concluded. All he wants is twenty head. How many hundreds of cattle graze your range, Mr. Ward?"

"I have no idea," said Ward. He was still belligerent, but he'd gotten the message that Burnett was trying to convey—close a deal with Barlow and get him out of the way. "Very well, Lieutenant. If you want to spend your money on beef to fill Apache stomachs, that's your business. I'll sell you twenty head. In fact, my men will round up a hundred head tomorrow and you can pick the twenty you want."

"Fair enough. I'll also need a couple of your vaqueros to help me take them into the Mogollon."

"Fine. And I trust that after tomorrow—"

"Lieutenant!"

It was Kathleen. Poised in the doorway, radiant with joy, she beamed a delighted smile across the room at Barlow. Then she rushed forward—and for one moment of complete panic Barlow thought she was going to throw her arms around him and give him a kiss in front of her father and the others. But she exercised a little restraint, and settled for simply grabbing his hand, holding it in both of hers as though she would never release it.

"What a wonderful surprise!" she gushed. "I was wondering when I would see you again."

"Kathleen!" snapped Ward, displeased by the warmth with which his daughter was welcoming Barlow.

"Yes, Father?" Kathleen turned her smile on Ward, an expression of sublime innocence on her lovely face, but she knew why her father was annoyed and she defiantly retained her control of Barlow's hand.

Ward grimaced. "If you'd be kind enough to show the lieutenant to the guest room. He'll be staying over until tomorrow."

"Oh, I'd be delighted. Perhaps you would have the time to ride with me in the morning, Lieutenant."

"Well, I . . ."

"Well, come along then. I'll show you to your room. I'm sure you must be very tired."

She started out of the room, refusing to relinquish her hold on him, and towed him into the main hall and up the staircase, chattering cheerfully about her horse—which was wonderful—and the weather—which had been awful—and several other things that were not of the slightest interest to Barlow. But at the top of the stairs she suddenly whirled and put her hands on his chest and pushed him against a wall and planted a firm, passionate kiss on his lips.

"You shouldn't be here," she whispered, her lips still so close to his that he could feel the heat of her breath on his face. "You're in terrible danger!"

"Am I?" he mumbled, his senses clouded by the passion of the kiss, by the scent of her, by the pressure of her lithe young body against his.

"Those men downstairs. Don't you know who they are?"

"I—"

"They are Confederate agents! They are your enemy."

Barlow's head cleared. "How do you know they're Confederate agents?"

"I keep my ears open. I know what is said in this house. Most people make the mistake of thinking I'm just some flighty girl without a thought in my head. And sometimes, because they think of me in that way, they get careless in their talk when I'm around. Those men are here to buy a large herd from my father and take it back to Texas to feed the Rebel army."

"And how do you feel about that?"

"Oh, I don't care about all of that," she said impatiently. "But I do care about what happens to you. As happy as seeing you again makes my heart, you mustn't stay here. It isn't safe. Sssh!"

Ward and Burnett were emerging from the dining room, talking. Burnett's associates followed. Kathleen shoved Barlow into a doorway and pressed against him to conceal them both in the event that one of the men at the bottom of the staircase happened to look up.

"We'll talk more tomorrow, then," said Ward, shaking Burnett's hand.

The three Confederates left the house, and Ward returned to the dining room.

"Come with me!" whispered Kathleen.

Taking Barlow's hand, she led him to a door farther down the upstairs hall, guided him into the room, and closed the door softly behind them. Leaning against it, she heaved a sigh of relief. "They've been here before, you know."

"How long ago?"

"About two months past. I got the impression they had just arrived from Texas."

"What was said?"

"My father talked to them mostly about the Apaches. Cochise and his people, in particular."

Barlow nodded. That was roughly the time when he had first visited the Chokonen village, with the Indian Bureau representative, Grenville—the occasion on which he and his troops had been fired upon by unknown assailants. He was pretty certain now that those assailants had been Clay Burnett and his associates.

"You don't need to worry about me," he assured her. "That Burnett fellow is too smart to make trouble. He'll let me get what I came for and leave unharmed."

"What *did* you come for?"

"Twenty cattle."

"And, um . . . didn't cross your mind at all?"

Barlow winced. "Well, yes, I thought about you." It was a lie, and he hoped he had told it convincingly. The truth was that he had forgotten all about Kathleen—and Kathleen's infatuation with him.

She smiled pensively. "You're not a very good liar. But I do care about you, Lieutenant. I know you must think I'm very young. Too young. But I'm not really. My mother was sixteen when—"

"Kathleen . . ."

He was on the verge of telling her about Oulay, then thought better of it. To tell her that he was in love with someone else was probably the right thing to do. Certainly it wasn't right or fair to let her continue to believe that there was any chance of a lasting relationship between them, when there was no such chance. But he discovered that he was too much the coward to hurt her, even if the hurting was necessary.

She held up a hand. "I know what you're going to say. But it doesn't matter. Even if you don't love me, that doesn't change the way I feel about you. Just know that I would do anything for you. I would die for you."

It was a perfect moment for a melodramatic exit, and she took it, giving him one last sweet, sad smile before slipping silently out of the room.

Barlow breathed a sigh of relief. His aching body cried out for rest, so he stretched out on the bed. A few minutes later, though, he was on his feet again— long enough to wedge a chair under the doorknob. He was fairly confident that he was right about Burnett, and that the Confederate agent was smart enough to recognize that his agenda was best served by letting Barlow ride out alive. Still, there was no point in taking unnecessary chances. Barlow returned to bed and, within a minute of lying down, was sound asleep.

John Ward was as good as his word. Early the next morning he sent his vaqueros out to round up a hundred cattle, and by midday the herd was available to Barlow, who picked out twenty cattle that he deemed—though he was by no means an expert on the subject—to be the healthiest of the lot. The rancher informed him that the vaqueros had drawn cards to see which two would accompany him into the Mogollons, and the two who had drawn low cards, named

Menendez and Ochoa, were prepared to leave immediately. "It isn't that they don't like you, Lieutenant," said Ward wryly. "They just know better than to trust the Apaches. A lesson you may not live long enough to learn."

They completed the transaction, with Barlow giving Ward full payment for the cattle at nine dollars a head. That left him pretty close to flat broke, and there would be no reimbursement of those funds from the army or any other source. Barlow didn't care. The main thing was that Chokonen children would not go hungry, and thus Cochise might restrain his angry young bronchos from striking out against the Pinda Lickoyi. At least, for a while. Barlow had no delusions about the prospects for a long-lasting treaty with the Apaches. Cochise would keep his end of the bargain, but the United States would not keep theirs. So Barlow was well aware that all he was really doing was postponing the inevitable.

The deal done, there was then no good reason for Barlow to linger at the ranch. Even though he considered himself divorced from the United States Army, and the duties and responsibilities of an officer of that army, he was still a citizen of the United States and a believer in the Union and what it stood for, and he didn't like the idea of Burnett taking a herd to Texas to provide food for Rebel forces. But what could he do about it?

Barlow set out for the Mogollons early in the afternoon, and even while he knew that Oulay waited at the end of this trail, he couldn't help but dwell on Kathleen Ward. She had not shown herself all day, and he had thought to pay her the courtesy of saying goodbye. The opportunity, however, did not present

itself, and as he rode away from the ranch, he worried
about her state of mind and hoped, for her sake, that
she would soon forget about him.

"Ask me, we should've killed him."

This was Carney, sitting with his body leaning forward, hands clenched into fists on the table, his chin
jutting defiantly as he looked at Burnett and Heller
and John Ward in turn. The four of them were again
sitting at the table in the dining room, and Ward, who
had thought that the purpose of this meeting was to
continue the business interrupted by Barlow's unexpected arrival, was startled and dismayed by the Texan's comment.

"That would have put me in a bad spot," said the
cattleman. Yesterday he had lost his temper with Barlow. Today, having had time to calm down and think
the matter through, he could see that Burnett had
been right—the best way to resolve the problem of
Lieutenant Barlow had been to give him what he
wanted and send him on his way.

"He knows who we are," said Carney. "I could tell
just by the way he was lookin' at us. And he'll go
back and tell his superior officer and before you know
it we'll have a whole passel of bluecoat soldiers
breathin' down our necks."

"I doubt that," said Ward. "His superior officer,
Colonel Lyman, is an acquaintance of mine. While the
colonel is a Union man all the way, he has his hands
full with the Apache situation, and I seriously doubt
that he will make any trouble for us."

"But you don't know that for a fact," persisted Carney. "Why take chances?"

"I'm with Carney on this one," said Heller.

"So you don't want him killed on your land," said Carney. "I can understand that." He turned to Burnett. "Just let me and Heller go after him. We'll make sure no one will connect his death to Mr. Ward."

Ward looked across at Burnett. He wasn't going to make any further effort to dissuade these men from killing Barlow. He didn't care what happened as long as he wasn't implicated. And he was smart enough to realize that his opinion really didn't matter that much anyway—in a decision of this type, Burnett was the one who called the shots.

Burnett shrugged. "Fine. If you want to kill him that bad, go ahead. But don't take too long."

"It'll take no more than two or three days to round up the cattle you want," predicted Ward.

"And on the fourth day, I aim to be starting home," said Burnett.

Carney grinned. "Don't worry. We'll be back. And the world will be shy one Yankee lieutenant."

"Now," said Ward, "we should settle on a price for the cattle . . ."

Pressed against a wall in the hallway just beyond the dining room door, Kathleen Ward began to tiptoe slowly, quietly backward, sliding along the wall to the staircase. As she neared the bottom step she turned—and stifled a yelp as she found herself virtually nose to nose with her brother.

Linus was curious. "What are you—"

Kathleen clamped a hand over his mouth with such force that the boy's eyes widened. He began to resist, making loud, muffled noises, but she wrapped an arm around him and lifted him bodily and started up the stairs. "Be quiet!" she hissed. She carried him all the way up to the second floor—a feat that Linus hadn't thought his slender and somewhat frail-looking older sister would be capable of. Only then did she release him, casting one last, anxious look to the downstairs hall, not quite believing her luck, since it seemed that none of the men inside the dining room had heard the commotion she and Linus had made.

"What is going on?" asked Linus crossly. He didn't like being manhandled, especially by his sister.

"Keep your voice down!" she warned in a fierce whisper, wagging a finger in front of his nose.

"Oh yeah? Make me."

Kathleen promptly grabbed him by the throat and pressed him back against the nearest wall.

"I'm not in the mood to play games," she hissed. "Those men down there with Father are planning to kill Lieutenant Barlow."

Linus could do no better than a strangled sound.

"You promise not to make a sound?" she asked.

He nodded frantically.

"Cross your heart and hope to die?"

He nodded again.

Kathleen let him go. He rubbed his throat ruefully and watched her move hurriedly along the hallway. He had to run to catch up with her.

"They're planning to do what?" he asked.

"You heard me." Reaching her room, she marched inside, and Linus followed. Throwing open a trunk at the foot of the bed, she took out a riding skirt of sturdy brown serge, and a short jacket to match.

"Why would they? Where are you going?"

"I must go warn him."

"The lieutenant?"

"Of course," she snapped, exasperated. Suddenly she was coming at him again, and Linus backed up quickly, throwing up his arms to defend himself. "Get out," she said, "so I can change into these clothes." She tried to push him out the door, but he resisted.

"I'm going with you!" he said.

"You most certainly are not."

"Yes, I am. You can't go alone. Who's gonna look out for you?"

She stopped tussling with him, and had to smile. "Oh. So you are going to be my protector. My pint-sized protector."

Linus scowled. "If you don't let me go, I'll tell Father."

In a flash she was angry at him all over again. "This is not a game. The lieutenant's life is in danger."

"Then stop wasting time arguing with me. I'm going and that's that."

"Oooh!"

Furious, she grabbed him by the arm and swung him around and then gave him a hard shove and he fell into the big trunk and she slammed the lid shut, sitting on it with arms folded tightly across her chest. Trapped inside the trunk, Linus shouted and banged his fists on the lid, and it wasn't long before Kathleen realized that this wasn't a solution to her problem, since he was making entirely too much noise. Standing, she lifted the lid, and helped him out. As soon as the lid swung open, Linus ceased the ruckus. With a gravity she had never seen in him before, he stood up and looked her right in the eye and said, "I can't let you go by yourself, sis."

"Fine," she said, her anger gone as quickly as it had come. "Slip out to the barn and saddle two horses. I'll be along. Now hurry! There is no time to lose!"

Chapter 11

They got away from the ranch house without being seen, which Kathleen decided was nothing short of miraculous. Their timing had been fortuitous. The segundo, Sanchez, was breaking a horse in one of the corrals beyond the barn, and the handful of vaqueros who weren't out looking for cattle had gathered to watch the show. Their attention was glued to the violent struggle of wills between man and horse, and they didn't see the two Ward children slip away from the barn.

Finding the tracks left by Barlow, the two vaqueros, and the twenty head of cattle was easy enough, and Kathleen set out with high hopes that they could catch up with the lieutenant in a matter of hours. He didn't have much of a head start on them, and she figured they would be able to make much better time since they weren't having to work to keep twenty ornery cattle, half wild after a winter of being left to their own devices on the open range, together and moving in concert.

They'd gone just a few miles when they ran into the Apache Netdahe.

For once Goyathlay had miscalculated. He did not know that he was so close to the Ward ranch house. He and his followers were looking for some of Ward's cattle, which they intended to kill; then they would leave the bodies of the two Chokonen hunters somewhere near the carnage. Goyathlay was aware that the plan had its flaws. A man more bound to calmness and reason than John Ward might wonder who had killed the two Apaches. But Goyathlay doubted Ward would trouble his mind with such a question. He would find his slaughtered beeves, and then he would find the Chokonen corpses—and he would have the excuse he wanted to make trouble for Cochise. Goyathlay was confident that the plan, flawed though it might be, would work.

He was also aware that this time of year the vaqueros would be popping the brush and rounding up the cattle, and he was hopeful that he and his Netdahe might be fortunate enough to stumble on a few of the Nakai-Ye. If so, they would kill the vaqueros, and then it would be assumed that the two Chokonen had been killed in a firefight.

The last thing Goyathlay was expecting was to run into Ward's children.

Seeing the Apaches appear, suddenly, right in front of them as they circled a large clump of ocotillo that stood twice as tall as a man, Kathleen and Linus checked their horses and stared. The Netdahe did likewise, and for a heartbeat, no one moved. Then Linus shouted a warning, his young voice breaking, and whipped his pony around to make a run for it, kicking the animal in the ribs for all he was worth. Kathleen followed suit, and the Netdahe, recovering from their shock, gave chase.

In front of the others, Kiannatah drew his pistol and fired a single shot. He hit his mark. Kathleen's horse went down, dying on its feet and throwing its rider.

Linus had gotten a good jump on the Netdahe, and the horse under him was sound and swift. He might have made good his escape. But the shot made him look round, and when he saw his sister fall, he immediately checked his mount so sharply that the animal seemed to slide on its rump. Fumbling with the flap of a pannier strapped to the back of his saddle, Linus brandished a Walker Colt. The fourteen-inch pistol was almost more than he could handle. He tried to get his horse to turn and go back, but the animal balked, so Linus leaped to the ground and rushed to his sister's side. Stunned by the fall, Kathleen was having trouble standing up. Linus tried to help her, but she fell sideways, and he could not hold her. Realizing that the Netdahe were circling him, Linus swung round and scanned the fierce bronzed faces of the bronchos. Using both thumbs, he got the hammer of the Walker Colt pulled back.

Kiannatah had already leaped from his horse. As Linus struggled to cock the big pistol, the Netdahe moved toward him, completely unfazed by the fact that the Colt's barrel was aimed, albeit unsteadily, in his direction. As the boy's finger tightened on the trigger, Kiannatah reached out and swatted the gun down. It went off, and the recoil knocked Linus off balance. Kiannatah grabbed the pistol then, and wrenched it easily from the boy's grasp. But Linus wasn't giving up. He launched himself at the broncho. A backhanded swipe sent him sprawling. Dazed, he lay there, and Kathleen crawled on her hands and knees to huddle beside him, her arms around him. They stared fearfully at Kiannatah, and the bronchos arrayed behind him. Kiannatah's eyes were dark and cold and harbored no compassion. He aimed the Walker Colt at the girl, and was about to squeeze the trigger when a sharp command from Goyathlay stopped him.

"These are the children of John Ward," said the Netdahe leader. "I have seen them before."

"Good," said Kiannatah. "I will kill them both, and we will leave the Chokonen bodies nearby."

"No," said Goyathlay. "We will take them with us."

"Why? Of what value are they to us?"

"We will take them alive," repeated Goyathlay, more firmly. "And we will leave the Chokonen bodies here. John Ward will think Cochise has taken his children. Then he will surely go to war against the Chokonen."

"He would just as surely go to war if he found his children dead," reasoned Kiannatah.

Goyathlay tried to stifle his anger, but it was there in his voice as he snapped a command to two of the other bronchos. These men dismounted and went to Kathleen and Linus and grabbed them roughly, hauling them to their feet. A third broncho approached the horse Linus had been riding. The animal shied away from him, but the Netdahe spoke horse talk, calming it. *"Ho-shuh, ho-shuh,"* he murmured, and the sound seemed to have the horse allow him to come closer—close enough for the broncho to grab the bridle. The hands of the captives were bound with strips of rawhide, and they were placed together on Linus' horse. Kiannatah watched all of this with a faint expression of disdain. He did not understand why Goyathlay was so insistent on keeping the two Pinda Lickoyi alive. It was not from some humanitarian impulse on the Bedonkohe's part. Goyathlay was no humanitarian, and Kiannatah doubted that he had any compassion for the two young captives. Certainly, keeping them alive was no act of mercy. Kiannatah could see it in their eyes—especially in the eyes of the nahlin. They knew they were going to die, and he saw no reason to postpone the inevitable. Still, Goyathlay was the leader of the Avowed Killers, and Kiannatah did not care *that* much about whether the prisoners died now or later that he was willing to challenge the jefe. So he belted the Walker Colt and remounted his pony. The corpses of the two Chokonen were cut loose from their horses, and left on the ground. Then the band of Netdahe rode south at a rapid pace.

Barlow and the two vaqueros made good time that first day, reaching the river that ran along the base of the foothills to the Mogollon Range, where they made camp. The river was running fast and high due to snowmelt, but the vaqueros knew of a good crossing only a few miles upstream. They got the twenty head across without mishap. Barlow calculated that they would reach the Chokonen village by late tomorrow. Then, at long last, he would see Oulay again. The prospect lifted his spirits.

But they had only just put the river behind them when one of the vaqueros called out, and when Barlow glanced his way, the man pointed behind them. Barlow saw a rider in the far distance. He produced his field glasses, and took a closer look. The battered stovepipe hat gave the rider's identity away. It was Short Britches. Barlow had a hunch he wasn't going to be the bearer of good tidings.

When the old scout arrived, he looked grim. Barlow

had never thought of Short Britches as being an expressive man, but it was obvious that today he was deeply troubled.

"John Ward's children have been kidnapped," he said.

"What? By who?"

"Apache."

Barlow's blood ran cold in his veins. It couldn't be. There had to be some mistake. "When did this happen?"

"Yesterday. Not long after you left the ranch, they were discovered to be missing. We rode out with John Ward, following their trail. We came soon to the place where they had been taken. Two bodies were found. Chokonen bodies."

Barlow realized then what had happened.

"Two Chokonen men disappeared days ago, while I was with Cochise," he told the old scout.

Short Britches nodded. "I told John Ward that the two had been killed some time back. But he will not listen to me, or to anyone. He is loco. He vows to kill Cochise and all of the Chokonen. Every man, woman, and child."

"Obviously Cochise had nothing to do with this," said Barlow. "Somebody is trying to manufacture a war. Surely you found sign."

Short Britches nodded. "Six or seven horses. Unshod. Heading for the mountains."

"What are you doing here?"

"I have come to warn you. Stay away from the Chokonen village, Lieutenant."

Thinking of Oulay, Barlow said, "I can't do that. You've got to slow Ward down. Buy me twenty-four hours."

Short Britches just looked at him.

"I know," said Barlow. "You're wondering why you should help me. But you know that the Chokonen had no hand in business. Ward is making a mistake. You may be loyal to him, and you may not care if there's a war or not, but I can't believe you would stand by and do nothing with innocent women and children in danger."

"And what will you do?"

"Warn Cochise. When Ward reaches the che-wa-ki he won't find any Apaches to kill."

Short Britches heaved a sigh. "You wouldn't have any tobacco on you, would you?"

"No. But I'll buy you a year's supply if you'll do this."

Short Britches scoffed. "You're broke. You could not buy a single twist of tobacco."

"I'll find a way."

The old scout took a moment to think it over. "If John Ward finds out, he will kill me."

"That's not a good reason. You're not afraid of him or anybody else."

There was the ghost of a smile on the man's face. "I will do what I can. But I can promise nothing."

"I'll settle for that."

Short Britches nodded, and began to turn away.

"You know," said Barlow, "if he wasn't so hell-bent on attacking Cochise, Ward might be able to catch up with the ones who have his children."

"I figure it was the Netdahe," said the old scout as he rode away. "But John Ward believes he will find his children with the Chokonen. When he finds out that he is wrong, it will be too late."

Barlow didn't have to ask too late for what. If Short

Britches was right, and the Netdahe had been the ones who'd kidnapped Kathleen and Linus, then if the young Wards weren't dead already they soon would be. He thought about the towheaded boy, so bright-eyed and excited by the arrival of soldiers when Barlow and his troop had paid their first visit to the Ward ranch. And he thought about Kathleen too, the pretty, passionate young woman who had pressed her body against his in the upstairs hallway of the Ward house. He was sickened, and overcome by a helpless rage, and he would have set out to find them himself—even though, realistically, there was hardly any chance that he would be able to do so and, if he did, that he would survive long enough to be of any help to Kathleen and Linus—but for the fact that his first priority was Oulay. The woman he loved stood directly in the path of a storm of violence—and she had no idea that death was coming her way.

He told the two vaqueros to continue pushing the herd into the Mogollon. One of them, Ochoa, who spoke a little English, explained that only Barlow knew the location of the Chokonen village. Barlow wasn't about to tell them exactly where to find the che-wa-ki. They were John Ward's employees, after all.

"Just take them up to the Rim," he said. "If I haven't caught up with you by then, hold them in a likely looking spot until I *do* show up."

The vaqueros were clearly not happy with this assignment. They had heard the news conveyed by Short Britches. They knew that war was coming, and no one in the Mogollons would be safe.

"Your padrone told you to do what I told you," said Barlow curtly. "Nothing has happened to change that. This is what I'm telling you to do. Will you see it through or not?"

Ochoa nodded. "*Sí*, senor. We will do as you say." With a glance at his *companero*, he added, "But we will not wait on the Rim forever."

"Fair enough," said Barlow, and left them.

When Carney and Heller caught up with the small herd of cattle Barlow was delivering to Cochise, it was dark, and from their vantage point on a rocky ridge they could look down and see the dying fire of a campsite, with the twenty cattle grazing quietly in a swale nearby. There were two men in the camp, and two horses picketed at the edge of the firelight's reach. This much they could see, but they weren't close enough to identify the two men.

"There's supposed to be three," muttered Carney, nervously.

"Hell, don't you think I know that?" Heller was already peering warily into the darkness behind them. "Don't see a night guard on the herd."

"Shuddup. He might be close."

Carney was silent for a while, straining to hear any telltale sound that might betray the whereabouts of the missing third man, and watching the camp—and the herd—in hopes that the man might appear down there, which would be a great relief. But he didn't hear anything, or see anything, and eventually his nerves got the better of him.

"Maybe we better just ease back a ways. We'll catch up again tomorrow, when it's light."

"The hell you say," whispered Heller fiercely. "I ain't movin' until I know where that third man is. Or until the sun comes up. Whichever's first."

Carney sighed, and sat tight. Down below, the fire burned down to embers, and the two men in the camp rolled up in their blankets and went to sleep. Had all three men been in camp, Carney would not have hesitated to slip down off the ridge quiet as you please to kill Barlow—and the two vaqueros too if they made any trouble. Even if they *were* Ward's men. Like many Anglos from Texas, where conflict between the races was generations old, he had no use for "greasers."

Now, though, he had to spend an uncomfortable night hunkered down among the rocks and the cactus, shivering because of the cold—and his nerves— praying for daybreak to come. This was an eventuality he simply hadn't thought to prepare for, and he predicted, bitterly, that sooner or later Heller would get around to mentioning that Clay Burnett never had this problem—that Burnett always seemed prepared for anything that could conceivably happen.

Daybreak did come, finally, after what Carney decided was the longest night of his life. And in the morning light, they stared down at the camp and realized that there wasn't a third man. The two vaqueros were there, brewing up some coffee and cooking beans for breakfast. But there was no sign of Barlow. Carney cut loose with a string of curses, and Heller listened for a while, then told him to shuddup again. Finally Carney stood up, a Bowie knife in hand.

"I'm gonna go down there and start carvin' the flesh off some greasers till they tell me where Barlow made off to," he declared.

"Hold up," growled Heller. He was in a particularly foul mood after an all-night vigil on the cold, windswept rim; he had spent most of the time thinking he'd been a fool to go along with Carney on this mission. "I rode with you because I figured the smart thing was to kill the Yankee lieutenant. Well, he ain't here, and I'm not gonna be a party to killin' anybody else—especially men who work for John Ward."

"Greasers are cowards, every last one of them," sneered Carney. "We won't have to kill 'em. They'll talk after they get one look at this here knife."

"You can go down there if you want," said Heller, heading down the far slope for the horses that had been tied up down below. "Me, I'm going back to the ranch. Burnett said he was going to Texas right soon and I aim to go with him. To hell with that Barlow fellow. It's clear as day that he ain't headed for Fort Union, so by the time he tells anybody about us—if he ever bothers to do that—we'll be long gone."

Carney watched Heller disappear down the hill. Casting one last look at the camp of the vaqueros, he muttered a curse, sheathed the Bowie knife, and followed his companion down to the horses. Despite his contempt for the fighting prowess of Mexicans, he wasn't about to take on the two vaqueros all by himself.

When he reached the Chokonen che-wa-ki, Barlow was relieved to see that Ward had not yet arrived, and that life was being carried on in normal fashion. His arrival evoked a great deal of curiosity—it seemed that the whole village turned out to see him—but there was no overt hostility. As Barlow neared the center of the village, Cochise emerged from his cowah, followed by Nana. And then Oulay came out, and Barlow's heart flip-flopped in his chest. Her beautiful face brightened at the sight of him, and she moved as though to run to his side as he dismounted, but then she remembered her place, and remained discreetly behind her father. Her eyes never strayed from Barlow. For his part, Barlow found it difficult to take his eyes off her.

Cochise summoned Nachita, his translator, and asked Barlow about the cattle he had promised to bring.

"They're on their way," replied Barlow. "But so is John Ward, with a small army of vaqueros, armed to the teeth and wanting to spill Chokonen blood."

The Chokonen jefe absorbed this news without any change in expression.

"Ward's children were kidnapped," continued Barlow. "And the bodies of two Chokonen men were found near the scene."

Nana made a sound that combined anger, disgust, and surprise. He began to speak, loudly, to Cochise, but the jefe silenced him with a curt gesture.

"For a long time John Ward has wanted a war with the Chokonen," he told Barlow, by way of Nachita. "We will give it to him."

"It would be a mistake to stand and fight," said Barlow. "If you do, you're just playing into the hands of men like Ward, who want a war between the Apaches and the white man."

"What would you have us do? Tuck our tails between our legs and flee like dogs?"

"I would have you keep the peace. It's peace, after all, that you want for your people, isn't it? That's why you signed the treaty paper."

Cochise grimaced. "I am beginning to think that was a mistake."

"No, it wasn't a mistake," insisted Barlow. "Take

your women and children and fade into the hills, so when Ward gets here all he will find are empty cowahs."

"That will not stop him. He will never stop hunting us if he thinks we took his children. But you must know, Lieutenant, that we did not."

"I know you had no part in it."

"It was Goyathlay and his Avowed Killers," said Cochise angrily. "They live only for war. And they would not hesitate to kill two of their own people."

Barlow was aware that some of the Chokonen bronchos had closed in around him, and now he could feel their hostility. They had heard the news, and as far as they were concerned, he was now the enemy. At a sign from Cochise, they would kill him.

"Even if you kill Ward and his men, you'll lose. You would have the United States Army to deal with then. And it wouldn't matter that you had fought to defend your women and children, or that you had no hand in the kidnapping of the Ward children."

Cochise was silent for a moment, staring at Barlow, considering all that had been said.

Finally, he nodded, and said, "I know that you speak from the heart and that you are a friend to the Chokonen. I will do as you say. We will go up into the mountains. But hear me well, Lieutenant—if John Ward follows, we will not run very far."

Nana protested explosively, but Cochise spoke sharply to him, and the broncho lapsed into sullen silence.

"All I need is a little time," said Barlow. "I'll go back to Fort Union to tell Colonel Lyman the truth of what has happened. Maybe Ward can be stopped."

Cochise did not respond. He had made his decision,

and now proceeded to put it into action. He spoke to the gathered Chokonen, and they immediately responded, dispersing to their cowahs. Cochise entered his own cowah, followed by Nana and Nachita. The entire village—save one—seemed to have forgotten that Barlow existed. Oulay stood there, an island of calm in all the tumult, gazing at Barlow as he climbed back into the saddle. He guided the horse closer to her, and as he drew near, she reached out to touch his leg. He put his hand on top of hers.

"Don't worry," he said, even though she could not understand his words. "I will find you. No matter where you are, I'll find you."

It might have been his imagination, but in her smile he thought he detected evidence that she comprehended his meaning. Regretfully, he turned the horse away, and left the Chokonen village.

Chapter 12

Fort Union was two day's ride from the Mogollons. Barlow covered the distance in a day and a half. He traveled through the night, and pushed his horse—and himself—to the limits of endurance. Immediately upon arrival, he was brought before Colonel Lyman.

"Before I have you thrown in the guardhouse," said Lyman, struggling to contain his anger, "I would like to hear your explanation for why you disobeyed my orders, which were to deliver the cattle to Cochise and then return to this post. Instead, as I was informed by Sergeant Eckhart, you abandoned your command in the field and took it upon yourself to call on John Ward. Is that right, Lieutenant?"

"Yes, sir."

"Just who the hell do you think you are?"

"I'm an officer in the United States Army, Colonel. As such, it is my responsibility to see that the terms of a treaty entered into by my country are adhered to. Ward didn't fulfill his end of the bargain. The cattle he delivered here should have been put out of their misery, not delivered to Cochise. I wanted to see if

Ward had even an ounce of integrity. He didn't. Not surprisingly."

"He honored his commitment."

"Maybe the letter of the agreement, but not the spirit."

"Damn it, Barlow. If you had a complaint, you should have brought it to me."

"I did complain to you, sir, and it didn't do any good."

Lyman fumed. "You are insubordinate, sir. And I must add that you are one of the worst officers I have ever had the misfortune of encountering in twenty years of service."

"That may be so, sir, but I'm the least of your troubles at the moment."

The colonel's eyes narrowed. "What is that supposed to mean?"

Barlow told him how Ward's children had been kidnapped, probably by the Netdahe, who had arranged it so that the blame would fall on the Chokonen, and how Ward and all his men were riding into the Mogollon dead set on some blood spilling.

"I've talked to Cochise. He still wants peace. And for that reason, he is abandoning his village and hiding in the mountains. But Ward won't give up. Sooner or later he'll find the Chokonen. And that's when the war starts. But you may have time to stop it, Colonel."

Lyman had listened to Barlow's narrative with horror growing on his face. Now he sat down in the chair behind his desk, like a man made weak-kneed by too much bad news.

"And how do you propose that I stop it?" he asked.

"That's easy, sir. Find Ward before he finds Cochise."

"There'll be no stopping him," muttered Lyman.

Barlow couldn't believe his ears. "So you're not even going to try?"

"You could be wrong. The Netdahe might not be involved at all. Maybe the Chokonen *do* have his children."

"No." Barlow was adamant. "Cochise would not be a party to that."

"It's no secret where your sympathies lie, Lieutenant," sneered Lyman.

"Or yours, Colonel. And by the way, I forgot to mention that John Ward is in collusion with three Confederate agents. He's selling them a herd of cattle that will go to feed the Rebel army."

Lyman surged forward in his chair, slamming the palm of his hand down on the desk in front of him. "This is outrageous. What is the basis for your accusation?"

"I was there. I heard them. I saw them."

"I don't believe you."

"Of course not," said Barlow dryly. "You only believe what you want to believe."

"Lieutenant, I am going to give you one last chance, and that only because your father was one of the army's finest officers. You will have no further contact with Cochise and his people. And henceforth you will stay away from John Ward. Until further notice you are confined to this post."

"Then I have no choice but to resign my commission, sir."

Lyman stared at him. A man for whom the army was life itself, he could not comprehend how someone in Barlow's position could throw away a career in such cavalier fashion. But there had been nothing cavalier about Barlow's pronouncement. Ever since he'd suffered the shame of delivering Ward's castoff beeves to Cochise the possibility—no, make that the likelihood—that he would have to take this fateful step had been in the forefront of his mind. As he looked back over the events of the past few months, it seemed that fate had steered him, inexorably, to this point. Even during his years at the military academy he'd had his doubts about the wisdom of pursuing a military career. He'd known that he lacked the kind of passion for it that his father had manifested. And then he'd been sent into a situation so ambiguous that he'd wondered if he was on the right side of it. Most of all, there was Oulay. At this moment, standing before Colonel Lyman, he felt possessed of second sight—he could see into the future well enough to be sure that he could never have both Oulay and a career in the army. There would be war—a war unlike any other conflict involving Indians that the United States Army had ever fought, a war in which no quarter would be given, in which women and children would be targets. The kind of war that would not permit a white man and an Apache woman to have a life together. So he'd been prepared to make a choice.

"Well," said Lyman, at long last, "I can't help but think that the army is better off without you as an officer. I will accept your resignation. But bear in mind, mister, that just because you will no longer be an officer does not mean you are no longer in the army. I have nothing further to say to you. You're dismissed."

Barlow saluted, turned on his heel, and left Lyman's office. He crossed the parade ground in long strides. As usual, the troops were being drilled. He saw Trotter and Hammond with their commands. Hammond saw him too and steered his horse across the parade ground to intercept him.

"Joshua! I thought for sure the old man would have you clapped in irons by now. How did you get out of it?"

"It was easy."

"You'll have to tell me all about it—later. Glad you're back, my friend."

Barlow nodded, forced a smile, and continued on his way, as Hammond returned to his cavalrymen, shouting abuse in a voice that pierced the din of two hundred men and horses in motion all at the same time.

Entering the quarters he shared with Hammond, Trotter, and Summerhayes, Barlow went directly to the trunk at the foot of his bunk, threw open the lid, and began tossing his meager personal belongings onto the bunk. Belatedly he realized that he wasn't alone. Summerhayes was in his bunk on the other side of the room; propped up on one elbow, he was watching Barlow's every movement, bewildered.

"What are you doing in here?" asked Barlow, stuffing his belongings into panniers.

"I'm sick." Summerhayes swung his legs off the bed and sat there, shoulders hunched, head hanging. "At least that's what I told the surgeon. But there's really nothing wrong with me. I'm just a shirker, you know." He stood up and went to the window and gazed out at the activity on the parade ground. "I should be out there with my troop, but my heart's not in it." He glanced apologetically at Barlow. "I wouldn't expect you to understand."

"Actually, I do."

"I have no business trying to be a soldier," admitted Summerhayes. "But there's a family tradition to consider. My father, and his before him. Both officers."

"Not unlike my situation," said Barlow.

Summerhayes looked surprised—and immediately more at ease. "I didn't want to join the army. I wanted to get married and become a storekeeper. I fell in love with this young lady . . . completely unacceptable to my family, of course. My father issued an ultimatum. I should have stood up to him then and there. But I gave in, instead. Ran up with the white flag without even a skirmish." Summerhayes laughed bitterly. "You see, my family was confident that by the time I got back, my feelings for the young lady in question would have faded. Or that she would have found another. So here I am. The last place I ever wanted to be. But at least I'm doing what's expected of me."

"I'm sorry, Charles."

Summerhayes shrugged. "A coward can hardly expect better luck. What are *you* doing, anyway?"

"Don't ask. You'd be better off not getting involved, believe me." Slinging the panniers over his shoulder, Barlow stuck out a hand. "Goodbye, Charles, and good luck."

"Goodbye? Where are you going?" Summerhayes took the offered hand, shook it—and then held on to it, as though he was considering trying to keep Barlow from walking out the door.

Barlow simply smiled. "Goodbye." He pulled his hand free, and turned toward the door. Then he paused, and turned back. "I don't consider myself an expert, by any means, Charles, but I think you'll find that if you really love that young lady, and she's really in love with you, that time and distance won't matter at all."

Summerhayes nodded, staring gratefully at Barlow in a way that made it plain he took the words to heart, and understood the sentiment Barlow was attempting to convey.

Once outside, Barlow headed for the gate, his stride long and purposeful. He was counting on the likelihood that the colonel's restriction regarding his movements had not yet reached the officer of the day and, through him, the sentries at the gate. They let him walk through without a challenge. Passing through the scattering of Indian lodges that stood beyond the fort's entrance, he bent his steps toward the tent town, a quarter mile to the east.

The denizens of that community—the prostitutes, the card sharps, the saloonkeepers, the cutthroats—took notice of his arrival. But Barlow avoided them all, making straight for the livery, where he knew that a man named Hoskins traded in mules and horses. Most of the latter were swayback nags; he finally settled on a coyote dun shaggy with its winter coat, an animal that wasn't much to look at but seemed to be fairly sound. Hoskins quoted him a price of fifty dollars. Barlow got him down to twenty-five, with a saddle thrown in as part of the deal. Even at that, Barlow thought he was paying too much. But the dun was probably the best mount he could get in the tent town. While he might have been able to make off with his cavalry mount, he didn't want to give Lyman more ammunition against him. It was bad enough that his actions could brand him a deserter; he wasn't going to add horse theft to the charges that might be brought against him.

Hoskins was a bearded, dirty, big-bellied man who

smelled of rotgut whiskey—but he was no man's fool. He had his suspicions about Barlow, and when the latter asked him if he could provide some civilian clothing, he voiced those suspicions.

"You're a deserter, ain't you?" he asked. It was a rhetorical question. "That means if I help you, I could have the whole United States Army breathin' down my neck."

Barlow was saddling the dun; now he turned to face Hoskins, and a pistol had materialized in his hand—a pistol that he now aimed at a spot right between the livery owner's eyes.

"You won't have any trouble with the army when you tell them that I took the horse—and the clothes, if you've got them—at gunpoint."

Hoskins was surprised, then frightened; then a slow smile creased his heavily jowled face. "Guess you're right about that, mister. I'll see what I can find in the way of clothes for you."

He returned a few minutes later with some stroud trousers and an old muslin shirt. Barlow offered to pay for them, but Hoskins declined. "They ain't worth nothin'," he explained.

"Neither is this horse, but you made me pay for it."

Hoskins chuckled. "Now you're wrong about that animal, mister. But I don't expect you to take my word on it. You'll find out for yourself, soon enough. If you live long enough, that is."

"What do you mean?"

"You're ridin' alone in Apacheria. That's just one step shy of suicide, in my book. Where *are* you headed, anyhow?"

Barlow smiled coldly. "If I told you, you'd go straight to Lyman and sell the information to him."

Hoskins looked offended. "What kind of man do you think I am?"

Barlow figured that was another rhetorical question. He finished saddling the dun, rolled the civilian clothes in his blanket, and mounted up. Hoskins wished him good luck, and watched him ride out of the tent town, headed east. Barlow kept to that course until he was a couple of miles away, then turned north, making straight for the Mogollons.

Riding into the mountains, Barlow kept one fact foremost in mind: Anyone he met was a potential enemy. Cochise had agreed not to stand and fight John Ward, but that didn't mean all the Chokonen bronchos could be relied upon to follow their jefe's lead. There could be some who had taken up their weapons and dispersed into the mountains, waiting for an opportunity to strike back against their enemies. And he couldn't trust Ward or the vaqueros, either. The best course of action was to avoid everyone. At the same time, he had to find the Chokonen hideout. All he knew was that it would be high up on the Rim, in the most inaccessible part of the mountains. His chances of success were not very good. But he had to find Oulay. Had to get her away, somehow, before the killing started. And since Colonel Lyman had no intention of interfering, Barlow now knew that war was inevitable.

He had no illusions about the sort of skills he would need to escape detection by Apache bronchos, not to mention vaqueros who had lived all their lives in this country—and about how lacking he was in those skills. What he would need in order to survive was luck, and a lot of it.

He got what he needed. Quite by chance he cut the

trail of three riders. It was fresh sign—they had passed this way only hours earlier. The horses were shod. That much he could tell. So they weren't Apaches, and since there were so few of them, he could not believe that they might be some of Ward's men. Surely the vaqueros were wise enough to stay together as they ventured into hostile territory. At first Barlow thought it possible that the three riders were the Confederates he had seen at Ward's ranch. For that reason, he followed the tracks the rest of the day. As darkness fell, he saw a flicker of light in the distance— a campfire. Approaching as close as he dared on horseback, he dismounted, tethered the coyote dun to a wind-twisted ironwood tree, and continued on foot. Climbing a rock outcropping, he found himself at a vantage point from which he could look down upon the camp of the three men he had been following. He was surprised to discover that they were Ward's men, after all. And one of them was Short Britches.

Barlow was perplexed. Why were these three traveling apart from the main body of vaqueros? In mountains known to be full of Apaches, that was asking for trouble. And why were they building a fire to warm their camp? The light cast by that fire could be seen for miles. It was as though they were inviting the bronchos to attack. But that didn't make sense. And surely Short Britches, of all people, knew better.

Intrigued, Barlow returned to where his horse was waiting, and spent the night there, sleeping on the ground with rein leather tied to his left wrist, and only his army greatcoat to shield him from the cold. He was up before the sun, and when Short Britches and the vaqueros broke camp, he followed at a discreet distance.

As he followed their trail that day, it struck Barlow
that the three men were making no effort to conceal
their progress; they did not try to use the rugged terrain to conceal themselves, and instead crossed open
ground and rimrock like men who didn't have a care
in the world. Barlow began to think that Short
Britches was *trying* to attract the attention of the
Apaches. By midday Barlow had decided it was time
to get some answers. And he could think of only one
sure way to get them. He rode right in on them.
Seeing him, the vaqueros brandished their long guns,
and they did it in a way that convinced Barlow they
meant business—even though they knew who he was
going to shoot. But a sharp word from Short Britches
stopped them. The old scout rode to intercept Barlow,
and they met out of earshot of the vaqueros, who kept
a wary eye on the proceedings.

"They want to kill you," said Short Britches, with
a nod in the direction of his two companions. "They
have orders to. From John Ward."

"He found the village."

"But the Chokonen were gone. That same day we
met Ochoa and Menendez with the cattle you bought
for Cochise. Now John Ward knows that you are the
one who warned the Apaches. That's why he ordered
his men to shoot you on sight."

"Why are you out here trying to get yourself
killed?"

"The padrone's idea," said the old scout, his tone
contemptuous. "Three groups of three men each. He
hopes Cochise will attack at least one of the groups.
If he does, we scatter. With luck, at least one of us
will survive to tell the padrone about the attack. Then

he thinks he will be able to track the bronchos back to the Chokonen hiding place."

"So he's willing to use his own men as bait." Barlow shook his head. "That amazes me. But what's even more amazing is that you people do what he tells you to do."

Short Britches looked at the pair of vaqueros. "These men will die for their padrone. That is part of their way of life. It is the way they think. They know no other way."

"What about you?"

The old scout looked surprised by the question. "I do not intend to die for anyone."

"Yet here you are."

"But I will not die," said Short Britches, with supreme confidence.

"Do you *know* where the Chokonen are?"

Short Britches shrugged, and cast his eyes up at the rim of the peaks that towered above them. "Somewhere up there."

Barlow rode higher into the mountains, seeking the Chokonen, aware of the likelihood that it would be the Chokonen who found him first. The question then would be whether they killed him on sight, or took him alive to their jefe. The prospects were daunting, but the stakes—Oulay's safety—were too high for him to turn back. Her life was more important to him than his own. That, of course, denied all logic—and he knew that it did. He had seen Oulay only three times, and had spent no more than an hour altogether in her presence. They could not speak each other's language, and a kiss had been their most intimate contact. Yet he knew, with absolute conviction, that she was his conviction, that life without her wouldn't be worth living.

Late on the same day that he had confronted Short Britches, Barlow was jumped by Apaches.

The first he knew of their presence was the impact of a body hurled at him from atop a boulder as he was guiding his horse through a narrow, serpentine passage between huge rocks. The impact carried him off the coyote dun, and he landed on his left side, with the weight of the broncho on top of him, and the wind was knocked out of him. Though he was dazed, and wheezing desperately to get air back into lungs that no longer seemed able to function, Barlow found the strength to throw a backhanded blow that connected solidly with his attacker's jaw. The broncho's head snapped back, and he slumped backward. Barlow scrambled to his feet and clawed for the pistol holstered at his side. His attacker was getting up, recovering quickly from the blow. Barlow figured he was Chokonen, and he didn't want to shoot the broncho unless he had to. So he leveled the pistol at the Apache but did not fire. In that instant he heard the distinctive sound of a carbine's lever action behind him. He threw a quick glance over his shoulder, and saw the second broncho then. This one was standing atop another boulder, the carbine up to his shoulder now, and aimed rock-steady at a spot between Barlow's shoulder blades. *I'm a dead man,* thought Barlow.

The first Apache called out to his companion, then turned his attention back to Barlow.

"Put down the gun or you die," he said, in English. The wrong decision would be fatal—but Barlow made up his mind instantly, and threw down the pistol. He had been ambushed, and that alone seemed to indicate that the bronchos meant him harm. But it occurred to him that they could have killed him from hiding. He knew enough about fighting Apaches to know that they did not ordinarily expose themselves to unnecessary risks. So maybe they had never intended to take his life.

The first Apache picked up the Colt revolver and nodded to Barlow—a silent acknowledgment of this Pinda Lickoyi's courage. No one knew better than an Apache that sometimes it took more courage to keep living than to die.

"Come with us," he said. "We will take you where you want to go."

Chapter 13

Short Britches had been right—the Chokonen hideout was on the Mogollon Rim, remote and accessible only, as far as Barlow could tell, by means of a ledge scarcely wide enough for a horse and rider to negotiate. Beyond the ledge was a snow-covered saddle with steep rock faces on both sides, dotted with caves. They were about as high up as a body could get in the Mogollons; the wind howled through the crags, cold and cutting to the bone, and low-slung clouds clung like cotton to the rocky slopes. Looking at the situation with the eye of a military man, Barlow thought it was a highly defensible and perhaps impregnable position. But he thought the Chokonen people had to be suffering from the brutal conditions under which they were now forced to live. The entrances to the half dozen caves that Barlow could see were filled with Apache men, women, and children watching his arrival. Cochise ventured out, wrapped in a blanket as protection against the incessant wind. He was accompanied by Nachita.

"The army isn't going to interfere," said Barlow. He had nothing but bad news to deliver, so he got straight to the point. "And you're not going to get those twenty cattle I bought from Ward. You're on your own."

"It has always been so," said Cochise.

"Ward has been to your village. Now he's sending out small parties, hoping you'll attack one of them and provide him with the opportunity to track your bronchos back here."

"All that you have told me I expected to happen," replied the Chokonen jefe. "Now I must decide. Do we stand and fight here in the mountains that have always been our home? Or do we seek sanctuary in the Cima Silkq. It is far from where we want to be, but at least we will be safe there. As safe as the Apache *can* be in the world today."

Barlow shook his head. "I'm sorry."

"You have proven yourself to be a true friend of the Chokonen. You have nothing to be sorry for."

"Yes, I do. I'm sorry for what I'm about to ask. I want to take your daughter away. Take her somewhere safe."

"Come with me," said Cochise, and turned away.

Barlow followed him to one of the caves, where about thirty of the Chokonen were sheltered. Oulay was among them. Cochise walked to the rear of the cave, motioning for his daughter to join them there. Nachita accompanied them to continue in his role as translator. The rest of the Chokonen, however, remained a respectful distance away, out of earshot. Cochise spoke gravely to Oulay, and though Barlow could not understand his words, he understood the look of surprise, mixed with joy, that Oulay gave him as she listened. When Cochise was finished, she spoke briefly, her eyes downcast, her voice scarcely more than a whisper. Though he tried to remain inscrutable, Cochise could not entirely conceal the pain he experienced. He looked gravely at Barlow.

"Why do you imagine I would let you take my daughter away from me?" he asked. "She is the source of the greatest joy in my life."

"Because I'm in love with her. And I believe she's in love with me. And also because you care about her—you care too much to want to see her live the life of a fugitive."

"You think she would be safer with you than with her own father at her side."

"Under the circumstances, yes, I do."

Cochise was silent for a moment. Barlow struggled to maintain a calm exterior. If Cochise refused, what could he do? He would not try to steal her away; even if he were the sort to attempt such a thing, he could not succeed. And he doubted that the Chokonen would tolerate his presence if he tried to stay there with her. Yet he would not be able to turn his back and walk away—not when she was in so much danger. It would be an impossible situation if Cochise said no.

The Chokonen leader again spoke to his daughter. With tears in her eyes, Oulay wrapped her arms around her father's neck and embraced him tightly. Barlow had his answer. Despite his joy, he felt a sadness, for he knew there was a very real possibility that Oulay would never see her father again.

His decision made, Cochise wasted no time in seeing his daughter off. A horse was provided, and more supplies than Barlow thought the Chokonen could spare. A half dozen heavily armed bronchos would provide an escort until they were out of the Mogollons. Barlow made no objection. The supplies and the escort were

Cochise's conditions, and if he wanted Oulay to go with him he would have to accept them.

But before he left, Barlow felt obliged to make a last appeal for peace. Through Nachita, the translator, he urged Cochise to take his people to Mexico at once. "Don't give John Ward what he wants. Even if he dies in these mountains, he wins because the Chokonen will never be at peace with the United States again. They will be hunted down until every last Apache is dead or behind bars. And that's what Ward wants. He wants it so much he's willing to die to see it happen."

"John Ward will have his way," replied Cochise. "I have always known this to be so. Even when I signed the treaty paper, I knew that my people would soon die. But at least we will die with rifles in our hands, and our heads held high. You cannot run forever from your destiny, Lieutenant. Now go. Take care of my daughter. I will see her again, on the other side of the mountains."

The six Chokonen bronchos escorted them as far as the foothills to the east of the Mogollon Range, a journey during which they saw no sign of John Ward's vaqueros. The sun was setting when the Apache men took their leave without a word spoken. Barlow had gotten the impression that they weren't very happy with them. They didn't like the idea of Oulay going away with a Pinda Lickoyi—especially one they thought was still a yellow-leg, a soldier. It was quite possible that one or more of the bronchos had entertained notions of making Oulay his own. But Cochise had assigned them the task of protecting Barlow, along with his daughter, and as distasteful as they might find the first part of that assignment, they carried it out.

Once out of the mountains, and free of his sullen escort, Barlow breathed a sigh of relief. But that relief was short-lived, for now he faced another dilemma. Where would he go? He hadn't really given that much thought, since just getting to this point had been such a long shot. Now there he was, with Oulay at his side, and the responsibility for her safety and happiness resting squarely on his shoulders. His pockets were empty, he had no home to offer her, and there was a good chance that the army considered him a deserter.

The first priority was to find shelter. The Ward ranch house was a few hours away, but that wasn't an option, even though the rancher and all of his men were in the Mogollons trying to find Oulay's people. Clay Burnett and his fellow Confederates remained a big question mark. Barlow didn't know where they were, but he did know that they posed as great a threat to him as Ward and Lyman and the Netdahe renegades whom he was convinced had been the ones responsible for the disappearance of Kathleen and Linus Ward.

They spent that night under the stars. Though down on the flats the days had been growing warmer, the nights remained bitterly cold, yet in the mountains, Barlow did not dare risk a fire. He spread several blankets out for Oulay's bed, and while she slept, he kept vigilant guard until sunrise. The next morning they continued in an eastwardly direction and, before midday, happened upon an adobe building nestled between a couple of low hills. The corral next to the house was empty, and Barlow saw no sign of life around the place, even though he spent nearly an hour observing it from a distance with his field glasses. Finally, using hand signs to bid Oulay to stay where she was, he ventured closer alone. Once inside the adobe he knew that the structure had served as a line shack, a temporary home for the men who rode the outer edges of the land John Ward had claimed as his own. Behind the corral he found a spring bubbling up out of a rock outcropping. The place wasn't much, but it would do.

They spent the rest of the day cleaning the place out—and it needed a lot of cleaning. That evening they had a decent meal, using some of the provisions Cochise had provided. Barlow built a fire in the fireplace. He couldn't help noticing how beautiful Oulay looked by firelight. He wanted her, but couldn't bring himself to make a move. That was odd, because he had never before been particularly shy around women. Like many other cadets at West Point, he had regularly gone "over the wall" to visit the women of loose virtue who plied their trade out of wagons parked in the nearby woods. And he'd been quite bold where Jennie Randolph was concerned too—although she made it easy for him to be that way. Jennie was adept at playing the role of the shy, timid Southern belle in public, but when they'd been alone together she had turned into a wildcat. She had been the kind of woman who made it easy for a man to come right out and say what he wanted.

Yet here he was, with the most beautiful and desirable young woman he had ever known, a woman he loved more than life itself, and one who loved him back just as intensely it seemed—yet he was acting like a schoolboy who wanted to steal his first kiss. In an agony of embarrassment and uncertainty he did nothing, and said nothing, but rather merely sat there on the hard-packed floor, gazing into the fire, while she sat beside him, her legs drawn up against her body and her arms wrapped around them and her chin resting on her knees. Eventually, Barlow started to get drowsy; he got up and fetched the blankets and made a bed for her, then laid out a blanket for himself a respectable distance away. With a halfhearted smile he bid her good night and stretched out on the blanket, covering himself with his greatcoat, hoping he could end his torment with the narcotic of sleep.

But sleep, of course, eluded him. Gradually the fire died down, and when it was very nearly dark inside the adobe, Oulay moved her blankets next to his. As he turned, she slid under the greatcoat with him, and the touch of her warm, silken skin made him gasp with wonder and desire. They kissed with rising passion, and she tore feverishly at his clothes. When they became one, he knew that his life had changed irrevocably and that he would never again be content unless Oulay was at his side, within sight, within reach, just a smile away.

Barlow woke the next morning with a premonition of danger. Oulay slept soundly in his arms, her legs tangled up with his. He managed to untangle himself without waking her. Pulling on his trousers, he picked up the carbine and stepped outside. Seeing movement out of the corner of an eye, he whirled, bringing the rifle to bear—on Short Britches, who was sitting on his heels with his back against the adobe wall of the line shack, eyes narrowed against the slanting light of the sun just now rising over the eastern horizon.

"You," said Barlow, disgusted. "Like a bad penny, you're always turning up."

"John Ward is dead," said the old scout, without emotion. "Thought you'd like to know."

Barlow lowered the carbine. "Dead. What happened?"

"Cochise happened. Some of his bronchos attacked one of the padrone's scouting parties. One of the vaqueros got away, just like the padrone had planned. He led the rest of us back to the site of the ambush. We found the trail of the bronchos, and we followed it. I told John Ward that the trail was too easy to follow. I was pretty sure they wanted us to follow. That we were riding into another ambush."

"But he wouldn't listen, would he?"

Short Britches pursed his lips, and kept staring at the rising sun. "They hit us an hour before sundown, yesterday. It was all over in a matter of minutes. The padrone was one of the first to fall. Only a few of us managed to get away."

Barlow leaned the carbine against the wall of the line shack and sat on his heels beside the old scout, trying to sort through his feelings. He had never liked Ward, but he was sorry to hear of his death—not to mention the deaths of the men who had followed him. It was all such a terrible waste. And he was sorry too because Cochise and his people would never have peace. They would be hunted down and killed. Their fate was inevitable. War was inevitable.

"What are your plans now?" asked Barlow.

Short Britches shrugged. "Find somebody else to work for." He looked across at Barlow. "How about you?"

"I don't know."

"Here's the thing. Now that the padrone is dead, there are hundreds of cattle in these parts that don't belong to anybody. By now his heirs are dead too."

"You can't be certain of that."

"I'm certain—and so are you."

Barlow tried, with mediocre success, to banish thoughts of Kathleen and Linus—and the terror they must have experienced in their final hours—from his mind.

"So what you're getting at," he said, "is that I might as well claim some of Ward's cattle as my own. That I should stay put here."

"I'm not saying anything in particular. Just that there are a lot of free cattle around. Sooner or later, somebody is going to put his brand on them. Now that you mention it, why not you?"

"I'm not alone."

"Oh, I know."

Barlow wondered how he knew—but decided not to ask. "She's Chokonen. How do you think she would fare in these parts—especially now that we've got a war coming?"

"Wars don't last forever," said Short Britches. "And she will fare as well here as anywhere. As you say, she is Apache. Where in the white man's world will she be made to feel welcome? Where will she be safe?"

Barlow had to allow that the old scout had a point. He had it in mind to take her far from this place, far from the conflict between Apache and Pinda Lickoyi. But she would not be accepted no matter where he took her. And neither would he, for no other reason than that he had chosen to associate with an Indian.

The Mogollons were not far—Barlow could see them from where he stood, on the porch of the adobe line shack; they were a narrow, ragged-edged line of blue along the western horizon. This was the land of Oulay's birth. Perhaps she would feel better remaining here.

As for putting his brand on some of John Ward's cattle, he had no reservations. Short Britches was right—now that the rancher and his family were dead, his property belonged to anyone who could grab it and keep it.

"Let's say I decide to stay," Barlow said. "Are you offering to work for me?"

"Long as you keep me in tobacco, I'll work for you."

"It'll take more than just the two of us."

Short Britches nodded. "I can find you more men."

Barlow gazed at the old scout for a moment. He didn't trust Short Britches. The man was loyal only to himself. The vaqueros who had followed their padrone to their deaths had been fiercely loyal to John Ward. But Short Britches wasn't like that. He hadn't been willing to die for Ward. *And he won't stick his neck out very far for me, either,* mused Barlow. But there was no getting around that the man knew this country—and its dangers—like the back of his hand. He would be a liability, but he'd also be a great asset.

"All right," said Barlow. "I'll stay."

He didn't have any place else to go.

Short Britches left the line shack a few hours later, and he was back late the following day with three vaqueros. Barlow recognized two of them as men who had once ridden for John Ward—in fact, Ochoa, one of the vaqueros who had been chosen to help Barlow take the twenty head of cattle to Cochise, was among the three. As for the third man, Barlow assumed he had also been one of Ward's men.

"I found them at the ranch house," explained Short Britches. "They were about to go back to Mexico, but I talked them into coming here. They say they will work for you, if you want them to. They are hard workers, and you can rely on them. Best of all, they know this land and the cattle."

"Tell them I have no money to pay them—nor do I expect to have any for some time," said Barlow.

"They have already talked about that. They know you bought the twenty head for the Chokonen, so they figured you were broke. But this doesn't matter to them. They know you are an honest man and that you will pay them a fair wage when you are able to do so."

"Fine," said Barlow. "As you can see, we're going to need more accommodations." He had no intention of sharing the line shack with anyone but Oulay. "The first order of business will be to build a bunkhouse."

Short Britches spoke to Ochoa and the others in Spanish. They were all grins, and immediately set about debating among themselves the best location for the new structure.

The old scout waited until they were out of earshot before speaking again. "I found something else at the ranch house," he said. "The three men from Texas."

Barlow's eyes narrowed. "The Confederates. What are they up to?"

"I'm not sure. They did not talk to me, and I said nothing to them. When we left the ranch house we rode south, then swung wide around to come up this way. I wanted the men from Texas to think we were going to Mexico. But Ochoa tells me that one of them asked him about John Ward. So they know that the padrone is dead."

"They're going to gather up a herd and take it back to Texas with them," said Barlow.

Short Britches shrugged. "Maybe. But there are plenty of cattle to go around."

Barlow knew what the old scout was really saying. Live and let live. Let the Confederate agents have their herd. What did it matter? Barlow was no longer an officer in the United States Army. The war between North and South was no longer his concern. With the Texans gone, he would have one less thing to worry about.

That all made perfect sense. And yet it rankled Barlow to think that Clay Burnett and his associates were on the verge of succeeding in their mission. He knew what his father would do, in his place. Because whether he was in the army or not, he was still an American, and he still believed in the Union and what the Stars and Stripes stood for. Southern-born though he was, he considered the Confederates traitors, and he couldn't just stand by and let them have their way.

And there was a more personal component, one that had to do with his father. If he did what Short Britches was suggesting, Timothy Barlow would probably never know that his son had let his country down. But Timothy Barlow had fought and bled for that country, and for no other reason than that, his son knew that he was going to have to stop the Confederate agents. There were plenty of cattle, more than enough to go around. But Barlow had but one conscience, and he had to live with it every minute of the day.

"I'm not going to let them," he told Short Britches. "I want you to stick around here and look after things until I get back."

"Three against one—those are bad odds. I will go with you."

"This isn't your fight."

"No. But if I don't go, you will end up getting killed, and then the vaqueros and I will have to find someone else to work for."

"Suit yourself." Barlow walked over to Ochoa—the only one among the vaqueros who spoke English, as far as he knew—and told the man that he and Short Britches had some business to attend to and that they would be gone for a few days. "You're to make sure that nothing happens to the woman in there," he added, pointing to the line shack.

"Do not be worried," said Ochoa. "We will guard her with our lives."

"You'd better," said Barlow, turning away, "because if you don't, I'll kill you."

He headed for the line shack. Now came the hard part, telling Oulay that he was going to have to leave her. She would accept the news without a display of emotion. That was the Apache way. But she would feel sad and lost while they were separated. He knew this, because he knew that he would feel the same way.

Chapter 14

While John Ward led his vaqueros into the Mogollon Mountains, and Goyathlay led his Netdahe, with their two prisoners, southward on a roundabout route, avoiding open country and frequently used waterholes, Burnett and his two fellow Texans awaited developments at the Ward ranch house. Carney wanted to ride with Ward for no other reason than that he was aching for a fight. Knowing that this was not a good enough reason, he tried to convince Burnett that the reason he wanted to go was because it would make Ward beholden to them, which could only benefit them later. But Burnett said no. For one thing, he could see right through Carney; he knew that his companion's only true motivation was a desire to experience the thrill of battle. Nonetheless, he went to the trouble to explain why they didn't need to ingratiate themselves to John Ward.

One of Burnett's attributes was a sharply honed ability to read people. He knew that Ward would not, for example, cut them a better deal on the cattle they wanted just because they'd helped him against the Apaches. Most other men might have felt a sense of obligation, or friendship, in such circumstances. But John Ward was the type who would cut a friend's throat if there was a profit in it. He didn't care about friendship, or obligation. That was one reason, he explained to Carney, why they weren't going to buy into the cattleman's little war with the Apaches.

There was another reason too. Their assignment had been to stir up trouble between the Apaches and the United States Army. The idea being, of course, that if the Union had to deal with an Indian uprising in the Southwest, they would have no recourse but to expend men, money, and matériel to put it down— men, money, and matériel that would not be brought to bear against the Confederacy. This was why they had tried to disrupt the visit by the man named Grenville to the Chokonen village, because they had been aware of Grenville's intention to negotiate a treaty of peace with Cochise. Now, it seemed, an Apache war was in the making—and, ironically, not as a result of their efforts but rather thanks to John Ward's hatred of Indians and the actions of some of the Apaches themselves. In other words, Burnett told Carney, that part of their assignment had been accomplished. Why risk their necks to stir up trouble when there was more than enough trouble stirred up already?

No, said Burnett, they would sit tight and bide their time; they would wait to see if John Ward survived his fight with the Chokonen.

Heller piped up and said he agreed with Burnett— which came as no surprise to Carney, since Heller *always* backed Burnett. That was a source of great annoyance to Carney, because Heller had been his saddle pard for years before either one of them had ever heard of Clay Burnett. They had been in just about every saloon and jailhouse in a large portion of Texas together before the war broke out. Carney had thought Heller to be a man he could count on. Then came Burnett, and Heller started acting like every word he spoke was something Moses had brought down from the mountain. Heller actually admired Burnett, and had said as much.

Carney had to admit that he wasn't as smart as Burnett. He assumed this was why Burnett had a commission in the Confederate Army, and why Burnett had been put in charge of this mission. Burnett had book learning, but more than that he was just one clever son of a bitch. Most of the time he seemed to know what people were going to do or say even before they did or said it. In every instance he seemed to be able to plan for every eventuality. And everything he had planned seemed to work out more or less the way he'd planned it. Carney thought that maybe he admired Burnett too. Yet he wasn't about to say so out loud, not to Heller, and certainly not to Burnett himself. And just because he might admire the man didn't prevent him from resenting the hell out of him. Admiring somebody and liking him were sometimes two different things.

So they waited, twiddling their thumbs around the ranch house and having the place pretty much all to themselves, since all of those who worked for Ward, aside from one very old Mexican and his plump daughter, had ridden against the Apaches. The Mexican was blind in one eye and his daughter was slow in the head, but they maintained the Ward house. Since the Texans were still guests of the padrone, the pair kept Carney and the others fed. Heller acted like he wanted to bed the girl, even though she was slow, and about as pretty as a cow patty, but then that was Heller for you. As long as it was female, he wasn't one to discriminate. But Burnett expressed his disapproval, and that was all Heller needed in the way of motivation to keep his hands off the girl.

Several days passed, and then a half dozen of Ward's vaqueros returned. A couple of them were wounded. All of them looked like lost souls in a limbo of despair. Since Burnett spoke fluent Spanish, he was able to learn what had happened. The vaqueros stuck around just long enough to tell him, and to gather up their personal belongings; the next morning they had all vanished. Later that day, the old Mexican and his daughter headed south in a rickety wagon. The padrone was dead, killed by the Apaches, who had also killed the other vaqueros. Apparently, no one believed that the two Ward children would ever be seen alive again.

"Well, boys," said Burnett, quite pleased with the way things had turned out, "looks like we can start thinking about going home. All we have to do is gather up as many cattle as we can handle and head east."

"We're gonna steal the cows?" asked Heller.

"You can't steal property that doesn't belong to anyone. It's finders keepers now that Ward is dead."

"What if they're wrong?" asked Carney. "What if he's not dead?"

"He is." Burnett was supremely confident. "Look, those vaqueros were loyal to him, and they wouldn't have made for the tall timber if he was still alive."

"He's right, Carney," said Heller.

"Shut up," said Carney crossly. "How are just the three of us going to push a herd all the way to Texas?

We were counting on Ward to lend us some of his men, or at least to help us round up a crew."

"We'll take only as many as the three of us can handle."

"We could have tried to hire on the vaqueros who were just here," said Carney. "That would mean more guns for when we have to pass through Comanche country."

Burnett shook his head. Just because the surviving vaqueros had pulled up stakes didn't mean their fierce loyalty to John Ward had been forsaken. He wasn't sure how they would react to his making off with some of the padrone's cattle, and he wasn't going to take any unnecessary chances.

They went to work immediately. Finding the cattle wasn't difficult. Not even Ward had known for sure just how many head grazed on land he claimed, but the number was in the thousands. During the winter the cattle were allowed to roam more or less at will; line riders tried to keep most of them within the boundaries of the ranch. During the spring, the vaqueros would round them up and brand any mavericks or calves they could find. Now Burnett and his companions had their own roundup. Burnett picked a spot less than a mile north of the ranch house as a holding ground. While one of them remained there to watch over the cattle already rounded up, the other two set out together to find more beeves. Carney had some experience with cattle, having been involved at an early age with a gang of rustlers in the Devil's River country of Texas. He knew how to "run iron" but Burnett wasn't interested in changing the Ward brand. Instead, as he told Carney and Heller, he would draw up a bill of sale and forge Ward's signature on it.

For all intents and purposes, they would appear to be returning home with a legally acquired herd of cattle, and who would there be to say otherwise?

When Carney heard this, he immediately thought of the gold Burnett carried—the hard money they had been given to make the purchase: five thousand dollars' worth of gold, in fact—enough to buy twice as many head of cattle as the two or three hundred Burnett thought they could handle by themselves. He had what he thought was a good idea.

"Since you're tryin' to make this look like a genuine sale," he told Burnett, "then we might as well keep some of that gold. Just tell 'em you paid it out for the cattle. Nobody will ever be the wiser."

But Burnett said no. They were going to be returning with fewer cattle than were expected, and to offset that shortcoming he intended to give back every last gold coin. Carney was incensed. Even Heller seemed to be of a mind to side with Carney in this case. Not that it mattered if both of them wanted the gold, because Burnett fully intended to have his way whether they liked it or not. He had the gold, and they would have to kill him to get it, and after thinking long and hard, Carney came to the conclusion that he wasn't prepared to do that. Clay Burnett was not only a smart man—he was also very dangerous. Carney had to admit to himself that he was no match for Burnett when it came to killing. That didn't mean, though, that he was giving up on the idea of taking some of the gold for himself. Carney had learned one lesson above all during his misspent life: If you kept your eyes open and watched for an opportunity and were prepared to grab it if it came, then you could end up getting what you wanted even though the odds were against you.

They gathered up more than a hundred cattle on the first day, and nearly as many on the day after that. On the third day it was Carney's turn to stay with the herd. Burnett and Heller rode out at first light. Carney rode a slow circuit around the herd. The days had been warming up and the snow on the ground was melting, so the cattle were busy looking for the first green sprigs of grass. Carney was relaxed. He didn't expect any trouble, from the beeves or anything else. But an hour after the departure of his companions, he spotted a lone rider, far off in the distance, coming in from the north in a hurry. Carney was on the south side of the herd, and his first thought was that this had to be either Burnett or Heller, so he expected the horseman to circle wide around the holding ground to avoid spooking the herd. A minute passed, then another—and Carney began to frown. He still couldn't identify the rider, but it was beginning to look as though the man intended to ride straight through the cattle. Carney kicked his horse into motion, even though he knew it was too late to cut the man off.

The horseman plunged straight into the holding ground. The cattle scattered. Carney shouted a curse. Then the rider drew a pistol and fired. Carney wasn't sure at first whether the man was firing at him, or just making smoke in order to spook the cows—it occurred to him that maybe somebody else had designs on John Ward's cattle, and had been waiting for him and his companions to do all the gathering before he came in and stole them away. But when the rider fired a second time Carney heard the bullet buzzing past, and he realized then that he was the target. He whipped his horse around and made a run for it. There was a rise to the south, and he thought that if he could get to the other side of it, he'd have just enough time to dismount and unlimber his long gun and be ready to pick the attacker off as he reached the rim.

It didn't work out that way. Carney was nearly to the top of the rise when a second horseman suddenly appeared before him, uttering a bloodcurdling cry that nearly made Carney jump out of his skin. The horse under him balked and reared, just as Carney involuntarily choked up on the reins. Both the horse and Carney went down. The horse got up immediately, and ran off, bucking. Carney was a little slower in recovering. Dazed by the fall, he groped for the pistol on his hip. The distinctive sound of a carbine's lever action being worked froze him in middraw. He looked up at Short Britches, still mounted and aiming a long gun at his head.

"Go ahead," said the old scout cheerfully. "I don't care one way or the other."

The first horseman arrived. Carney turned to identify him—and his jaw dropped when he recognized Barlow.

"You!"

"Where are your friends?" asked Barlow.

"Go to hell."

"I told you," remarked Short Britches. "Can I go ahead and kill him?"

"Yeah," said Barlow. "Go ahead."

Short Britches braced the carbine's stock against his shoulder.

"No! Wait! They're . . . they're out looking for more cows."

"Which way did they ride?"

"East. They rode east." To Short Britches: "Put the gun down."

"How long ago did they leave?" asked Barlow.

"Couple of hours ago."

"When are they due back?"

"No way to tell. Whenever they find some cattle."

Barlow glanced at Short Britches. "Don't kill him yet."

"That's a mistake," commented Short Britches, but he lowered the carbine. "His life is of no value to us."

"I'm not in the habit of shooting men down in cold blood," snapped Barlow.

"You don't have to. I'll do it."

"I said no, damn it."

Short Britches shrugged. "You're running the show. So what do we do with him?"

"We're not far from the ranch house, are we?"

"Not far. Maybe a mile yonder."

"We'll take him there. When his friends get back and find him gone and the herd scattered, they'll also find our tracks. My bet is they'll follow."

"They won't come for me," said Carney. "Not Burnett."

"Yes, he will. He won't leave you behind, for fear you might talk. He'll either want you free or dead."

Carney didn't respond. He felt his heart hammering inside his chest because he realized that Barlow was right.

The first night the Netdahe had spent running, putting as much distance as possible between themselves and the scene of their crimes. But on the second night Goyathlay made camp. The horses were tired. He

would not allow a fire. As far as he could tell, they
were not being pursued, but there was no point in
taking chances.

Kiannatah was impressed by the bravery of their
two young prisoners. Now and then the girl would
weep, but she did it quietly, and was quick to regain
her composure. The boy was defiant. He had a brave
heart for one so young. He looked the Netdahe
straight in the eye and did not flinch. It was a shame,
thought Kiannatah, that they were both going to die
soon. Their deaths were inevitable. Goyathlay would
never let them go, and trying to ransom them was not
an option. Kiannatah still believed that Goyathlay had
erred in preventing him from killing both of the children as soon as they had been discovered. He assumed
Goyathlay wanted the blame for their deaths to be
attributed to the Chokonen, and he believed that this
would happen regardless of when or where the bodies
were found. Kiannatah tried on several occasions to
broach the subject with Goyathlay, but Goyathlay was
sullen and tight-lipped and would not talk to him.

That night the other bronchos raped the girl. This
Kiannatah had anticipated. At first she fought back,
but doing so was futile. She was beaten brutally, and
then used. The boy was bound hand and foot, and
was powerless to help his sister. He shouted until he
lost his voice, and then, realizing that he could not
stop the nightmare, he shut his eyes and turned his
face away. Unfortunately, he could not shut his ears
to the moaning and whimpering of his sister as, one
by one, the bronchos took a turn with her. Goyathlay
had walked a short distance from the camp before the
attack began—Kiannatah could see him standing on a

rock a stone's throw away, a dark shape against the star-filled sky. Although Kiannatah was sure Goyathlay could hear what was happening, the other man did not move. For himself, Kiannatah sat to one side and watched the goings-on with hooded eyes. When one of the other bronchos invited him to join in, he simply glared at the man. For nearly an hour, he sat there. Then, abruptly, he rose, in one fluid motion, and approached the boy. The boy looked up and saw the knife in Kiannatah's hand, and his eyes glimmered with the terrible knowledge of what was about to happen. Kiannatah killed him quickly, cutting his throat.

The other bronchos were surprised, and when Kiannatah rose and approached them, they backed away, uncertain of his intentions. His features betrayed nothing. The girl lay on her belly, her torn clothing in shreds around her.

She was trying to crawl. Kiannatah pinned her down with a knee between her shoulder blades. He grabbed a handful of her yellow hair with one hand and lifted her head. The blade bit deeply, opening up her throat. Her body tensed, convulsed, and then was still. He let go of the hair and rose, wiping the blade clean with a remnant of her clothing before returning it to the sheath at his side.

Standing, he turned to look at the bronchos again. They had recovered from their surprise, and now a couple of them were resenting what he had done. They had not finished with the girl. Kiannatah had nothing but contempt for them. He had witnessed rape before, but never participated. In his mind, rape demonstrated a weakness, and he did not tolerate weakness, either in others or in himself. The purpose of the Netdahe was to kill the enemies of his people, nothing more and nothing less. It was certainly not to indulge one's lust.

He did not feel the need to explain any of this to the other bronchos. He didn't care if they understood why he had killed the two children. He didn't care if they hated him. With the possible exception of Goyathlay, he was not afraid of any of the other Avowed Killers. And none of the others challenged him, or even went to Goyathlay to complain. They could have done so—it was, after all, Goyathlay's place to decide the ultimate fate of their prisoners, not Kiannatah's.

Some time passed before Goyathlay returned to camp. Kiannatah was sitting where he had sat before. The other bronchos were gathered in a surly group on the other side of the camp. Goyathlay sat down near Kiannatah and gazed for a moment at the two corpses.

"They had to die," said the Netdahe leader, at long last.

Kiannatah didn't say anything.

"I have seen you cut the eyes from an enemy's head," said Goyathlay. "I have seen you cut the skin from his body. Why does it matter that these two suffered during their last hours? They were Pinda Lick-oyi, after all."

Still Kiannatah said nothing. He wasn't surprised that, of all his companions, only Goyathlay understood why he had slain the children. Only Goyathlay knew that it had been an act of mercy, rather than one of brutality.

Chapter 15

The Ward ranch house and outbuildings were a ghost town. It was odd, thought Barlow, that even though the buildings had been unoccupied for only a few days, they looked as though they'd been abandoned long ago. There was a forlorn air about the place, as though the structures themselves were somehow aware of the tragedy that had befallen their former occupants. Seeing them brought Kathleen and Linus to Barlow's mind. He didn't mourn the passing of John Ward, but Ward's children were another matter entirely. And even though there was a slight chance that they might still be alive, and might even survive whatever ordeal they were now suffering, he knew, deep down, that he would never see either of them again. There was the ultimate tragedy, he thought glumly: Innocent children, so full of life and promise, had become victims of a needless war.

Short Britches assumed that Barlow would want to move the prisoner into the main house, but Barlow chose instead one of the bunkhouses. Once inside, he gave the place a thorough going-over. There was one door and four windows—two of these on the front wall, providing a view across an expanse of hard pack of the main house, and one on either end. All the windows were provided with heavy-timbered shutters, and these sported gunports. Short Britches informed him of a floor hatch, located in a back corner under one of the narrow bunks. This, he said, allowed a man to drop down to the ground and crawl out from under the building. It was obvious that the bunkhouse had been built to double as a fortress in the event of an attack. The walls were adobe, a foot thick, and capable of stocking any round. The one shortcoming was the timbered roof. The best way to flush defenders out of such a fortress, mused Barlow, would be to set the roof on fire.

They used a lariat to bound Carney hand and foot and laid him out on one of the bunks. Even though the Confederate hadn't uttered a word since his capture, Barlow gagged him anyway. After that, there wasn't much to do apart from wait. Short Britches took up his station at one of the front windows while Barlow took the other.

They didn't have long to wait. A little more than two hours later, the old scout called Barlow's attention to two riders coming in slow from the east. The horsemen passed the big house and checked their horses to give the place a careful survey. Barlow headed for the bunkhouse door.

"What are you doing?" asked Short Britches. "I can knock at least one of them down from here."

"No, not yet. I want to talk to them first."

The old scout was mystified. "What is this? You just *trying* to get yourself killed?"

"I'm just trying to do this in a way I can live with."

"I've always worried more about just living than about living with something."

Barlow stepped outside, shutting the door behind him.

When the other men saw him, the two riders urged their horses forward. As they approached, they put some distance between one another, and when they checked their horses a second time, they were still a good thirty feet away from the bunkhouse.

"Lieutenant Barlow," said Burnett, with an amused expression on his face, "I should have guessed. Where is Mr. Carney?"

"Alive, and inside. My prisoner. I'm going to hand him over to the army."

"Is that right? Well, I don't think I can stand by and let you do that, Lieutenant."

"I don't think you can stop me."

Barlow glanced at Heller. The latter's eyes were narrowed into slits, and his hand rested on a thigh not six inches from the pistol on his hip. Here, thought Barlow, was a man who had killed before, and had no compunction about doing it again—and would commence the task upon a single word from Burnett.

"So what do you want?" asked Burnett, head cocked slightly to one side. He had scanned the bunkhouse, and seen the barrel of Short Britches' long gun jutting through the gunport of the window shutters. "You must want something, or you wouldn't have waited here for me to show up."

"I want to give you a chance to go back to Texas. Ward is dead, and I'm claiming his cattle. You don't get to have even one, Burnett. Just turn around and head for home and you can live."

"What gives you the right to claim Ward's cattle?"

"Nobody gave it to me. I'm taking it."

"You've got *cajones,* Lieutenant. I'll give you that," said Burnett admiringly. "But why let the two of us go when you're dead set on keeping Carney? Cut him loose and I'll consider your offer."

"No. Carney is going to tell people about the scheme you and John Ward were involved in."

"Why would you waste your time slandering the name of a dead man?"

"It's not slander. It's the truth."

Burnett nodded. "And then maybe nobody will much care if you take all his cattle. Is that it? Well, Lieutenant, I tell you what—I'll have to talk your offer over with my pardner, here."

"You do that."

"I'll get back with you." It sounded like a threat.

Burnett and Heller wheeled their horses around and rode away. They didn't look back. Barlow watched them for a moment before returning inside.

"They might leave without their friend," said Short Britches. "But that Burnett isn't going back to Texas without what he came for: cattle."

Barlow nodded. "I know. He made up his mind to fight. But he's not a fool. He won't come charging straight into our guns. That would be suicide. No, I expect he'll wait until dark. Try to get in close without being seen. Maybe try to set fire to the roof and smoke us out."

"That's what I would do," concurred Short Britches.

"So here's what we're going to do," Barlow said and proceeded to tell the old scout his plan.

When Barlow was finished, Short Britches thought

the plan over and nodded. "It might work. But doesn't sound like you'll be alive to find out."

"I'll be alive—unless you miss."

Short Britches grinned. "Not at that range. Not with this gun." He hefted the Big Fifty.

They had an hour until sundown, and they used that time to turn every bunk in the place into kindling. The shattered wood was piled up just inside the door. This they doused with kerosene from several lanterns, emptying two and keeping only an inch of fuel in the base of the third. Finally they moved the bunk that concealed the floor hatch in the back corner.

"Time for you to get into position," said Barlow.

Short Britches dropped through the hatch. Barlow went to one of the front windows and peered through the gunport, wondering where Burnett and Heller were holed up, wondering if they were watching, and wondering if they would see Short Britches headed for the main house and figure out that there was an ambush in the making. But Barlow never saw the old scout. And that brought to life the old doubts he'd had about the man. Could Short Britches be trusted? Perhaps, instead of making for the big house, he'd gone to the barn, where they had put their horses, and was at this very moment heading for the hills, leaving Barlow to his fate. And why shouldn't he do that? What did he have to gain from throwing his lot in with a lone deserter? One thing was certain: Barlow knew that if Short Britches abandoned him, he was done for.

Barlow dragged the bound and gagged Carney over to the corner of the room near the open floor hatch, and sat there in the darkened bunkhouse with his back against the wall and his carbine across his knees—and waited, the lantern, turned low, within reach.

A half hour later Carney turned his head sharply—he'd heard something that Barlow had missed, and was straining to hear it again. Barlow placed the barrel of his pistol against the Confederate's head. A moment later he heard the telltale creak of a loose plank on the bunkhouse porch. Someone was approaching the front door. Barlow tried to swallow. His throat was dry as dust. He reminded himself to breathe.

The door burst open, hurled back on its hinges by the force of Heller's kick. Barlow pistol-whipped Carney and was aware of the Confederate's unconscious form slumping down through the open hatch as he turned up the lantern and hurled it onto the pile of kerosene-soaked wood in front of the doorway. The wood exploded into flame. Still in the doorway, Heller threw up an arm to shield his face. A heartbeat later he was swinging his rifle in Barlow's direction. Barlow dived forward, triggering the pistol. His bullet struck Heller high in the shoulder. It didn't even knock the big man off balance. But in the next heartbeat Heller's chest exploded in a spray of blood and shattered bone—a gruesome sight followed immediately by the distant boom of a big-caliber rifle. Short Britches was in the main house, after all—and he'd been able to frame his target against the light from the blazing pyre inside the bunkhouse.

Barlow glanced upward, saw the flames licking at the rafters, and wasted no time in rolling to the floor hatch and dropping through. The space between the bunkhouse floor and the ground was no more than twelve inches, but it was enough; Barlow began to crawl, dragging the unconscious Carney along behind him. He was still under the bunkhouse when the old scout's Big Fifty boomed again. Emerging at the back of the bunkhouse, Barlow left Carney and circled round to the front. He took the corner cautiously. Heller lay faceup on the porch, his legs across the door's threshold. A second man—it had to be Clay Burnett—was crawling, slowly, across the hardpack, away from the burning bunkhouse. Barlow went to him. Burnett rolled over on his side and tried to bring his pistol up, but Barlow kicked it out of his grasp, and Burnett fell over on his back with a gasp of pain. By the light of the fire, Barlow could see that the front of the man's shirt was slick and dark with blood. Barlow knew in a glance that the man had only moments to live.

Burnett managed a pain-racked smile. "You . . . you don't play fair, Lieutenant," he whispered.

"No, I don't."

Barlow looked up to see Short Britches coming across the hardpack from the main house. Even in the night shadows it was easy enough to identify that bent stovepipe hat and his horse-warped amble. The Big Fifty was over one shoulder. When he arrived, he glanced down at Burnett and grunted.

"Huh. About an inch to the left of my mark," he said in a clinical, detached way, as though he were passing judgment on a shot fired into a bull's-eye rather than into a human being. Then he saw something, and knelt beside Burnett. Pulling aside the dying man's bloody shirt, he exposed a money belt secured around the other man's waist. The old scout glanced up at Barlow. "Well, what do we have here?" Opening one of the pouches, he brandished a gold coin.

"Confederate money?" asked Barlow.

"Not Confederate. Yankee. A lot of it."

"What he was going to pay John Ward for the cattle?"

Short Britches used his knife to cut the belt away from Burnett's body. Standing, he measured the weight of the belt for a moment, then offered it to Barlow.

"You killed him," said Barlow. "You take it."

"I have no use for gold," admitted Short Britches.

Barlow shrugged. He didn't care if Short Britches took the gold and rode away never to be seen again in this part of the country. His feelings where the old scout was concerned were confused. He was grateful for the fact that the man had backed him in his clash with the Confederate agents—without Short Britches, he wouldn't have stood a chance against Burnett. But he still didn't trust Short Britches. The man was a cold-blooded killer who might turn on him at any time. It was like living with a rabid dog.

Short Britches glanced at Heller's body, and asked, "What about the other one?"

"He's out cold, behind the bunkhouse."

"You really going to turn him over to the army?"

Barlow nodded. What he wanted to do was go home to Oulay—it was funny, but he thought of the line shack as home only because she was there. But he needed to find out what, if anything, Colonel Lyman intended to do about his unauthorized departure from Fort Union. Had he been branded a deserter. Was he subject to a court-martial and long years behind bars? If that were the case, he might never see Oulay again. Yet the alternative was to live out his life constantly looking over his shoulder, and that was no way to live.

He wanted a fresh slate with Oulay; the last thing he wanted to do was to permit a situation in which one day his past might destroy her.

"Well," said Short Britches, "that doesn't make any more sense to me than it did to him." He nodded at the dying Clay Burnett. "You wanted him for bait, and that worked. Now he's of no use to us. I'll kill him if you want."

"I've seen enough killing for one day," replied Barlow.

As soon as Barlow spoke, Burnett dragged one last ragged breath into his lungs and died.

"Let's get out of here," said Barlow.

"One last thing to do."

Short Britches edged closer to the bunkhouse—now a blazing inferno—and retrieved a chunk of timber that was aflame at one end. This he carried across the hardpack to the main house. A few minutes later he was back, and Barlow began to see the flickering light of the fires he had set through the windows of the house.

"Why did you do that?"

Short Britches gazed bleakly at the building across the way. "That place is filled with ghosts. They're all dead now, you know. The children along with the father."

"How do you know?"

"Like I said. Ghosts."

He walked away, leaving Barlow to wonder if the old scout actually expected him to believe that he'd seen the ghosts of Kathleen and Linus Ward.

Kiannatah waited with the rest of the Netdahe on a rocky ridge overlooking a year-round spring that was located only a couple of hours north of the Mexican border. Goyathlay had gone to visit an old Nakai-Ye sheepherder whose hut was located near the spring. This old man had lived his entire life in this region, and though he seldom strayed from his home, he knew everything that was going on. Travelers often stopped at the spring, and thought nothing of speaking freely in the presence of the old man, who never seemed to pay any attention to anything except his flock. Goyathlay wanted to know the extent of both the American and Mexican army activities along the border before he chanced a crossing, and the best person to ask about such things was the sheepherder. So he had gone down to speak to the old man, alone.

Without the burden of their two young prisoners to slow them down, the Netdahe had made excellent time in their flight south. The bodies of Kiannatah's victims had been left where they lay. Before long, the desert's scavengers would pick their bones clean. It was unlikely that their remains would ever be found.

The other bronchos were eager to make the crossing and continue on their way to the Cima Silkq. They were tired of being on the run, and the Sierra Madre mountains provided them a sanctuary where they could recuperate without fear of attack. Eventually, Goyathlay would lead them on another raid—hopefully, next time, against the Nakai-Ye villages. Those were easy pickings. They would kill some of the Nakai-Ye, rape some of the women, and steal some of their mules. Mule meat was a favorite repast for the Apache. Then, their grisly deeds done, they could simply fade back into the Sierra Madre, where not even the Mexican soldiers dared to venture.

Kiannatah did not share in their anticipation. He

was haunted by thoughts of Oulay, the daughter of Cochise. He sat there, apart from the others, brooding over what his next move should be. It seemed that the farther they got from the Mogollon, the more intense was his longing to possess the pretty Chokonen nahlin. He admired Goyathlay, and had always before thought he would remain content to follow the Netdahe leader wherever the man took him. But Goyathlay was leading him away from the object of his obsession.

Eventually Goyathlay returned from his visit with the old sheepherder. He told his followers that no American soldiers had passed this way in recent days. Nor was there any word of any out-of-the-ordinary activity by the federales on the other side of the border. Therefore, Goyathlay had decided they would cross immediately. At that moment Kiannatah made his decision.

"I am not going with you," he said.

The others stared at him. They looked surprised—all save Goyathlay. It was impossible to read his reaction to Kiannatah's pronouncement.

Having made his intentions plain, Kiannatah turned toward the horses. Goyathlay followed him.

"Where are you going?" asked the Netdahe leader.

Kiannatah saw no purpose in lying. He told Goyathlay that he intended to find the Chokonen and steal away the daughter of Cochise. Goyathlay looked even more somber than usual. For a moment he was silent, and during that interval Kiannatah swung with pantherlike agility aboard his horse.

"Cochise will know that John Ward did not kill those two Chokonen hunters," said Goyathlay. "I am sure that he suspects us, which means he will kill you."

"He will not get the chance."

"The reason for the things we have done is to force Cochise and Mangas and the others to fight the Pinda Lickoyi. Soon all the Apache will be at war with the White Eyes. When that happens, they will welcome us back into their cowahs, for they will have need of fighters such as us. Cochise will have to put aside his hatred for us so his people may survive what is to come. Once more Goyathlay will fight side by side with him, and with Mangas, just as in the old days against the Nakai-Ye."

Kiannatah watched Goyathlay intently, and said nothing.

"I have thought of you as a son, Kiannatah," said the Netdahe leader. "Of all the Avowed Killers, you are most like me. But if you do this, you will become my enemy. And if you enter the Cima Silkq, I will have to hunt you down and kill you. Then I will return to Cochise his daughter, and present him with your head as an offering of peace. All Apache must fight together if we are to defeat the Pinda Lickoyi."

"We cannot defeat the Pinda Lickoyi," Kiannatah replied flatly. "I do not kill my enemies for the sake of the Apache. I do not ride with you to bring about a war. I already have a war. It has been with me since I was a child, watching my family murdered by the Nakai-Ye in the village called Dolorosa. It makes no difference to me if Cochise and Mangas fight at your side or at mine. I do not need them. And I do not need you."

Goyathlay's eyes blazed with anger. "I will let you go now because of my feelings for you. But once you are gone, my heart will be hardened against you, and we will be enemies."

Kiannatah leaned forward slightly. "Do not try to hunt me down unless you are ready to die."

Goyathlay stared at the young Netdahe. He knew that this was no mere bravado on Kiannatah's part. The broncho was supremely confident that, if the day ever came when they fought one another, Goyathlay's death would be the outcome. And as he watched Kiannatah ride away to the north, Goyathlay experienced something entirely new: fear. Until today he had never been afraid of another man.

Barlow and Short Britches, with their prisoner, were about halfway to Fort Union from the Ward ranch when a half dozen Apache bronchos suddenly emerged from a nearby arroyo. They were mounted, and heavily armed. But it wasn't an ambush. Their weapons were not drawn. They merely showed themselves and then waited to see what the reaction of the three Pinda Lickoyi would be.

Carney gave a shout of alarm. With hands bound behind his back, he was acutely aware of how helpless he was—and how quickly he would die—if the Apaches attacked. He cried out to Barlow to cut him loose. But Barlow paid him no heed. While his hand involuntarily dropped to the pistol at his side, Barlow was quick to comprehend that these bronchos did not have murder on their minds. Had it been otherwise, the killing would have already commenced. Still, he was more than a little surprised that even Short Britches had been caught off guard—a fact manifested by the fervent *"Madre de Dios!"* that the appearance of the bronchos elicited from the old scout, and by the way the Big Fifty materialized in his hands.

One of the bronchos called out, raising an empty hand. Short Britches breathed a sigh of relief.

"He says they don't want a fight," he told Barlow.

"Glad to hear it. Find out what they do want."

Short Britches rode closer to the bronchos. He talked with the one who had called out to him. They conversed for some time—enough time for Carney to get so edgy he felt like he was about to come out of his skin.

"Damn it, Barlow, cut me loose and give me a gun. Give me a chance at least!"

"Shut up."

"It's a trap. All you got to do is look at 'em and you can see they're on the warpath. There're only three of us and six of them—at least six, probably more. The others are waiting for a signal, and when it comes, they'll be on us like ticks on a hound, and you gotta at least let me die like a man."

"I'm not going to tell you again."

Carney shut up.

A few minutes later, Short Britches motioned for Barlow to come forward. Barlow complied, towing Carney's horse along behind, with Carney looking like a man being dragged closer and closer to the gates of Hell.

"These men are from the White Mountain band," explained Short Britches. "This one is called Delgadito. He's what you might call the head honcho. They heard there was a war brewing out here, and they've traveled a long way to fight against the other Apache bands."

"Why would they want to do that?"

"There's plenty of bad blood between the White Mountain band and the other bands. It goes back a long way, many generations. There was a falling out, and the Chokonen and Bedonkohe and some of the other bands joined forces to drive the White Mountain band away. I'm not sure anybody still remembers exactly what started the trouble. But the White Mountain band had to move, and they carved a place for themselves in Comancheria, though it cost them many lives to do so. Ever since then they've harbored ill will toward the other bands."

"But why here and now?"

"The White Mountain band is apparently on good terms with soldiers garrisoned in that part of the country. Delgadito here says that an officer told him he should come out here and volunteer his services as a scout. He and the others jumped at the chance."

Barlow shook his head. "I'm afraid they're in for a disappointment. Colonel Lyman doesn't believe in using native scouts."

"Won't do any good trying to tell them that. They'll have to find out for themselves. But they've noticed your army coat. They want to ride with you to the fort."

"I guess that'll be all right. But make sure they understand I have no influence over the colonel. In fact, riding in with me won't help them in their cause."

Short Britches spoke again to Delgadito in the Apache tongue. Then he turned back to Barlow.

"I told him what you said. But they still want to join us."

"Then let's get moving," said Barlow. He was impatient, wanting to get to Fort Union—to find out what the future had in store for him.

Chapter 16

Lieutenant Charles Summerhayes was officer of the day when Barlow arrived at Fort Union with his prisoner, Short Britches, and the six White Mountain Apaches—a group who, naturally, drew a lot of attention. As he approached the fort, Barlow noticed that the scattering of lodges occupied by random Indians that had once existed outside the walls was now gone—or at least the Indians were gone and the remains of the lodges were piles of burned embers. The main gate was closed, and there were more than the customary number of guards on the walls. By the time he and his companions neared the gates, more than a dozen soldiers were on the rampart overhead, aiming their rifles at the Apaches. Barlow figured that the only thing stopping them was his presence. Though there were civilian clothes underneath, he still wore the army-issue greatcoat. Barlow identified himself and asked that the gates be opened. The men did not immediately comply with his request. Then Summerhayes appeared on the wall, poking his head out to peer down at Barlow in utter disbelief.

"Joshua?"

"Charles, let us in."

"Who are your friends?"

"I'll vouch for them."

Summerhayes hesitated, and Barlow realized that, considering his situation, the fact that he was willing to vouch for a half dozen Apaches might not be sufficient. But Summerhayes decided to trust his old messmate, and called down for the gate to be opened. This revealed another twenty or so heavily armed soldiers. Barlow glanced at Delgadito, but spoke to Short Britches.

"They need to know I can't protect them. I'm persona non grata myself."

Short Britches didn't know what persona non grata meant, but he could read the situation as well as anyone, and spoke to Delgadito. The latter listened gravely, scanned the soldiers beyond the gates and on the walls, and nodded. Short Britches turned back to Barlow with a shrug.

"He says they will follow you."

Barlow shook his head. He didn't want the responsibility, but he had no idea how to get out from under it. So he kicked the coyote dun into motion and rode into Fort Union. As soon as he and the others were inside, the gates were closed. Summerhayes came down off the wall and pushed through the semicircle of grim-faced troopers.

"What's going on, Joshua?" asked Summerhayes. "What are you doing here?"

"Tying up loose ends, I hope." Barlow surveyed the fort. "What's happening here, Charles? Something's not right."

"You mean you don't know about Trotter?"

"What about him?"

"He's dead. Along with forty-two men. Cochise ambushed them about a day's ride west of here."

Barlow was stunned. "When did this happen?"

"Two days ago. Sergeant Farrow and a few others survived, and just made it back this morning. The colonel sent Lieutenant Hammond out with your old troop and his own. That leaves us with about forty men in the garrison."

The cold reception they had received made more sense to Barlow now. War had come to Apacheria, and Cochise had won the first victory—hence the siege mentality he detected among the men who remained at Fort Union. Disaster had struck, and they were expecting it to strike again. And they weren't inclined to trust any Apaches, White Mountain or otherwise.

"I better see the colonel," said Barlow.

"I'm here."

The barrier of troopers parted to make a path for Lyman, who was accompanied by Major Addicks. Lyman looked at Barlow, then at Carney and Short Britches, and finally at the six Apaches. His gaze lingered there.

"Who are they?" he asked.

"White Mountain Apaches, Colonel. They've come a long way to fight the Chokonen. There seems to be a history of bad blood between the two bands, and these men want to volunteer their services to the United States Army, as scouts."

Lyman stared at Delgadito and the other bronchos for a moment—and nodded. "Excellent. Tell them they are most welcome."

Barlow blinked. He wasn't sure he'd heard right. Was this the same man who, not long ago, had been convinced that the army had no business employing

Indians in any capacity, much less as scouts, due to their untrustworthy nature? This was a philosophy Lyman had consistently espoused in all the time that Barlow had known him and, if anything, his change of mind gave Barlow an inkling of the seriousness of the situation the colonel now found himself in.

Short Britches was waiting for an okay from Barlow to relay Lyman's welcome to the White Mountain bronchos. Barlow finally gave him the nod. When Short Britches was finished, Delgadito and his companions conversed excitedly for a moment. They were clearly pleased with developments, and the manner in which they smiled and nodded enthusiastically at Barlow indicated that they were under the mistaken impression that he had been instrumental in securing that welcome from Lyman.

"And who is this man?" asked the colonel, indicating Carney.

"I'm an innocent man—that's who," said Carney.

"He's one of the Confederates," said Barlow. "One of the men I saw with John Ward. They were negotiating the sale of a herd of cattle, to be driven to Texas for the purpose of feeding the Confederate army."

Lyman scowled. There was a hint of defiance in Barlow's voice. Carney's presence was a vindication, of sorts, of his accusations regarding John Ward—and his doubts about the rancher's true allegiance—accusations that the colonel had dismissed out of hand.

"That's a dirty lie," protested Carney. "I never heard of anybody named Ward. I was just riding along, minding my own business, when all of a sudden—"

Lyman turned to Addicks. "Lock this man in the guardhouse. We'll deal with this later."

Realizing that further protestations of innocence

were pointless, Carney shut up. He scowled at Barlow as two troopers dragged him off the horse and hustled him across the parade ground.

"Barlow, I'll see you in my office. Bring your Apache friends with you."

He spun on a heel and walked away. As Barlow dismounted, Charles Summerhayes stepped closer.

"You shouldn't have showed up back here," warned Summerhayes. "I've never seen the colonel madder than when he found out you were gone. I think he was all set to send every last one of us out to hunt you down and bring you back to a court-martial. But then all this with the Apaches happened. Why'd you come back, Joshua? What happened to that Indian girl you were in love with? I thought the two of you would be halfway to Canada by now." Summerhayes smiled pensively. "I must admit, made me smile to think of it—at least one of us doing the right thing."

Barlow put a hand on his friend's shoulder. "Sorry, Charles. Guess you could say I found out that you can't run away from the past."

He handed the dun's reins to a trooper and, with a nod at Short Britches and the White Mountain bronchos, started across the parade ground toward the commandant's quarters.

Lyman was waiting for them in his office, pacing behind his desk, with hands clasped behind his back. Major Addicks stood to one side, as always tight-lipped and watchful. The bronchos and Short Britches arrayed behind him, Barlow stood in front of the desk and waited for Lyman to speak. Finally Lyman ceased pacing. Instead of facing Barlow, he stared at the territorial map on the wall.

"When word reached this post that John Ward and his men had been massacred by the Apaches, I sent Lieutenant Trotter with two troops to apprehend the Indians. Instead of—"

"Excuse me, Colonel," said Barlow. "I wouldn't describe what happened to Ward as a massacre. He was mistakenly convinced that Cochise was responsible for the abduction of his children, and he was leading a force of heavily armed men against the Chokonen village in the Mogollons. Cochise had no choice but to defend his people."

Lyman turned and stared angrily at Barlow. "Are you quite through, Lieutenant?"

"Just trying to set the record straight, Colonel."

"Instead of apprehending Cochise, Lieutenant Trotter apparently led his men into ambush. All but a handful lost their lives. This morning I sent Lieutenant Hammond, with two troops, to locate Cochise and his people. It is my opinion"—he turned and traced a route with his finger—"that Cochise will make for the border with Mexico. Once across that border, he has escaped us. We cannot pursue the Apaches onto Mexican soil, and we have no means to coordinate a campaign with the Mexican army. I suspect Cochise will be found somewhere . . . here. It is the quickest way from the Mogollon Mountains to the border."

Short Britches stepped forward. "Excuse me, Colonel."

Lyman turned. "Yes?"

"You wouldn't happen to have any tobacco, would you?" Short Britches eyed a wooden humidor on Lyman's desk.

Exasperated, Lyman pushed the humidor across the

desk and opened the lid. Smiling, Short Britches helped himself—taking several of the cigars the box contained.

"Thanks, Colonel. And by the way, it doesn't have anything to do with the quickest route. Cochise has several hundred people with him, and they need water. He'll have to go from one waterhole to the next. And he won't cross the border just anywhere."

"Is that right?" said Lyman. "Keep talking."

Short Britches ran one of the cigars under his nose and savored its fragrance. Then he glanced at Barlow, who nodded.

"Well," said Short Britches, peering at the map, "Cochise knows that all he's doing is jumping from the frying pan into the fire, so to speak. The Mexicans would rather keep the Apaches north of the border, and let us deal with them. So there are plenty of Mexican army patrols that Cochise will have to watch out for—except for one place."

He walked around the desk and pointed at a spot on the map.

"Right about here. It's called Apache Pass. It's called that because, for as long as anybody can remember, Apaches have used it to get through this stretch of mountains. So many Mexicans have died chasing Apaches into or out of that pass that they stay away from it now, for the most part. You won't find many Mexican officers willing to risk their commands, and their lives, patrolling the pass. And once Cochise is through the pass he can fade off into the hills all along here"—Short Britches moved his finger side to side—"until he thinks the time is right to scoot down this way—to the Sierra Madre. That's another place the Mexican army won't go, by the way."

"All the more reason," said Lyman grimly, "for us to do everything within our power to catch Cochise before he gets across the border."

"In my opinion," said Barlow, "you should just let him go. You don't want him here anyway, so let him go to Mexico. Once there, he won't bring his people back."

"Damn it, Barlow," growled Lyman. "I *know* where your sympathies lie. But you forget Cochise has dealt a severe blow to the honor of the United States Army. The ambush of Trotter's command cannot be left unavenged. If we let that happen, what message will we be sending to the other Apache bands?"

Barlow wanted to tell Lyman that he didn't believe for a minute that it was the honor and reputation of the army that the colonel was concerned about, but rather his own reputation. He didn't say so though. He didn't say anything.

"No," said Lyman, turning his attention back to the map. "We will stop Cochise. I have sent messages to Forts Keough and Scott, but I cannot be sure that they will act in time. Since that is the case, I intend to take command of another detachment and head for the border. For this Apache Pass. With luck, I'll be able to join forces with Lieutenant Hammond."

"You'd better," said Short Britches, "because I don't think you have enough men here to stop Cochise, Colonel."

"We'll see," said Lyman curtly. "As for you, Mr. Barlow, your commission will be reinstated, and you will serve, for the duration of this campaign, as my chief of scouts. You will take charge of these White Mountain men."

"No, thanks."

"I'm not making a request, Lieutenant," snapped Lyman. "You will either serve as my chief of scouts, or I'll have you clapped in irons and you can rot in the guardhouse until I have the time to convene your court-martial."

"These men," said Barlow, with a gesture at the bronchos, "owe me no loyalty. You don't need me to lead them."

"That's not how I see it. Besides, I would not trust you with the command of regular troops. No, you will take your scouts and you will locate Cochise for me. If it looks as though he will escape across the border before I can close with him, you will do everything you can to slow him down. You will leave first thing in the morning. I intend to leave tomorrow, as well. Lieutenant Summerhayes will be left in command of the fort. Those are your orders. Do you understand them, Lieutenant?"

Barlow fumed. He was trapped. If he defied Lyman, the colonel would lock him up and throw away the key, and hell would freeze over before he got to be with Oulay again—if he even survived the proceedings that Lyman would bring against him. On the other hand, he had no desire to take part in a campaign against Cochise, because the campaign was a mistake, and in his mind an attack against the Chokonen was a greater injustice than any that previously had been visited upon the Apaches.

"Yes, sir," he said coldly. "I understand."

Leaning on his desk, Lyman pointed a finger at him. "And if I even suspect that you are acting in a way that might aid and abet the enemy, I will have you standing in front of a firing squad."

Barlow looked at Short Britches. "Let's go."

He turned and left Lyman's office. Short Britches and the White Mountain bronchos followed.

"Well," said Short Britches, as they stood for a moment outside the commandant's quarters, "you found out what you came here to learn. It looks like we're going to fight a war."

"Not we. You're going to go back. Look after things until I return."

Short Britches was chewing on the tip of the unlit cigar. "You might need me. You don't know how to talk to these men."

"No, but there's a sergeant here who can speak their language. He can ride with me. I want you to watch over Oulay, and let no harm come to her."

"Right. And if anything happens to her, you'll kill me."

"Exactly."

"She will be there, waiting for you, when you get back."

Barlow nodded. He still had no real reason to trust Short Britches, but somehow he believed that the old scout fully intended to keep his commitment.

Barlow left the fort at first light, accompanied by the six White Mountain Apaches and Sergeant Farrow, one of the few survivors of the ambush that had claimed the lives of Lieutenant Trotter and most of the cavalrymen under his command. Farrow had received a slight wound to the head, but he jumped at the chance to ride out again, this time with Barlow. And he was obviously intrigued by the White Mountain bronchos. He spent much of that morning in conversation with the Apaches. When, along about midday, they stopped at a waterhole to let their horses drink, Farrow approached Barlow, pointed at the bronchos with his chin, and gave a satisfied nod.

"They're a good bunch," he said. "You couldn't ask for better in a scrape. And they'll back you all the way, Lieutenant. They've got this idea that they're getting to do this thanks to you."

"I had nothing to do with it. Colonel Lyman was desperate."

Farrow chuckled. "The colonel is worried. It won't look good that he sent Lieutenant Trotter out to get slaughtered. Now he's done the same for Lieutenant Hammond. If he doesn't pull off a miracle and save the rest of the command—and bring Cochise to heel at the same time—his career will be finished. Or at least that's the way he sees things."

Barlow nodded. "That was my impression too."

Farrow gazed at the horizon, and his expression was suddenly somber. "I tried to warn Lieutenant Trotter. The Apaches showed themselves. Just a handful of bronchos. One minute they were there. The next minute they were gone. Soon as he spotted them, the lieutenant ordered the charge. I told him it was the oldest Apache trick in the book, and that he was probably riding straight into a bushwhacking. But he wouldn't listen." Farrow sighed. "I saw a lot of good men die that day. Some were good friends. We didn't stand a chance."

"Why did Cochise do it?"

"That's easy. We were lucky. We were going to try to track them from the place where they had finished off Ward and his men. But we cut their trail before we even got to the Mogollons, and before you knew it, we were closing in on them. I guess Cochise figured we were getting *too* close to the women and children.

So he had to stop us. And that he did. All because Lieutenant Trotter wouldn't listen." Farrow peered at Barlow through eyes narrowed against the glare of the desert sun. "Was he a friend of yours?"

"Not exactly."

"Well, the thing about Lieutenant Trotter, he wanted to make a name for himself. He was a glory hunter. All he could think about was the fame that would come his way if he was the one who captured or killed the legendary Cochise."

Barlow didn't say anything. But he concurred. That sounded just like the Frederick Trotter he had come to know.

"And if you don't mind me saying so, the colonel is cut from the same cloth," added Farrow. "So if you were wondering, that's why I jumped at the chance to ride with you. Otherwise I'd be riding with him. And I don't want to push my luck. I'm not sure I'd be able to walk away from another ambush. With you, though, I figure the odds of coming out alive are pretty fair. I say that because I know you have something to live for. And it ain't glory."

"No," said Barlow. "We'll both come out of this alive, Sergeant."

Late the following day they found what they had been sent to find. The passage of hundreds of people, some mounted, some on foot, was impossible to miss. The White Mountain Apaches eagerly studied the tracks and conferred among themselves. Barlow and Farrow waited patiently for them to come to some decision as to the size of the group that had left the sign, and a calculation as to how long ago they had passed this way. A consensus was eventually reached, and Delgadito spoke to Farrow at some length. The sergeant, who had looked rather bored by the entire process, suddenly looked quite interested. He proceeded to study the tracks himself, walking back and forth, sometimes kneeling, sometimes touching the ground, and sometimes gazing off to the west. Try as he might, Barlow could not control a growing impatience.

"Well?" he asked sharply. "What's the verdict here, Sergeant?"

"There's no question these tracks were made by the Chokonen. Women and children among them. So this is the main bunch. This sign is maybe a day old. No more than that."

"They're not making very good time, then," mused Barlow.

"Cochise is moving as fast as he can. But he's got the very young and the very old with him, and he's not going to leave them behind, no matter what happens. And they're carting all their belongings with them too." Farrow stood, still staring, with brows furrowed, to the west. "But something's not right, Lieutenant. Delgadito and the others agree that there are maybe forty bronchos with this group. Cochise has more fighting men than that."

"What are you saying?"

"I guess I'm saying that most of the Chokonen bronchos aren't traveling with this bunch. But Delgadito thinks they're probably close by."

Barlow thought it over. Cochise was still several days away from the border. Fort Union was two days to the east, and presumably, Colonel Lyman was considerably closer than that, since he had departed from the fort on the same day that Barlow and his companions had set out. Lieutenant Hammond was somewhere to the north. And the majority of Cochise's bronchos were . . . Barlow felt a cold chill run down his spine. He was painfully aware that if he and his small group were caught out in the open by dozens of bronchos they were as good as dead. Even though he had visited the Chokonen village several times, he could not be sure how many men Cochise could muster, but he estimated their number to be more than a hundred—and possibly considerably more than that. That was a force large enough to crush Hammond's detachment as well as Colonel Lyman's column. The next step was obvious.

"We've got to find those bronchos, Sergeant," he said.

Farrow got back into the saddle. He smiled ruefully. "I was afraid you were going to say that, sir. I suggest we head that way." He nodded to the west.

Without another word, Barlow led the way.

Chapter 17

The desert was a vast and trackless place, but Kiannatah was confident he could locate Cochise and the
Chokonen people without too much difficulty. He
knew the desert like the back of his hand, having spent
many years as an outlaw and fugitive, constantly on
the move, constantly avoiding his enemies. He knew
where all the water holes were located, and that was
the key. While Cochise could not be counted on to
lead his people on the quickest, most direct route from
their Mogollon home to the border, he was restricted
in his movements by the necessity of providing hundreds of people with water. Kiannatah, then, had an
advantage over the several army detachments that
scoured the countryside looking for the Chokonen
band. He could confine his search to a specific area.

Indeed, it did not take him long to locate his quarry.
The warm days had swiftly melted the snow that had
only recently blanketed the arid flats, and it was impossible for a group the size of the Chokonen band
to avoid leaving a cloud of dust in the air during their
trek. Kiannatah spotted this telltale dust on the third
day of his quest. He approached with caution, finding

an outcropping of rock from which he could observe
the Chokonen from a distance with the aid of a pair
of field glasses—loot he had taken from the belongings
of a Pinda Lickoyi killed during a Netdahe raid on
one of the Butterfield stagecoaches. Kiannatah made
sure that the afternoon sun was behind him so that
sunlight could not reflect off the lenses of the binoculars and betray his location. One of the first things he
noticed was that Cochise had deployed scouts—there
were two riding well ahead of the main body, and two
far behind. For a long time, Kiannatah searched the
eastern horizon—a series of barren hills—and finally
spotted two more riders many miles away. This was
to reduce the chance that the main body would stumble into an enemy ambush. It also warned Kiannatah
that there had to be two more scouts nearby, to the
west of the main body, so he kept a watchful eye out
for them. But he didn't move. His horse was hidden
in the rocks below his vantage point, and it was unlikely that he would be discovered unless a scout thor-
oughly searched the outcropping. If that happened,
Kiannatah was fully prepared to kill. It didn't matter
to him that his victim would be another Apache. Even
though the Chokonen were making war against the
Pinda Lickoyi, and thus could be considered his allies,
Kiannatah knew that Cochise and his people were as
much his enemies as the Nakai-Ye and the yellow-leg
soldiers. Because he was there with one purpose in
mind—the abduction of the daughter of Cochise. Anyway, his war with the Americans and the Mexicans
was a personal one that he was content to fight alone.
He had no need of allies.

Kiannatah remained hidden in his vantage point all
day, watching the Chokonen passing several miles

away across the plain—too far for him to distinguish individuals among the tight mass of men, women, and children. Only when the sun had set and darkness spread across the land did he move, following the fugitives several miles until he found their encampment, within a narrow valley passing between two low hills. There were no fires, and Cochise had posted sentries, but Kiannatah was too alert to blunder too closely to the camp. Secure in the knowledge that the Chokonen had settled in for the night, he withdrew about a mile and made his own cold camp among the hills.

By daybreak Cochise was on the move again, and Kiannatah followed. He had spent the night before concocting a plan. To charge into the Chokonen and grab Oulay and make good an escape would be an impossibility. Not even the element of surprise would be enough to ensure success. But somehow he had to infiltrate the Chokonen, locate Oulay, and spirit her away. The plan he devised was a daring one, and the odds against success were steep. But there was a chance. And Kiannatah was not deterred by the likelihood that he would die in the attempt.

He approached from the rear, holding his horse to a walk, gradually closing in on the two scouts who rode more than a mile behind the main body. Before long he had been spotted by one of them. The Chokonen broncho checked his pony, turned it, and sat there for a moment watching Kiannatah's approach. The manner of that approach was calm, confident, and deliberate. How could a single rider, approaching in the open, without stealth or haste, pose a danger to the band? This, at least, was what Kiannatah was hoping to convey.

Eventually, the scout made up his mind to investigate. He put his horse in motion, riding to intercept Kiannatah. This brought Kiannatah to the attention of the other scout, who first noted that his colleague was no longer at his station, and, in scanning the flats to locate him, saw Kiannatah for the first time. This man also checked his horse, and turned to watch. But he did not approach.

When the first scout was within twenty yards of him, Kiannatah stopped. The Chokonen broncho did likewise, and waited for Kiannatah to speak. Kiannatah noticed that he was well armed—long gun, pistol, knife, bow and arrow. But the scout did not have any weapons in hand.

"I have come to see Cochise, with a message from Mangas Colorado," said Kiannatah.

The Chokonen looked him over, missing nothing. There was nothing that identified Kiannatah as a Netdahe, an outcast. But the headband that kept his shoulder-length hair out of his face, and the beadwork on his n'deh b'ken were clearly of Bedonkohe origin. The chief danger, as Kiannatah well knew, was that this man might recognize as one of those who had long ago arrived at the Chokonen che-wa-ki on the Mogollon Rim with Goyathlay, whom everyone knew was an outlaw. He studied the scout's eyes, but saw no sign that the man recognized him.

"Why does Mangas Colorado send a message to Cochise?" asked the scout, finally.

"We have word of what has happened to the Chokonen."

"Give me the message, and I will deliver it to Cochise."

Kiannatah shook his head once. "I gave my word to Mangas Colorado that I would not return until I had delivered his message myself."

The Chokonen scout spent a moment carefully surveying the desert behind Kiannatah. He was not, thought Kiannatah, suspicious so much as careful, wondering still if perhaps Kiannatah was not alone. For his part, Kiannatah waited patiently, for all outward appearances sublimely unconcerned.

"Come with me," said the scout.

He maneuvered his horse to the side, and gestured for Kiannatah to precede him. They rode at a canter, and were soon intercepted by the second scout. The first Chokonen relayed Kiannatah's story, and it was decided that he would escort Kiannatah to Cochise while the second scout remained at his post.

They rode, now side by side, at a faster pace, intent on catching up with the main body. Kiannatah was not surprised that the scouts hadn't demanded the surrender of his weapons. One did not disarm another Apache unless he was an enemy, and to do so when such was not the case would be a serious insult—one the Chokonen scout did not wish to direct at a man whom, he was by now fairly convinced, came as the personal emissary of the great Mangas. And if this turned out not to be the case—if, in fact, Kiannatah *was* an enemy—the scout was supremely confident in his ability to kill him at the first sign of hostility.

As they drew near the main body they were enveloped in the dust kicked up by hundreds of human feet and the hooves of mules and horses—dust that seemed suspended in the breathless air. Kiannatah looked back once, just to confirm that the second scout had remained far behind; he was scarcely able to make the man out because of the distance and the thickening dust. So far, thought Kiannatah, with satisfaction, his plan was working.

A few minutes later he made his move. He was just beginning to make out the shapes of the Chokonen who brought up the rear of the main body. And without looking over his shoulder again, he assumed that now the dust was thick enough to completely obscure him from the view of the scout who had remained behind. Surreptitiously drawing the knife from its sheath at his side, he edged his horse closer to that of his escort. As he came right alongside, the Chokonen broncho glanced at him. Kiannatah looked straight ahead. Out of the corner of his eye he could see the Chokonen look away, and just as the latter began to guide his pony to the left to put some distance between himself and Kiannatah, the Netdahe struck. Turning the blade sideways so that it could easily slip between the ribs, he stabbed the Chokonen in the chest, aiming for the heart. His aim was true. The Chokonen gasped but did not live long enough to cry out. Dying almost instantly as the point of the blade pierced his heart, he slid sideways off his pony. Kiannatah gathered up the riderless horse and kicked his own mount into a canter. Within seconds he was in the midst of the Chokonen. He had to work on the assumptions that in a few minutes the second scout would arrive in the vicinity of the dead man—and that he would spot the corpse. Then the alarm would be sounded, and if he hadn't found Oulay by then, or reached the side of Cochise, he would surely die.

Some of the Chokonen were mounted, but the best ponies were being used by the bronchos, and many of the people were traveling on foot. Mules, dogs, and

even people pulled travois laden with their belongings.
All of them had been pushed to the limits of their
endurance. This was evident in their shuffling gaits
and dull stares. Some glanced at Kiannatah, but none
demonstrated more than mild curiosity—while most
would recognize that he was not one of their own, no
one would be unduly alarmed; they would assume that
he couldn't have gotten past the scouts if he posed a
threat. Kiannatah looked for Oulay. In the process he
noticed that there were relatively few bronchos among
the women, children, and old men. That puzzled him.
Where was the balance of Cochise's warriors? The
Netdahe told himself that this was not his concern. In
fact, their absence simply made his task simpler. A
bigger question concerned Oulay. Where was *she*? Kiannatah assumed that Cochise would be riding at the
head of the column. Perhaps he was keeping his
daughter near his side. Cognizant of the fact that he
was running out of time—that before too much longer
he would be found out—Kiannatah hurried forward.

As he drew nearer the head of the main body, he
saw Cochise, surrounded by a handful of bronchos,
including Nachita. But no Oulay. With grim resolve
etched into his gaunt face, Kiannatah continued into
the midst of the warriors who guarded the Chokonen
jefe. The first one to look at him shouted an alarm
and steered his horse across Kiannatah's path,
blocking him. Kiannatah turned his pony away, and
found himself side by side with Nachita, who looked
startled. Kiannatah reached out and grabbed Nachita,
dragging him off his horse and across the haunches of
his own. Nachita started to struggle—until the sharp
edge of Kiannatah's knife caressed his throat.

Taking Nachita hostage, though, was not going to

stop the other bronchos. Several guns swung in his direction, and those guns would have been fired had Cochise hesitated in ordering them not to shoot. He didn't hesitate—and the bronchos did not hesitate in obeying. They lowered their weapons slightly, but did not put them aside.

"What are *you* doing here?" asked Cochise angrily.

"I have come for your daughter, Oulay."

The Chokonen jefe's eyes narrowed. "Let Nachita go."

"I am not a fool, Cochise," admonished Kiannatah. "Do not take me for one. If I release him, you will have me killed. You may have me killed anyway—but if that happens, your friend will die with me. I can promise you that."

Cochise glanced at Nachita, and his expression revealed that he believed the Netdahe. Nachita was one of the jefe's oldest friends and most trusted advisers. Kiannatah had been betting on the fact that a threat to Nachita's life would be far more productive than a threat directed at Cochise. The Chokonen leader would not give up anything—least of all his daughter—to save his own life.

For a moment they all sat their horses, with no one speaking a word. Behind them, the rest of the main body had also come to a stop. Those near the front could see what was happening, and were quite still; the ones farther back were already beginning to speculate about the reasons for the unexpected halt. It wasn't like Cochise to stop while there was light left in the sky. What was the matter? Was the enemy near? Were they about to be attacked? A ripple of anxiety and restlessness began to move through the Chokonen. Kiannatah could hear this—he could *feel* it—but he kept his attention focused on Cochise and the bronchos, who were ready to kill him at the command of their leader.

"You," said Cochise, venomously, "you and Goyathlay are responsible for all of this. It was you who killed two of our people and left their bodies on the land of John Ward. Because of you we have been forced to leave the mountains that have been our home for more generations than I can count."

"You lost your home the day the Pinda Lickoyi first came here," replied Kiannatah. "In your heart, you know this. And it was not John Ward's land. It was the land of the Chi-hinne. It has always been our land."

Cochise scoffed. "You care nothing about the Chi-hinne, or our land. You only care about killing."

"I have not come to speak of these things," said Kiannatah disdainfully. "I am here for Oulay."

"Even if she were here, she would never go with you. I would never let her. No matter how many throats you cut before you died."

"Where is she?"

Cochise defiantly lifted his chin. "I will tell you, because then you will know that you have come for nothing. She has been taken far from here by a soldier of the Pinda Lickoyi."

Kiannatah stared at him. His first impulse was to accuse Cochise of lying. But Cochise did not lie. And the explanation for Oulay's absence was so bizarre, so unbelievable, that it had to be true. Had Cochise been inclined to lie in order to save Nachita—and Oulay— he would have devised a more believable scenario. No, as incredible as it sounded, what Cochise said had to be true. The Chokonen jefe had concluded that Oulay would fare better in the care and keeping of a yellow-leg soldier than she would with her own father, a fugitive in her own land, always on the run, in danger every moment of the day and night.

"Who is this soldier, and where did they go?"

"I do not know where they went. I did not want to know. And I will not tell you his name. Now let Nachita go. If you do not, you will die. If you free him, I will let you live, and you may go without fear that I will follow."

Kiannatah thought the offer over. Clearly he had learned all that he would ever learn from Cochise. His agile mind immediately formulated another plan.

"I will take Nachita with me. If, at sundown, I see no pursuit, I will let him go. But if anyone comes after me, he will be the first to die."

Cochise knew that this was the best bargain he was going to get. He nodded curtly, and snapped another command at the surly bronchos who surrounded Kiannatah. They moved, making a path for the Netdahe, who promptly turned his horse and rode away, Nachita still draped over his horse with a knife to his throat. One of the bronchos rode ahead to warn off the scouts. Before long, Kiannatah was deep within the rugged hills to the east. He continued on for an hour, then another, constantly checking behind him. The hatred Cochise harbored for him was strong, and there was a possibility that the Chokonen leader would decide to sacrifice Nachita in order to kill the Netdahe he blamed for the woes of his people.

Long before sundown Kiannatah stopped his horse and shoved Nachita to the ground. Nachita's legs buckled, and landed clumsily. Before he could recover, Kiannatah had vaulted from the back of his pony and was straddling him, the knife once more to his throat.

Fear clutched at Nachita's heart. He looked beseechingly into Kiannatah's eyes—and saw no mercy there. Even though he knew that an Apache did not beg for his own life, Nachita did just that. He couldn't help himself.

"Please," he gasped. "You gave your word. Do not kill me. What good would it do you to kill me?"

"I am Netdahe. What is my word worth to an Apache who would do nothing but heap scorn on my name, were it not for my knife at his throat?"

"What do you want? Please. I'll do anything. Just don't kill me."

Kiannatah's contempt for Nachita was so powerful that it made him tremble. It was all he could do to refrain from slashing the man's throat just to silence his whining voice.

"Tell me where the yellow-leg took Oulay."

"I don't know!"

Kiannatah pressed the knife harder against Nachita's throat, and Nachita cried out as the blade cut deeply into his flesh.

"You lie," rasped Kiannatah. "Tell me!"

"If I tell you, Cochise will kill me."

"Cochise will not know unless you tell him yourself. Now speak!"

"He had with him the one known as Short Britches," said Nachita, "the one who rode with John Ward. They did not say where they were going, but since Ward is dead, we assumed it would be to the land he had claimed as his own. There are many cattle there who now belong to no one."

Kiannatah decided that this made sense. "What is the soldier's name?"

"Barlow. He is a lieutenant."

"Why did Oulay go with this Pinda Lickoyi?"

Nachita tried to swallow the lump in his throat, afraid that the truth would so enrage Kiannatah that the Netdahe would kill him on the spot. But he dared not lie. This man would know if he was lying.

"She is in love with him."

Kiannatah's smile chilled the blood in Nachita's veins. "We will see how long her love lasts when this man is dead," said the Netdahe.

He contemptuously pushed Nachita down on his back, and Nachita squeezed his eyes shut, thinking that this was the end. Instead, Kiannatah turned abruptly away from him. When Nachita dared to open his eyes again, the Netdahe was riding away, to the northeast, still leading the Chokonen pony.

Nachita lay there for a moment, filled with a shame so immense that he could scarcely breathe because of it. He had betrayed his friend Cochise and placed Oulay's life in jeopardy. The only way to redeem himself, to prove that he was not a complete coward, was to admit to Cochise what he had done. He rose and began the long walk back, telling himself the entire time that he would do the honorable thing and confess. But he knew, down deep, that he wouldn't, that he would keep the secret of this terrible shame until the day he died.

Chapter 18

As it turned out, Sergeant Farrow was right.

They hadn't traveled far before they came upon the sign of numerous unshod horses. The trail led south, parallel to the route taken by the main body of the Chokonen. The White Mountain scouts were sure that these were bronchos and that there were no women or children in this group.

"So what do you reckon Cochise is up to, Lieutenant?" asked Farrow.

"He's got most of his men shadowing the main column," replied Barlow. "They're close enough that they could hear gunfire. If the main column is attacked, they ride to the rescue, presumably attacking the attackers from the flank or rear. It's a daring strategy. One might even call it desperate."

Farrow nodded. "Cochise must be a desperate man by now. He's got to know that the whole country is crawling with detachments looking for him. But I got to wonder which group he's with."

"I don't wonder about that," said Barlow. "He's with the women and children. They are at the greatest risk, and he will share that risk with them. He and a handful of men will have to hold off any attackers until this bunch can reach the field of battle."

"What do we do now?"

Barlow glanced at Delgadito and the other White Mountain Apaches. They were talking excitedly among themselves.

"They're not going to like what we're going to do next," Barlow told the sergeant. "But you're going to take three of them and head back toward Fort Union. The colonel should be somewhere between here and there. You tell him what we've found here. I'll take the other three and ride north. Hopefully I'll be able to find Lieutenant Hammond's command."

He didn't bother adding that, in his opinion, it was likely that his friend Hammond was a lot closer to the fleeing Chokonen than Lyman. And he had to be warned about the trap Cochise had set.

"Well, you're right—they won't like it, not one bit," agreed Farrow. "They're working up a hesh-ke now. A killing craze. They can almost taste the blood and smell the gunpowder and they've got a powerful ache to strike back at the Chokonen."

"They'll have to wait a while."

"You take Delgadito with you. He's a smart fellow. Even though you don't speak his language, he'll probably have a good idea what you want him and the others to do, most of the time."

Barlow agreed. He liked the idea of having Delgadito ride with him. Though he hadn't seen Delgadito in action, his hunch was that the White Mountain broncho was the type of man you wanted siding with you in a scrape. Farrow's assessment of the man was right on the money.

And so they parted company, with Farrow and three

of the bronchos headed east, while Barlow, Delgadito, and the remaining two White Mountain Apaches turned north. Since they were riding *away* from their enemy, the Chokonen, whom they had come such a long way to kill, the latter three didn't look too happy. Barlow had half expected them to abandon him on the spot and set out after Cochise's people. But Delgadito seemed to reason with the other two; he appeared more willing than his brethren to trust Barlow's judgment and to follow his lead. Barlow felt bad about that too because Delgadito had come to fight the Chokonen, while Barlow intended to do everything in his power to avoid just that.

They found Hammond's column as the day was winding to a close. It was visible from miles away, thanks to the cloud of dust that marked its passage across the desert.

The cavalrymen had the look of men who had been too long on the trail. They were haggard, bearded, their eyes sunk deep in the sockets, their clothes stained with grime and coated with pale dust, and they had that faraway gaze of men who were weary to the bone. The horses they rode looked no better. But every man in the column perked up a bit when they saw the Apaches riding with Barlow. This was something none of them had ever seen—or ever expected to see.

Hammond was as haggard and dirty as the rest, but he was grinning from ear to ear when he saw Barlow. They shook hands, and Barlow realized that he had actually missed this man's company.

"What the hell are you doing way out here?" asked Hammond. "To be honest, after you snuck off the way you did, I never expected to see or hear from you again."

"I'm the new chief of scouts, believe it or not," said Barlow ruefully.

"The colonel did that?" Hammond couldn't believe it. "I thought for sure he'd just lock you up and throw away the key if he got the chance."

"That was my other option."

Hammond laughed and then, just as quickly, his grin faded. "You heard about Trotter?"

Barlow nodded. At that moment, Sergeant Eckhart arrived, checking his horse alongside Barlow's.

"Beggin' the lieutenant's pardon," said the noncom, "but I wanted to pay my respects to my former commanding officer, sir."

"Hello, Sergeant," said Barlow.

"Lieutenant." Eckhart was trying, without much success, to suppress an ear-to-ear grin—one that couldn't be undone even as he gazed, with no little suspicion, at the Apache warriors behind Barlow. "If you don't mind me askin', sir, what have you got here?"

"White Mountain Apaches. They've signed on to scout for the army against Cochise and his people."

"And Colonel Lyman went along with that?" Hammond shook his head. "What is the world coming to?"

"It just means, sir," drawled Eckhart, "that no dog is too old to learn a new trick."

Hammond glanced wryly at the noncom. "As usual, Sergeant, you're right on the line of insubordination with a remark like that."

"It was just an observation, Lieutenant," said Eckhart laconically.

Barlow was amused. "Lieutenant Hammond is an expert on that line."

"Speaking of the colonel, where is he?" asked Hammond.

"Day or two east of here. Trying to catch up with Cochise before he crosses the border."

"I've been on his trail for the past two days," said Hammond. "My men are worn-out, but I think I can push them enough to catch Cochise before it's too late."

Barlow told him then of the trap Cochise had in store for any pursuit. Hammond expressed heartfelt gratitude for the information.

"I know he's got us outnumbered," he said. "But knowing what you've told me, I might yet have the advantage. After all, he's got his women and children to worry about." He gave Barlow a look that the latter couldn't decipher. "I have a pretty good idea what you're thinking, Joshua. But I do actually intend to carry out my orders to the best of my abilities. And after seeing what was left of Frederick Trotter and his men . . ." Hammond just shook his head and looked away.

"My advice would be to wait until the colonel joins up with you."

"If I do that, Cochise gets clean away."

"He didn't start this."

"That may be true. But after what he and his men did, we've got to do our damnedest to catch him."

Barlow nodded, and gestured in the direction of the White Mountain bronchos. "You can take them with you. They're wanting a fight in a bad way. And you can trust them."

"I'll take your word on that. What about you?"

"I'm going to find the colonel. Tell him what the situation is."

"Then take Sergeant Eckhart with you. Isn't smart to travel this country alone if you can help it."

"That's a good idea."

"I have another one," said Hammond, pitching his voice low so that only Barlow and the sergeant could hear him. "I have a pretty good idea how you feel about Cochise and all of this in general. So take my advice and take an extra day or so bringing the colonel. You'll be doing us both a favor."

"How do you figure that?"

"Because you don't want to fight Cochise, I know. And frankly I'll stand a better chance against the Apaches without the colonel."

"You're walking that line again, John."

With a nod, Hammond solemnly extended his hand. "I'll see you, Joshua."

Barlow shook his friend's hand again, then turned to Delgadito. He pointed at the Apache, then at Hammond, and then to the south, in the direction of the Chokonen. Raising both hands, he pretended to aim and fire a rifle. Delgadito nodded that he understood, and spoke rapidly to his two companions.

"You're chief of scouts and you can't even speak their language," said Hammond, laughing.

"Shut up, John," said Barlow, trying not to smile.

A moment later he was riding east, accompanied by Eckhart.

They had been traveling for less than an hour when they wandered straight into an Apache ambush.

The first Barlow knew of it was a rifle shot, followed instantly by a blood-chilling sound from Eckhart's horse, which went down headfirst, throwing its unsuspecting rider a good fifteen feet through the air. Bar-

low didn't have time to check on Eckhart—in the next
instant an Apache was springing up out of the ground
directly in front of him. The broncho had dug a shallow hole and, after lying down in it, covered himself
with dirt. The manner of his appearance spooked the
coyote dun, which reared. Barlow felt himself sliding
off the saddle. He grabbed for the carbine in the saddle scabbard, secured beneath his left leg, and as he
fell, he drew the long gun. For a split second the dun
was between him and the broncho, then the horse
bolted out of the way. But it was enough time for
Barlow to lever a round into the carbine's breech and
bring the rifle to his shoulder. He fired at point-blank
range. The bullet punched the Apache in the chest
and knocked him backward.

Barlow looked around for Eckhart. The fall had
stunned the sergeant, he was slow getting up. And
when he finally managed to regain his feet, he took
one step and fell down again. Only then did Barlow
notice the shattered bone jutting from Eckhart's torn
trouser leg.

A shout made him turn, in time to see three more
bronchos—all of them on foot—rising up out of an
arroyo about fifty yards away. All three began shooting. Bullets sounded like sharp peals of thunder as
they passed him in close proximity. Barlow was on
the move, running to Eckhart. He grabbed the injured
sergeant around the waist and half lifted, half dragged
him to the dead horse. They fell behind the animal's
carcass, pursued by the Apaches' bullets. Eckhart let
out a groan, and Barlow regretted the rough treatment, but there hadn't been time for anything else.

"Can you shoot, Sergeant?" he asked. He spoke

loudly, firmly, and the query seemed to bring Eckhart around.

"Just watch me," growled the noncom, brandishing a pistol.

Barlow braced his carbine across the dead animal's haunch and snapped off a shot at a broncho diving for cover behind desert scrub. He missed. So did one of the other bronchos, who fired at Barlow's head, striking the horse instead; the bullet plowed a deep furrow in the animal's side and sprayed Barlow's face with blood. When he could see again, all of the Apaches had disappeared from view. They didn't stop shooting though.

"They're gonna try to keep us pinned down until it's dark," said Eckhart through teeth clenched against the pain from his broken leg. "Then they'll sneak in and finish us." He got off a shot at a puff of powder smoke. "And the one you killed, Lieutenant—he's not Chokonen. He's Bedonkohe."

Barlow stared at him. "Are you sure?"

"I've been out here a long time. There're ways you can tell the difference, if you know what to look for."

Barlow didn't say anything. He didn't even want to contemplate all the possible implications of what Eckhart had just said.

For the next half hour they traded lead with the Apaches, and not once in that time did Barlow catch even a glimpse of one of the bronchos, so adept were they at using the available cover to conceal themselves, and they moved after every shot, so eventually he grasped the futility of firing at the powder smoke—in essence, they were shooting at an enemy that was already gone. But the idea was to keep the bronchos at bay, and so he kept answering their fire.

The sun sank below a distant range of mountains, and the long shadows of night crept across the plain, making it even less likely that they would catch sight of a legitimate target.

"I'm running out of ammunition," Eckhart told him grimly. "I've got five rounds left. How about you?"

Barlow checked. "I've got one in the carbine, five in my pistol."

"This damned horse was always on'ry," muttered Eckhart, his tone betraying the fact that, despite his words, he grieved the death of the animal. "And now it's lyin' on top of my carbine and a pannier full of ammo. I could reach that gun from right here 'cept for the thousand pounds of horseflesh that's in the way."

One of the bronchos fired again. The bullet thudded into the carcass that shielded them. Eckhart rose up to squeeze off a shot. But Barlow grabbed his gun arm before he could do so.

"Wait. Don't shoot."

"I ain't got anything better to do, Lieutenant."

"There might be a way out of this."

Eckhart's glance was full of skepticism. "Do tell."

"We stop shooting back. They may figure we're out of ammunition, and decide to come in before it gets dark to finish us off. That might give us a chance."

Eckhart stared at him for a moment, mulling over the plan. "Maybe," he said, dubiously. "I guess we might as well give it a try. What have we got to lose?"

"Exactly."

"But since it probably *won't* work," continued the sergeant, "I want to say that it's been an honor to serve with you, Lieutenant."

"We're going to get out of this alive, Sergeant."

"Spoken like a man who has a lot to live for," murmured Eckhart, with a pensive smile.

"There's just one small problem," said Barlow. "I have this hunch that one of the Apaches has circled around behind us? For a while now it's been sounding like only two are firing at us."

Eckhart looked apprehensively over his shoulder. They were backed up to a stand of ocotillo that blocked his view of the terrain behind them.

Another gunshot—and this time the bullet whined over their heads. They stayed low, and didn't shoot back. The bronchos fired several more rounds at them, and then stopped firing.

"I think they'll be comin' now," whispered Eckhart.

He was right. But they came from the flanks. One broke cover not twenty feet from Eckhart, who rolled over on his side and fired. His first bullet only winged the Apache, who came on. His second staggered the broncho, but did not drop him. Eckhart muttered a curse, and expended a third round. This time the Apache dropped to his knees, clutching at his chest. His last act was a shout of defiance at Eckhart—right before he pitched forward on his face.

Almost in the same instant, another Apache charged in from Barlow's side, firing a pistol as he ran. The latter sat up and fired the carbine without bringing it up to his shoulder—and the shot went wide. Tossing the empty long gun away, Barlow brought his pistol to bear. His first shot caught the Apache high in the shoulder. He didn't get off another one before the broncho was on him, aiming his own pistol at Barlow's head as he closed in. Barlow fell back, lifted his legs, and kicked the Apache in the midsection, spoil-

ing his aim—the pistol roared and spat flame so close
that Barlow could feel flecks of errant gunpowder
burning his cheek, but the bullet plowed into the
ground inches from his head. Barlow's two-legged kick
sent the Apache staggering backward, and Barlow
fired two more rounds into the broncho's chest. The
Apache spun and fell—tried to get up, then collapsed.

The third Apache was crashing through the ocotillo
right behind them, and Eckhart rolled over on his
back and shot at the broncho as he came into view.
The Apache kept coming, and Eckhart took aim once
more. Before he could get off a shot, though, the
broncho hurled his knife. The blade entered the sergeant's body right below the sternum. Eckhart's back
arched in a paroxysm of pain, and his finger spasmed
against the trigger. The shot went wide. With a savage
cry of triumph the Apache pounced, driving the blade
deeper into Eckhart, and twisting it. He lived just long
enough to know that he had killed the yellow-leg soldier, for Barlow, having just dispatched the Apache
attacking from his side, whirled and fired at point-
blank range, the barrel of his pistol only inches from
the temple of Eckhart's killer. The bullet exited the
man's skull in a spray of pink mist, and the Apache
slumped across Eckhart's body.

Barlow shoved the Apache corpse off the sergeant,
checked frantically for a pulse. But there wasn't one.
Eckhart was dead. Dazed, Barlow sat there for a while,
leaning against the carcass of the horse, dead men
strewn all around him. It was only then that he realized
he was wounded. A bullet had grazed his rib cage. It
was a painful wound, but not a serious one. He assumed
it had been inflicted by the last Apache he'd killed, who
had come out of the brush firing a pistol.

As night closed in around him, Barlow roused himself. He used an Apache knife to dig a grave. That took hours, and he hardly had the strength to finish the job, but he was determined to bury the sergeant—he wasn't about to leave Eckhart's remains for the scavengers. When at last he was done, he placed the body in the shallow hole and covered it with dirt. Then he piled rocks on top of the grave, to discourage the coyotes from exhuming the corpse. By the time this was done he barely had enough left in him to stand. Despite his exhaustion, he started walking east—the direction he and Eckhart had been traveling prior to the ambush. He had no water and no food, and his only weapon was his own pistol and one he salvaged from the body of the first Apache he had shot. He didn't give much for his chances. But it wasn't in him to give up. Because Oulay was out there, waiting for him, loving him.

He hadn't gone far before he heard the thunder of horse's hooves. Dropping into a crouch, he whirled, pistol at the ready. But it wasn't another Apache broncho. The coyote dun emerged from the darkness. Seeing Barlow, it stopped running, and whickered softly, tossing its head.

Barlow thought maybe, just maybe, his luck was about to change.

Chapter 19

Barlow traveled east the rest of that day and well into night, thinking a little luck might come his way and that he could possibly see from a fairly long distance the campfires of a column the size of Colonel Lyman's. But Lady Luck was still spurning him. In the early morning hours he simply couldn't go any farther. He was tired and cold, hungry and thirsty—he'd drunk the last of his water hours ago, and while the Apache bullet had only grazed his rib cage, the wound still hurt like hell. Stopping the coyote dun, he slid out of the saddle and went immediately to the ground, clinging to the reins and, without benefit of blanket, curled up under his horse and went immediately to sleep.

He woke with a start—and found himself staring down the barrel of a carbine. The man with the long gun was on foot, looming over him. He had a companion, still astride his horse. The morning sun was directly behind both of them, and momentarily blinded Barlow. For an instance he thought that they might be Apaches, and that he was as good as dead. Then he realized that Apaches would have killed him while he slept. He narrowed his eyes and took a closer look—and just as the man with the carbine spoke, he noticed that they were soldiers.

"Lieutenant Barlow?" The man straightened, relaxing, and lowered the carbine. "Beggin' your pardon, sir. A man can't be too careful out here."

"Those 'Paches are sneaky bastards," said the mounted man.

Barlow recognized them, but didn't know their names—they were part of the garrison at Fort Union but hadn't been assigned to the troop he had once commanded.

"What are you doing out here, sir?" asked the first man.

Barlow tried to swallow, but it was too painful. "Water," he croaked.

"Throw me your canteen, Lew," said the man with the carbine, and his companion complied. Barlow drank gratefully. After he took a few swallows, the first man took hold of the canteen and firmly pulled it away.

"Not too much, sir. You'll get waterlogged if you drink too much all at once."

"A little for my horse," said Barlow.

The man nodded. Barlow poured a small quantity of water into the crown of his hat and let the coyote dun drink from it.

"He's been shot, Henry," said Lew, for as Barlow turned he saw the blood-soaked shirt.

"Just a flesh wound," said Barlow. "You men are riding with the colonel, I take it."

Henry nodded. "Yes, sir. Lew and I pulled flanker duty today."

"I'm guessing you run into some Apaches, Lieutenant," said Lew. "How many was there?"

"Four. But you don't need to worry about them."

"Good for you, sir," said Lew enthusiastically. "That makes four *good* Indians, I say."

Barlow's expression made it plain that he didn't share in Lew's cheerful assessment. "How far is the main column from here?" he asked.

"Less than a mile to the south, sir," replied Henry.

"I must report to Colonel Lyman at once."

Lew was acutely curious, but he couldn't just come out and point-blank ask to be made privy to information meant for his commanding officer. "You haven't seen any more Apaches besides the ones you converted, have you, sir?"

"No, but they're out there."

"You'd better go along with the lieutenant, Henry," said Lew. "Make sure he gets to the colonel."

"I'll find my way," said Barlow. "The two of you stick together. Watch each other's backs."

He climbed stiffly into the saddle, gave the two cavalrymen a nod, and turned the coyote dun toward the south.

Lyman was at the head of the column, accompanied by Major Addicks and a young bugler. The colonel noticed right away that Barlow had been wounded, but he made no comment on that subject.

"Well, Lieutenant, did you find Cochise for me?"

"I found his trail," said Barlow, as he pulled his horse alongside Lyman's, and proceeded to relay all the events that had transpired since he and Farrow and the White Mountain scouts had found the Chokonen sign. He spoke of the deception Cochise was trying to pull off, with most of his bronchos riding parallel to the main column, placed there to strike any force attacking the main body from the rear. He spoke also of finding Hammond, and of his friend's insistence upon hotly pursuing Cochise, even though he was out-matched in the number of fighting men he had compared to the Chokonen jefe. And finally, with deep regret, he told of the ambush by the four Bedonkohe Apaches and the gallant death of Sergeant Eckhart.

"Eckhart was a good man," allowed Lyman. "He'll be sorely missed. But you said *Bedonkohe*?"

"The sergeant was certain of that."

Brows raised, Lyman glanced at Major Addicks. "This is completely unexpected." He turned back to Barlow. "Do you think Mangas Colorado has opted for war against us, Lieutenant?"

"I have no idea," said Barlow. "I don't know what kind of man Mangas Colorado is. I do know that Cochise would never ask him to buy into this trouble. If he's in it, he's in it on his own accord."

"Or it might be just a handful of Bedonkohe bronchos," said Addicks. "If they decided to fight, Mangas couldn't stop them, even if he was of a mind to."

"That's right," concurred Barlow.

"A handful or a host, the fact remains that Lieutenant Hammond has no idea that they are behind him, does he?" asked Lyman.

"Not a clue," agreed Barlow.

Lyman was silent for a moment, scowling and deep in thought. Barlow knew what the colonel was thinking. He was thinking that he had already lost a third of his command—Trotter's detachment—and now he was poised on the brink of losing one-third more, Hammond's column. If that happened, the Apaches—especially if the Chokonen and Bedonkohe bands were united in war—would have a relatively easy time of it if they decided to attack his force. The only chance of averting disaster would be to join up with Hammond before the enemy struck.

He turned his gaze upon Barlow. "In your opinion, Lieutenant, can I catch up with Lieutenant Hammond before it's too late?"

Barlow didn't feel the least bit sorry for Lyman. In fact, he blamed the colonel, in part, for this unnecessary war. John Ward was the principal culprit, but if the colonel had listened to reason, and comprehended what would come of delivering old, sick cattle to the Chokonen—and in so doing demonstrating a cavalier disregard for the very treaty the Chokonen were expected to adhere to—none of this would have happened. Ward had insisted on tangling with the Apaches—and he'd ridden to his doom. So be it. But it hadn't been necessary for Lyman to launch a campaign against Cochise to avenge the death of the cattleman.

"You might," said Barlow, finally. "But it'll be a close-run thing. Cochise is maybe a day and a half from the border. If Lieutenant Hammond makes good time, he'll catch the Chokonen before they cross. But the Bedonkohe are probably only hours behind the lieutenant."

"How many men can Mangas muster against us, Major?"

Addicks shook his head. "I'm not sure, sir. More than two hundred, I should think."

"So, if they're all on the warpath, Lieutenant Hammond won't stand a chance."

"No, sir."

Lyman made his decision—and nodded. Barlow knew what it would be before the words passed the colonel's lips. There really was no other choice. Not for Lyman—and not for him. Hammond was a friend, and as much as he disliked being a participant in this bloody charade, he wasn't about to check out of the game at this stage.

"A small detachment will return to Fort Union with the mule train," Lyman told the major. "The rest of us will proceed as rapidly as possible to the aid of Lieutenant Hammond."

"Yes, sir!"

Barlow checked the sky. Black-bellied cumulus clouds were scudding across the sky from the southeast. Here and there across the desert expanse, some of the clouds were dropping gray curtains of rain upon the land. He calculated that by day's end there would come a deluge. That was all he needed on top of being hungry and tired and cold and in pain. But he didn't complain. Now was not the time to dwell on rest and recuperation. He was headed straight into what he had most wanted to avoid—a fight with Cochise and the Chokonen.

All day long the vaquero named Ochoa had watched the clouds coming up from the southeast. They seemed to gather on this side of the distant Mogollons, and as they thickened they also grew angrier; by midafternoon he could see the jagged yellow fingers of lightning plunging suddenly to earth, followed by the distant peals of thunder rumbling across the arid flats. This would be the first rain of the spring season. Being a man who had spent his entire life outdoors, Ochoa didn't mind the weather. Still, he thought it was a shame that the storm was coming so soon, before he and his fellow vaqueros had finished

•

the adobe that Barlow had directed them to build, and which would be their shelter. He wasn't young anymore and had in fact become somewhat accustomed to spending inclement nights in the bunkhouse at the Ward ranchhouse.

Since Barlow's departure they had been working steadily, and made good progress, with one wall completely up and another partially so. First they had built the wooden molds, and then mixed the mud and straw—a mixture that went into the molds and, when hardened, was left out in the sun to bake. These were then put in place and secured with mud. In preparation for the coming storm, they had stretched a tarpaulin between the two walls. At sundown they'd ceased their labors, cooked some beans and tortillas, and eaten their fill. Then Manolo had brought out his guitar, as he often did in the evenings, and begun to play and sing. For a time Ochoa sat near the fire. Its warmth soothed his aching bones and made him drowsy. The rain began to fall, gently at first, and then with a steadily increasing intensity, until it became a downpour that thundered against the tautly drawn tarpaulin that sheltered them. Occasionally, bolts of lightning would presage a crack of thunder.

Ochoa eventually roused himself from the fire. It had become his custom to go to the line shack and bid the Apache woman *buenos noches* every night before he rolled up in his blankets and went to sleep. Although she apparently did not know his language—just as he did not know hers—she seemed to understand the sentiment behind his well-wishing, and appreciated his courtesy. Ochoa did not do this because of Barlow, but rather because he had come to like the young woman, even though she was an Apache. Oulay was quiet and, at first glance, looked fairly frail, but Ochoa had learned to look beneath the surface of the people he met, and in Oulay he saw a woman of great inner strength and bravery. She was also kind and compassionate. She had spent most of the past few days working side by side with Ochoa and the other vaqueros. This was not something that she had needed to do or that had been expected of her. Ochoa got the impression that she worked not only because she didn't like to stand idly by while others labored, but also because she was bored and lonely and did not want to sit all day in the line shack and think about the man she loved, now absent for nearly a fortnight.

As he looked out into the darkness and the rain, he wondered about Short Britches. The scout had shown up yesterday. He had told a worried Oulay that Barlow was well, and that he would be back as soon as he tended to a little unfinished business that had something to do with the gringo army. That was all the explanation he gave for Barlow's continued absence. He remained around the line shack for a few hours and then rode away, assuring Oulay that he would be back soon and that he would never be far away. Oulay knew this was so. While in the employ of John Ward, Short Britches had never done any of the work that was expected of the vaqueros. He did not herd or brand cattle, break mustangs, or perform any of the myriad duties expected of a ranch worker. All he did was ride the range, keeping his eyes open for anomalies, for potential dangers to his employer and his employer's property. That had been fine with John Ward, and in fact most of the vaqueros, Ochoa included, felt better just knowing that Short Britches was out there, like some grizzled guardian angel look-

ing over them. They all knew that the old scout rarely
missed anything. If there was trouble brewing somewhere, he usually found out about it. As far as Ochoa
could remember, Short Britches had not spent a single
night under a bunkhouse roof in all the time the two
of them had worked for John Ward. Even on a night
such as this, the scout preferred sleeping under the
open sky.

Ochoa pulled his hat brim down low over his face
and hunched his pancho-covered shoulders as he
stepped from beneath the shelter of the tarpaulin. The
other two vaqueros watched him, but neither had to
ask where he was going. They knew. As Manolo continued to play the guitar, Ochoa circled round to the
front of the line shack, out of their sight.

He made it to within three strides of the door before he died.

Kiannatah had been watching the three vaqueros
for four hours from a distance of less than two hundred yards. He had seen Oulay working with the
Nakai-Ye, and then, as night fell, she had gone into
the house. Under cover of night, the Netdahe crawled
closer, making no more sound than would a ghost. He
might have been able to slip into the house unnoticed
by the vaqueros. He might have been able to spirit
Oulay away without their knowledge. He was highly
skilled at remaining unseen. But he had already made
up his mind that he was going to kill the Mexicans.
After all, they were Nakai-Ye, and long ago, on that
fateful day in Dolorosa when he had watched his family being murdered, he'd vowed to slay as many of the
Nakai-Ye as he could. He considered the presence of
Ochoa and the other vaqueros as an unexpected but
fortuitous turn of events. For this night not only would

he take into possession the woman who had haunted his thoughts all these months, but he would also have an opportunity to slake his thirst for revenge.

Even though Kiannatah knew from experience that this was one thirst that he could never slake. He had lost count of the Nakai-Ye he had killed since that day in Dolorosa. It had to be more than one hundred. But his hesh-ke—his killing craze—burned so fiercely inside him that when he killed it only made him hunger for more killing. It was never enough. He thought of it now as the reason he had been brought into this world. To kill Mexicans was his destiny. To strike fear into the hearts of the Apaches' perennial enemies was the purpose for his existence. It was why Ussen, the Apache god, had permitted his parents and little sister to meet their terrible fate—and permitted him to witness every horrible moment. This, in order to forge him into the perfect instrument of vengeance against the people who had persecuted his people for so long. For that reason it was not only his pleasure, but also his duty, to kill all Nakai-Ye who crossed his path. That was why the three vaqueros had to die.

Kiannatah had arrived at the ranch house of John Ward to find the place reduced to a pile of charred timbers. He had searched the ground for sign, and found the tracks of two riders, coming from the north on shod horses. This was the only clear sign he could discern, and for that reason he had decided to track the two riders. Their trail had led him here.

When he saw one of the vaqueros leave the shelter of the tarpaulin and head for the line shack, Kiannatah also moved. He had no idea what the Nakai-Ye had in mind where Oulay was concerned. All he knew for sure was that it would be preferable to kill the man before he got inside the house, where he would be far more difficult to get to.

Ochoa did not see Kiannatah, nor did he hear the broncho. The rain had turned the hardpack around the line shack into mud, and the raindrops made loud smacking sounds as they struck the earth. Even if Kiannatah had been so careless as to make a sound audible to human ears, Ochoa would not have heard. But a man who had survived in Apacheria as long as Ochoa developed an instinct, a kind of sixth sense. The vaquero felt a tingling at the base of his spine, and wisely responded to the warning. He turned just in time to catch a glimpse of Kiannatah's fierce features emerge from the gloom of the rainy night, and just in time to see the blade of the big knife in the broncho's hand. He opened his mouth to shout and fell back, but he wasn't quick enough to save himself. There was an excruciating pain, and then Ochoa realized that he could no longer breathe, could no longer draw air into his lungs. Kiannatah's knife had not only sliced open his jugular, but had also severed his windpipe. Gagging on his own hot blood, Ochoa toppled forward into blackness. The man became a corpse in the time it took him to hit the ground.

After making the killing stroke, Kiannatah didn't bother to look again at his victim. He had killed enough men to know that his aim had been true; the Mexican would perish within seconds. He glanced momentarily at the door to the line shack, only a few feet away. Oulay was beyond that door, almost within his grasp. Now, at long last, he would make her his own. But he restrained himself—remembering that the killing wasn't done. Bypassing the line shack, he broke into a crouching run as the other two vaqueros, illuminated by the firelight, came into view. They, however, did not see him until he was upon them. The one who wasn't playing the guitar uttered a strangled cry of fear and lunged for his carbine, which leaned against the half-finished adobe wall. His hand never touched the weapon. Kiannatah hurled the knife, imbedding it in the Nakai-Ye's back, right between the shoulder blades. The broncho altered the angle of his run and made for Manolo. The latter, rising and falling back at the same time, swung his guitar in a desperate defensive effort to fend the broncho off. Kiannatah was too quick and agile; he ducked under the instrument and plowed into the Mexican. Once he had his victim on the ground, the Netdahe rolled him over and slammed his face into the mud. Manolo writhed, but Kiannatah was straddling him, and he could not escape. A moment later he stopped struggling; he died of asphyxiation, his mouth and nostrils clogged with mud.

Kiannatah stood for a moment over his last victim, a fierce exultation fixed upon his lean features. But the feeling was only momentary, leaving him thirsting for more. It was a shame, he thought, that there had been only three. And it was a shame too that the soldier who had taken Oulay away was not here. He had possessed her, and since she belonged to Kiannatah, that was a trespass for which he would have to pay with his life. But not tonight.

Netdahe retrieved his knife, returned to the line shack, and kicked in the door. Oulay had been seated on the floor, near a fire that blazed in the adobe's heart, when the door burst open. She leaped to her feet with a gasp, recognizing Kiannatah, remembering him from his single visit to the Chokonen village.

Cochise had sometimes spoken of him in conversations with other men—conversations that she had
overheard. She knew a lot about what was going on,
because she had learned how to remain discreetly in
the background, forgotten by her father and the men
with whom he discussed important issues. It was assumed that such matters were of no interest to women,
anyway. Kiannatah was Netdahe, an Avowed Killer,
an outcast, a man who rode with Goyathlay. The broncho stood for an instant framed in the doorway, his
gaze fixed upon her, and Oulay felt fear creeping
through her body. He had a knife in hand, and she
assumed that the three Nakai-Ye had been killed. She
was alone—but not defenseless. Barlow had left her a
pistol. It was still on the table—there, between her and
the door—right where he had put it prior to leaving.
Sometimes she had sat at the table and stared at the
pistol, wondering if the man she loved was well or
in danger and forced to resort to the other weapons
he carried.

Kiannatah saw her eyes move to the pistol, and he
was ready when she lunged for the table. He reached
it a split second before she did, and overturned it. The
gun fell and went skittering across the floor. Now the
overturned table stood between her and the weapon,
but Oulay did not hesitate—she vaulted over the table
and dived for the gun. Kiannatah dived too, catching
her around the knees and bringing her down, the gun
inches away from her outstretched fingers. She twisted
in his grasp, striking at him with a fist. It was a solid
blow, but Kiannatah wasn't fazed. With one arm still
wrapped tightly around her knees, he reached out with
the other and grabbed one of her arms above the
elbow before rolling her over on her back. He tried

to straddle her, but Oulay would not relent; her legs now free, she brought one up and kicked Kiannatah in the back of the head. This time the blow stunned him long enough for her to writhe out from under him. Once more she tried for the gun. But the Netdahe was quick to recover. Anger surged within him, and he struck her a powerful backhanded blow that sent her sprawling—away from the pistol. Rising, Kiannatah picked up the weapon, and as he turned to face Oulay, he contemplated the weight and balance of it in his hand in such a way that, for a moment, she thought his intention was to use it on her. Still she would not relent, and she was too proud to cringe or beg for mercy. Instead, she gathered her feet under her and prepared to lunge once more at her assailant. If he was going to kill her, she would die fighting.

Kiannatah saw her coiling her lithe body, making ready to attack him—and admired her spirit and courage. These attributes had their place, and she would most certainly need them in the life that he envisioned for her—as the woman of a Netdahe who had no home, who was always on the run, always attacking the enemy. Still, she would have to learn that he was the master; now was as good a time as any for the first lesson. He put the pistol under the broad leather belt that held the himper he wore around his narrow waist, and then used both hands in a gesture that encouraged her to come on.

She gladly accepted the offer, throwing herself at him, and Kiannatah even let her land another blow to his face, one that was surprisingly powerful from a woman so slight in build. He rocked back on his heels, then hit her again, hard enough to drive her to her knees. She was dazed and felt blood from her cut lip trickle down her chin. Kiannatah stood over her, waiting to see what she would do. Eventually Oulay felt clearheaded enough to get to her feet. She looked him in eye—and spat blood on the front of his himper. The Netdahe looked at the blood on his shirt, raised his eyes to hers, and smiled.

"You will come with me," he said.

"I will die before I go anywhere with you."

"No. You will not die. You will live and be my woman. I knew this when I saw you in the cowah of your father, Cochise."

"I will *never* be your woman," raged Oulay. "Never. My heart belongs to someone else, and it will be so until my last breath."

Kiannatah hit her, and Oulay didn't even see it coming. Her world turned suddenly black. Unconscious, she began to slump toward the floor, but the broncho caught her. With ease, he tossed her over a shoulder. With a last look around the line shack, he went out into the night and the rain.

Chapter 20

When Short Britches cut the sign of the solitary rider, he immediately knew that there was trouble.

The horse that left the tracks was unshod, which meant it was an Indian pony, most likely an Apache pony. And an Apache traveling alone in this neck of the woods—the range formerly claimed by his deceased padrone, John Ward, was an anomaly. The rider was traveling swiftly, like a man on a mission, and he was using the contours of the desert plain to best advantage in terms of keeping out of sight. A white man looked at those flats and assumed it was impossible to move across them without being seen by anyone who might be on the lookout. But an Apache knew better. For all these reasons, the old scout concluded that the lone rider was an Apache broncho, and since he was traveling by himself, he was, most likely, a Netdahe.

And he was heading straight for the Ward ranch house.

Short Britches followed the sign, which he judged to be only a few hours old. Reaching the site of the ranch house, which now was nothing more than a pile of charred timber (thanks to him), he noticed that the broncho had ridden in circles around the place, looking for sign. He then followed old tracks northward. Short Britches was pretty sure these were the tracks he himself had made, along with the three vaqueros he had rounded up and taken to Barlow. So this meant that the broncho was heading straight for the line shack. Straight for Barlow's woman too—whom Short Britches had vowed to protect.

Alarmed, the old scout urged his mule to greater exertion. But while the animal had many fine attributes—it was as sure-footed as a mountain goat on high country trails, and it had the necessary stamina for long, hot, dry treks—it wasn't a very fast mount. Short Britches knew he would not be able to intercept the broncho before the latter reached the line shack. He could only hope that Ochoa and the other vaqueros would be able to deal with the broncho if, as he suspected, the Apache was up to no good. But the old scout was not altogether confident that this would be the case. If it was the case that this lone Apache was an Avowed Killer, the vaqueros would be no match for him, even if they did enjoy a three-to-one advantage.

The old scout traveled through the night, hunched over in his saddle against the cold rain that fell. It was fortunate that he had already reached a conclusion regarding the broncho's intended destination, because the storm was enough to erase the tracks he had been following. He arrived at the line shack at first light. He knew even before he reached the place, however, that something bad had happened. The vultures were already circling in the sky. He approached with all due caution, the Big Fifty rifle at ready. The vultures were feeding on the remains of the three vaqueros. Desert scavengers wasted no time. Oulay was nowhere to be seen. It was only drizzling now, but at times during the night the rain had become a deluge, and as a result, there was nothing that the ground could tell Short Britches. He had to assume that the broncho had kidnapped Oulay, else her body would have been feeding the vultures just like those of Ochoa and the other vaqueros. And the broncho had taken nothing else, not even the vaqueros' horses. So he had come for one reason and one reason only: Barlow's woman.

More than ever, Short Britches was convinced that the lone Apache was Netdahe. How he had known Oulay and known where to find her were questions that the old scout knew he would find no answers to until he had caught up with the Netdahe. But following an Avowed Killer was a difficult prospect under the best of circumstances. With the rain continuing to obscure or blot out entirely any sign the Apache might leave, Short Britches had a large problem. He could take heart, at least, from the fact that the Apache had already made a mistake, something that was rather uncharacteristic of a Netdahe—even had he not wanted the horses of the vaqueros, he should have killed them. Short Britches switched his saddle from the mule to Ochoa's horse, a white-maned bay that, in a glance, the old scout could tell was a notch above the other horses. Then he was gone, traveling south. He had to rely on some guesswork now—and he was betting that the Netdahe would make for the Mexican border. There was only one true sanctuary for an Avowed Killer, and that was the Cima Silkq, the mountains that the Mexicans called the Sierra Madre. The old scout had been in the Cima Silkq only once, and that had been many years ago, when he'd been a much younger—and more foolish—man. The mountains were not safe for anyone who was not Apache. The man he was following would have the advantage of familiar ground, assuming he reached the Cima Silkq before Short Britches caught up with him.

Not once did Short Britches seriously consider not giving chase to the Apache who had stolen Barlow's woman. It wasn't that he feared Barlow, or the consequences that Barlow had spelled out should harm come to Oulay. Nor did he feel any loyalty or friendship toward the Chokonen woman. What he did have, though, was a personal stake in her well-being, because he *was* loyal to Barlow. He wasn't sure why this was so, and he realized that Barlow did not entirely trust him. The old scout had thought that maybe his loyalty to Barlow stemmed from the fact that the lieutenant was an honest man—a man who tried to do right by all he encountered and who played fair even if it cost him. In short, he was endowed with attributes that Short Britches lacked, and for that reason, mused the old scout, Barlow was a person who deserved his admiration.

Whatever the reason, Short Britches was determined to find the Netdahe and attempt to rescue Oulay. Even if it took him into the Sierra Madre. Even if it cost him his life. He had the Rollingblock rifle and about sixty rounds of .50 caliber ammunition to go with it. He also had the gold that Barlow had allowed him to take from the body of the Confederate agent he had killed at the Ward ranch house. And finally he had a lifetime of experience in hunting dangerous men, and the wiles and wisdom that many years in the desert imparted to anyone resilient enough to survive them. He wasn't sure if this would be enough; he couldn't say whether he was a match for an Avowed Killer. But he was willing to take that chance.

With Oulay as his captive, Kiannatah traveled all through the night and the following day. He was tireless, and so was his horse, even though it carried two people now instead of one. It was a feat of endurance that few men, and few horses, could have achieved. But Kiannatah was accustomed to such feats. As a Netdahe, he knew it was sometimes necessary to do such things—things that the men who wanted to hunt him down and kill him were not capable of doing. He could go days without food or water or sleep and thought nothing of it.

What impressed him was that Oulay did not once complain, even though she too went without food or water or sleep for nearly twenty hours. By the time he stopped, Kiannatah was more sure than ever that Oulay was meant to be his woman. She had the strength, the fortitude, the resilience, to survive as the woman of an outcast broncho. This, in addition to that serenity of her soul that had proved so alluring to him that he was willing to forsake Goyathlay, his mentor, and even the crusade to which he had dedicated himself.

It had rained on and off during the day, and Oulay was soaked to the skin, but he did not build a fire, and she did not ask for one. She didn't ask for anything, neither food nor drink. Kiannatah had not stopped for himself, or even for her, but rather to rest his horse. He gave it a little water, and then sat down, cross-legged, in the mud. Oulay stood there, watching him, and in the darkness of the overcast night he could barely make her out even though she was only a few paces away. With a curt command he bade her sit down near him, and she complied. He did not know what to say to her, so he said nothing else. Nor did she say a word; she asked him no questions: not where they were going or what her fate would be at his hands. But she wasn't resigned to her fate, and if she was afraid of him, she wasn't going to give him the satisfaction of knowing it. Kiannatah could sense her defiance, and that suited him. A woman who wept, begged, or gave up hope at this stage would not survive the life he had chosen for her.

He did not sleep that night. Oulay remained sitting up, within his reach, and eventually she lowered her head and closed her eyes and slept. When morning came, Kiannatah spent some time surveying the desert flats to the north. He saw no sign of pursuit. Where was the White Eyes soldier who had claimed Oulay for his own? He might have asked Oulay, but he doubted that she would provide him any information. When the soldier found out that she was gone, would he try to find her? Kiannatah couldn't imagine how any man would let a treasure like Oulay go without making an effort to get her back. But it really didn't matter, because in less than a fortnight he and Oulay would be deep within the Cima Silkq, and no White Eyes would find them there.

Confident that they could spare a little time, and wanting to show Oulay that he wasn't oblivious to the hardships of her ordeal, Kiannatah did not get under way immediately, but rather offered her some food— a piece of hard bread and a strip of salted beef. It was all he had. He knew she had to be famished, and she looked longingly at the food, but declined it. He shrugged, as though he were completely indifferent to whether she ate or not.

"You will eat," he said, "sooner or later."

"I will eat again when you have set me free," she replied.

His eyes narrowed as he studied her face, wondering if she was bluffing. Did she really intend to starve herself? Did she have the will? He decided that she did. She would kill herself rather than remain with him.

"You will eat," he said again grimly, as though simply by making the statement he could make it so. But he realized that he was powerless to prevent her from doing what she intended. He had expected resistance—she would not have been so appealing to him if she'd been the kind of person who lacked the will to resist—but this was something he had not anticipated. Angry, worried, and most of all, perplexed, he mounted his horse, pulled her up behind him, and continued southward.

Aware that time was running out, and that it was now just a matter of hours before Cochise and his people crossed the border into Mexico, Lieutenant John Hammond decided to act. He had devised a plan—the kind of plan people would call daring if it succeeded, and foolish if it failed.

He had closed with the main body of the Chokonen—he knew this thanks to reports from the White Mountain Apaches whom Barlow had brought to him. Apparently Cochise was unaware of his proximity. This amazed Hammond, but he reasoned that perhaps the Chokonen had lowered their guard now that sanctuary was almost within reach. He called his sergeants to him and explained what he had in mind. The entire troop would launch an attack on the main body of the Chokonen. But this would be a feint, and he stressed that the troopers were to avoid if at all possible the killing of women and children. The Chokonen would do one of two things: They would either turn and fight, or they would flee. Either way, Sergeant Billings, with a dozen men, would try to keep them occupied, while the rest of the command would turn quickly to the west and, establishing a defensive position, would meet the expected onslaught of the Chokonen bronchos who were shadowing the main body. The bronchos were expecting to have the element of surprise on their side; Hammond was hoping that if his men could inflict severe casualties on the bronchos, they would give up the fight. Like most other officers serving in Apacheria, Hammond didn't think the Apaches would stand toe to toe with his soldiers and slug it out. They preferred not to fight unless they knew they had the upper hand. If this was true, then they would lose heart and fall back. That would give Hammond an opportunity to turn his full attention once more on the main Chokonen column, and with a little luck Cochise might become convinced that, if he did not surrender, his people would suffer high casualties.

The men in Hammond's command were bone-tired. They had been on the trail of the Apaches for many days. But despite their weariness, they were eager for action, eager to bring the campaign to a close. They understood the risks inherent in their lieutenant's plan, but not one of them gave any indication that they disapproved. They liked John Hammond. He

possessed the dash and charisma that tended to inspire
loyalty in the ordinary soldier.

And so they eagerly followed him in an exhilarating
dash across a desert plain, with Hammond leading the
way, saber drawn, and the bugler sounding the charge.
The two bronchos who rode a quarter mile behind the
main body of Chokonen turned to face the bluecoat
onslaught. It was suicidal to stand and fight, but the
bronchos did just that. They dismounted, and let their
ponies go—they weren't going to need mounts
anymore—and used their rifles to good effect for the
few moments they had left to them, the handful of
minutes it took the cavalry charge to reach them. The
line of soldiers on their hard-charging horses swept
on, leaving the bodies of the bronchos behind.

The appearance of the soldiers threw the Chokonen
column into a panic. Some of the women and children
ran. Others fell to the ground, with mothers covering
their offspring with their own bodies. Though outnumbered, the Chokonen men turned to meet the charge,
hoping to at least blunt the attack. Cochise and a
handful of bronchos formed the core of this defense.

As soon as he saw the Chokonen bronchos begin
to form a living shield to protect the women and children, Hammond halted the charge. Sergeant Billings
and a dozen troopers dismounted and began firing at
the Chokonen men from a range of a few hundred
yards. Hammond led the rest of the troop to the west.
Up ahead, three Indian horsemen appeared suddenly
at the rim of a low rise. It was Delgadito and the other
White Mountain Apaches, who had been charged with
keeping an eye on the Chokonen bronchos who were
shadowing the main body. No signal was needed for
Delgadito to inform Hammond that the Chokonen

warriors were coming. The trio of White Mountain
bronchos were clearly on the run. Hammond called a
halt again, and deployed his troopers in a single line
midway up the eastern slope of the rise. No sooner
had Delgadito and his two companions joined the line
than a mass of Apache warriors—at a glance Hammond estimated their number to be more than three
score—came surging over the top of the high ground.
Hammond's command to fire was echoed by noncoms
along the line. A sheet of flame poured from the barrels of dozens of cavalry carbines, and a hail of bullets
tore into the charging Apaches. Hammond, walking
behind the line of troopers, gave the command to fire
at will. Through the drift of powder smoke he saw
that the initial volley had broken the Apache charge,
and that the bronchos who remained alive were disappearing back over the rim. So far, things were working
out just as he had planned.

But his elation was short-lived, because another
large force of bronchos suddenly appeared to the
north.

These bronchos hit Sergeant Billings and his detail
first, and Hammond watched in mounting horror as
the detachment, less than half a mile away across the
desert flats, was quickly overrun and annihilated.
Using his field glasses, Hammond saw the small band
of Chokonen bronchos fall back to herd the women
and children to the south. Meanwhile, the second
group of bronchos, which Hammond figured num-
bered more than a hundred and fifty, turned toward
his command.

"My God," he breathed, "we're done for."

He didn't have time to worry about where this second bunch had come from. He was now outnumbered

by a margin of better than two to one. Making a snap
decision, he shouted for the troopers to make for the
top of the rise. Achieving this goal, they formed a
circle with the horses held in the middle. To the west
of the rise they were taking fire from the scattered
remnants of the Chokonen bronchos. To the east, the
larger Apache force was closing fast. Hammond urged
his men to hold their fire. He hoped a volley might
slow or even stop the onslaught. When the bronchos
were within two hundred yards, he gave the order to
fire. The punishing volley thinned the ranks of the
bronchos, who immediately split into two groups, with
one circling to the north of the cavalrymen, and the
other moving around to the south. The Apaches began
firing, then. Caught in a cross fire, the knot of troopers
suffered greatly. All around Hammond men were falling, dead or dying. Half of the horses were cut down
in a matter of seconds. The top of the rise instantly
became a scene of carnage. Refusing to cower, Hammond stood tall, a saber in one hand, a pistol in the
other. He had soon emptied the latter. Delgadito appeared beside him. The White Mountain Apache was
wounded in the leg, but he didn't seem to notice. He
fired his carbine in one direction, then whirled to fire
in the other. Pausing to reload, he glanced at the
lieutenant.

"They are Bedonkohe," he said, in a voice that
Hammond thought was ludicrously calm considering
the desperate situation in which they found
themselves.

"Bedonkohe!" Hammond could scarcely believe his
ears. "What the hell . . . ?"

He didn't ask Delgadito if he was certain—there
was something about the White Mountain broncho

that made it pretty plain he wouldn't make such a statement if he wasn't sure of his information. So Hammond accepted that the second group of bronchos was from Mangas Colorado's band. He concluded that, while he had been chasing after Cochise and the Chokonen, the Bedonkohe had been chasing after him.

He looked at Delgadito and forced a smile. "I'm sorry, but I don't think this is going to work out the way I'd wanted."

There was no fear in Delgadito's eyes. He had already seen both of his White Mountain brethren fall. "We are both warriors," he replied. "We chose to die this way."

He raised the reloaded carbine and fired again, then moved away from Hammond, into the part of the circle where the casualties were the heaviest and the line was beginning to thin. The bronchos were circling now, pouring a hail of bullets into the cavalrymen. The Chokonen bronchos had regrouped and were eagerly joining the fray. Had he bothered to look across the plain to see what Cochise and the rest of the Chokonen were doing, Hammond's view would have been obscured by the thick pall of powder smoke that hung over the rise. Had this not been so, he would have seen the Chokonen women and children disappearing into the distance, racing for the border. But he didn't need to see this to know that he had failed. Taking solace from Delgadito's words, he followed the White Mountain broncho into the thickest of the fight.

Chapter 21

Barlow was feeling much the worse for wear. He had been in the saddle for more days than he could count. And even though his wound had been cauterized and field dressed, his body had not yet recovered from the trauma of being shot. Instead of much needed rest and recuperation, though, he was adding to his exhaustion by the hour, as he traveled with Colonel Lyman and his column, moving in a southwesterly direction, ever closer to the border—and to what the colonel hoped would be a final reckoning with Cochise. Confronted with the prospect of losing yet another portion of his command—namely, Hammond's detachment, Lyman didn't eat or sleep. And he apparently didn't think the men he was leading needed to, either. He pushed them hard, and they grumbled behind his back, but all they did was grumble, then kept on going, because they were soldiers in the Second United States Cavalry. And when that day Lyman had been longing for finally did come, and they heard the shooting way off in the distance, they forgot all about their aches and pains, their empty bellies and sore behinds, and gladly followed the colonel at double-quick time into battle.

To his credit, Lyman didn't plunge blindly into the fray. Reaching the edge of the desert plain, he paused the column and sought high ground, accompanied by his ranking officers, Addicks and Barlow. From that vantage point, they surveyed the ground before them with their field glasses.

Two things became immediately apparent to Barlow. John Hammond, about a mile off to the west, was in a bad way, surrounded by so many Apaches that Barlow figured he could safely assume some of them were the Bedonkohe. At that extreme distance he couldn't make out many details, but another safe assumption was that Hammond and his troop were about to be overrun; the determination and ferocity of the Apache attack was ample evidence in that regard. The bronchos could taste blood. They could smell victory. If this weren't so, they wouldn't be fighting out in the open like that.

And then, way off to the south, Barlow could see a column of dust—so much dust that it could only signify a great many people on the move. That had to be Cochise and the Chokonen women and children. He couldn't see them, but he calculated that they had to be getting close to the border. That was another reason the bronchos were fighting in such a determined fashion—they were buying Cochise time enough to get his people to safety. Barlow decided there was a very good chance they would succeed. The colonel would have no choice but to rush to Hammond's rescue. He would have to let Cochise go.

Lyman saw what Barlow had seen: Hammond in trouble and Cochise escaping.

"Lieutenant Barlow," he snapped, "you will take a detachment of twenty men and intercept Cochise before he gets to the border."

"But, Colonel . . ."

He fastened a steely gaze on Barlow. "And if he gets away, mister, I'll assume you let him go—and I'll have your hide."

"Colonel," said Addicks, "you can't be serious. You can't do this."

"I can't do what, Major?"

"There must be two hundred Apache warriors down there, sir. We need every last man if we're to save Lieutenant Hammond."

"The Apaches will run when we charge them," said Lyman.

"No, sir," said Barlow, "they won't—not this time."

"Damn it, Lieutenant, are you second-guessing me?"

"I agree with the lieutenant," said Addicks. "To divide this command at this point in time is . . . madness."

Barlow glanced at Addicks with a certain measure of admiration. He'd been surprised back at Fort Union when the major had lied to the colonel, denying that he'd been struck. And he was even more surprised now, because Addicks was openly questioning Lyman's judgment on the field of battle. It seemed the junior officers in the Fort Union garrison had been wrong about the major all along. He wasn't a sycophant. He wasn't Lyman's yes-man, after all.

Lyman was every bit as surprised as Barlow. He stared at Addicks for a moment, fuming. "Lieutenant Barlow," he said at last, "do you intend to obey my order?"

Barlow glanced again at Addicks. If the major was

willing to risk his career—perhaps even his life—by declaring Lyman unfit to command based on the order just given, Barlow was willing to back him because Addicks was right. It *was* madness. The colonel was so consumed with the desire to prevent Cochise's escape that he was risking not only the lives of John Hammond and the cavalrymen in his column, but also those of the men who waited down below.

But the major backed down. He nodded at Barlow, who, though disappointed by the major's decision, had already made up his mind what to do in the eventuality that Addicks backed down.

"Yes, sir," he said to Lyman briskly because he couldn't challenge the colonel by himself. If he defied Lyman, it would change nothing. The regiment would still be doomed. Hammond and his men were going to die, and so would Lyman and the troopers who followed him. The only ones who stood any chance at all were those sent off in pursuit of Cochise.

And Barlow was determined not to die. He would not become one of Colonel Hartwell Lyman's victims. He wasn't interested in sharing the kind of glory Lyman had in mind for the Second Cavalry. He had too much to live for. His future was waiting for him in an adobe line shack many days' ride to the northeast.

Of course, there was the possibility that he was wrong and Lyman was right, that victory could still be had and John Hammond would survive.

Barlow went down to the column and picked the first twenty men. Playing the part of God—deciding who would live among these men, and who would die (assuming that he was right about the outcome of the colonel's strategy) did not sit well with him. He was simply in the wrong place at the wrong time, and it was tempting to blame Lyman for his being there—after all, he'd tried to leave, and it was the colonel who had insisted on bringing him back into the fold. But there seemed little point in agonizing over all that now. He mounted up and led his twenty men south without so much as an explanation to the troopers, who were as bewildered and troubled by the division of the column as Barlow had been a few moments before.

Minutes later, moving across the flats, Barlow looked behind him—and noticed that many of the men in the detachment were doing the same—and saw Lyman's column, no more than fifty men, riding hard to westward, in the direction of the battle on the low ridge, where Hammond and his command were fighting for their lives. In spite of his determination to live, Barlow found riding away from that fight a difficult thing to do. But he had his orders.

As Lyman drew nearer the battle, Barlow couldn't resist stopping the column and using his field glasses for a closer look. The bronchos parted to let the new detachment of yellow-leg soldiers swarm up the slope and join the remnants of Hammond's besieged command. Then they closed ranks, and the melee continued, even more fiercely than before. *I should go back,* Barlow told himself. *I should disobey the colonel's orders and get into this fight.* If he survived the day they would call him a coward, even though he was doing what he'd been instructed to do, for the simple fact that the battle was over there and he was riding *away* from it. He didn't care about that for himself, but he couldn't help wondering what it would do to his father. Yet if he did go back, if he did engage the enemy, it was likely that the bronchos would react in the same way they had with Lyman's troops, and he would lead these men right into the trap that Lyman had so willfully fallen into.

Torn, he lowered the field glasses.

"What do we do, Lieutenant?"

Barlow looked at the sergeant—the only noncommissioned officer among the twenty men he had selected. He realized he couldn't remember the sergeant's name. The sergeant looked at him with an expression reflecting sympathy, as though he could tell that Barlow was in anguish, and why.

"We do what we're supposed to," Barlow said bitterly.

The sergeant wasn't sure what that meant—until Barlow wheeled his horse around and headed for the battle. Then the sergeant grinned, as did most of the men in the detachment as they unlimbered their carbines. They were warriors, and a fierce elation burned within them, and it didn't really matter that they might be riding to their deaths.

In the time it took for Barlow to lead the detachment across the flats and get within range of the bronchos, he came up with a plan that, he hoped, would improve their chances for survival. As they drew nearer the fight, he shouted a command, echoed by the sergeant, that transformed the tiny column of bluecoats into a single line of cavalrymen riding abreast. When they began to take fire from the Apaches, Barlow ordered a halt and dismount. They stood, a thin blue line, at the base of the long slope leading to the rise, where Hammond and Lyman and the rest of their comrades were encircled. Staying in the saddle, Barlow rode down the line, telling the men to fire at will. This had the effect of catching the bronchos in a cross fire, since the troopers who remained alive at the top of the rise were still producing withering fire of their own. Some of the bronchos charged Barlow's line, hoping to shatter it, but there was no concerted assault, and the troopers shot them off their horses. Two bronchos tried to circle round behind the line, but Barlow killed one with a lucky pistol shot at reasonably long range, then rode out to meet the survivor. The broncho fired his carbine as they closed, but hitting one's mark from horseback wasn't easy to do, and he missed. Barlow used his saber to strike the barrel of the Apache's rifle, knocking it down, and then tried to decapitate his adversary with a powerful lateral stroke. But the broncho was quick; he avoided the saber and launched himself at Barlow, trying to drag him from the saddle. Barlow punched him, slamming the saber's guard into his face. The broncho's grip loosened, and he slid down between Barlow's horse and his own, his feet dragging the ground. Barlow jerked the reins hard, wheeling his mount to the right, and the Apache lost his grip altogether then and fell. Barlow kept pulling on the rein leather, bringing his horse all the way round in a complete circle, and as the broncho got back on his feet, Barlow was in position to strike again with the saber. This time he was quicker. The blade bit deep into the Apache's neck, nearly severing the man's head from his body.

Barlow returned to his troops. The mass of Apache warriors between them and their colleagues atop the rise was thinning out. Dead and dying men and horses littered the long slope. Several of Barlow's men had fallen, but there were enough still to keep the pressure on, and a moment later, as Barlow had hoped, the bronchos broke and drifted over the rise and down the opposite side. At Barlow's order, his men charged up the slope on foot to join the survivors of Hammond's and Lyman's commands in chasing the bronchos with an unrelenting fire.

Gazing with mounting horror at the piles of blue-coated dead along the rim, Barlow spotted Delgadito. The White Mountain broncho was kneeling beside Hammond, who was on the ground, propped up against the carcass of a cavalry mount. Barlow leaped from his horse and joined Delgadito at his friend's side. Hammond had been hit in the chest, but a cursory examination gave Barlow hope—the Apache bullet had missed Hammond's heart.

"I'll be fine," rasped Hammond, through teeth clenched against the pain. "Just get the goddamn piece of lead out of me."

"We will," said Barlow. "Lay still."

He stood up, looked around for Lyman. He saw Addicks instead, and went to the major, trying not to step on the dead. The major's arm hung limp and bloody at his side. But Addicks didn't seem to notice. He was gazing down at the body of Colonel Hartwell Lyman, who lay staring with sightless eyes, an expression of surprise frozen on his face, and a bullet hole in his forehead.

"Thanks for coming back, Lieutenant," said Addicks. "I was wondering if you'd disobey that order."

"I almost didn't."

Addicks nodded. "I don't even want to try to explain all this. Or you."

"I didn't want to be here."

"I'm wondering now if any of us really did."

"*He* did," said Barlow, nodding at Lyman. "He's got his glory."

"Yeah." Addicks have him a long look, one Barlow couldn't read. "Now why don't you get out of here?"

Surprised, Barlow nodded. "Thanks. I'll do that."

He returned to his horse. Climbing into the saddle, he noticed that Delgadito was watching him, his face inscrutable. Barlow saluted the White Mountain broncho, turned the horse around, and rode down the slope.

There was no river to cross, no markers to signify that the border between the United States and Mexico had been reached, but Cochise knew when his people were safe. There were certain landmarks, even in this barren land, that, to the uninitiated, appeared to be void of distinguishing characteristics. His people knew, as well, but they had endured too much to be exuberant. Instead, there was a pervasive feeling of relief, mixed with gratitude for some, and with sorrow for others, as Nana and those bronchos who had survived the clash with the yellow-leg soldiers rejoined the main body. Even though dozens of Chokonen men had died that day, Nana was fiercely jubilant, for many more soldiers had perished, and he considered it to be a great victory for The People, especially since the women and children had survived. Cochise reminded Nana that they were far from the Mogollons, and that now that they had killed so many soldiers they would never be able to return home. That, as far as Cochise was concerned, could not possibly be construed as a cause for rejoicing.

Though severe losses had been inflicted on the yellow-leg soldiers who'd been pursuing his people, and he doubted that those who had survived would cause further problems, Cochise did not relax. They were in the land of the Nakai-Ye now. Their enemies were everywhere. The Cima Silkq, their only real sanctuary, was many days travel to the south. It would be a trek fraught with peril. Their chances of reaching the mountains without coming into contact with the Mexicans were very slim. Cochise knew that the border area was particularly well patrolled by soldiers. So the sooner his people moved deeper into Mexico, the better. They were tired and hungry—and many grieved the loss of son or husband in the battle that had just been fought—but they had to keep going. They were still fugitives on the run. Now they were at war not only with the Nakai-Ye but also the White Eyes. Cochise knew that his people were doomed. But they would keep on running and fighting until the day came, as inevitably it must, when the Chi-hinne were no more.

Epilogue

It was just pure bad luck that Sergeant Farrow and his three White Mountain companions missed Colonel Lyman's column—and ended up right in the path of the Avowed Killer named Kiannatah.

Although the sergeant and the trio of Apache scouts had made a cold camp, Kiannatah knew there was danger ahead long before he saw them. He had developed a sense about such things. This was an attribute that he could not explain. Goyathlay had once told him that to survive a Netdahe had to trust his instincts. A warrior might smell something or hear something that did not even register in his consciousness. A person might feel the hair at the nape of his neck stand on end, or experience a cold chill running down his spine, for no readily apparent reason. But such things *always* happened for a reason. Kiannatah thought that perhaps, even at a quarter of a mile, his ears had picked up the whicker of a horse, even though he could not say that he had actually heard it, or that he had caught the faintest whiff of gun oil, or even the stench of a Pinda Lickoyi. The White Eyes had a smell to them that Kiannatah could easily distinguish. It was an odor distinct from that of an Apache or even of a Nakai-Ye.

Kiannatah could not say what alerted him, but he knew better than to ignore his instincts. He and Oulay had just embarked on another day's journey, starting out before the rising of the sun. Immediately he dismounted, and helped her down off his horse.

"Make no sound," he warned her. "And do not try to run away."

He didn't have to threaten her with death if she failed to obey these commands. He had no need to issue threats of that sort. She knew perfectly well what the consequences of disobedience would be.

Of course, Kiannatah realized the danger in bringing her with him as he scouted ahead, since she apparently was willing to die rather than stay with him. But he could not—*would* not—leave her behind. He had gone to great trouble to possess her, and he wasn't about to let her out of his sight now.

They moved silently forward in the gray half-light of the moments before daybreak, when the shadows of night still lay in the creases and folds of the ground. Kiannatah led the horse with one hand, and carried his rifle in the other, while Oulay followed along behind. Eventually he left the horse, ground hitching it, secure in the knowledge that it would be there when he got back. He led Oulay down into a ravine and up the other side, stopping just below the rim of the cut bank to motion a silent warning to Oulay that she must be quiet. Then he peered cautiously over the rim of the embankment—and saw the White Mountain broncho, sitting on his heels some fifty yards away, almost invisible against the backdrop of a large clump of ocotillo. Oulay peered over the rim too, and at first she could not make out what had captured Kiannatah's attention. Kiannatah realized that this man had to be a sentry, which meant there was a camp nearby. He did not know that the sentry was a White Mountain warrior, but it didn't really matter what band he belonged to; at that point, Kiannatah considered even his own people to be potential enemies.

Leading Oulay, he moved farther down the ravine, then climbed out of it and, in a running crouch, moved several hundred yards to the west. She kept up with him, making no more sound than he did. Until she knew more about the situation, she wasn't going to act rashly.

Then they heard the whicker of a horse, and Kiannatah dropped to the ground. She stopped too, and he pulled her down on her belly. They crawled to an outcropping of rock; Kiannatah insinuated himself into this jumble of boulders, reaching a place from which he could gaze down into the camp made by Sergeant Farrow and the Apache scouts. The men in the camp had just wakened; two were preparing their horses, and the third, a Pinda Lickoyi, was rolling up his blankets. There was enough light for Kiannatah to make out the uniform that the Pinda Lickoyi was wearing. He wasn't surprised to see Apache warriors riding with a yellow-leg soldier. Goyathlay had once predicted that the White Eyes would turn Apache against Apache. It didn't matter to Kiannatah which band these men came from—they were traitors to their people, and as such, they had to die. That there were four adversaries there—three below his vantage point and the sentry somewhere behind him—did not deter Kiannatah. He had faced greater odds and prevailed. But as he raised his rifle, making up his mind to kill the

Apaches first—since they were more dangerous than the white man—Oulay laid a hand on his arm. He looked at her angrily, but she would not remove her hand.

"Why must you kill them?" she whispered. "We could slip past them before the sun rises."

Kiannatah shook her hand off his arm, but she put it right back where it had been before.

"Don't," she said. "Please."

"Do you know these men?" he asked suspiciously.

"No." She lied, without a second's hesitation, because she recognized Farrow as one of the men who had been with her lieutenant when they had come to her village with the peace treaty.

He lowered the rifle. She was asking something of him. What would it cost him to give her what she wanted? The sight of the Apaches riding with the Pinda Lickoyi had infuriated him, but her voice—and her touch—quelled his anger, and for the first time he considered the possibility that the course of action he'd been prepared to take would have put Oulay in jeopardy, and he reminded himself that he no longer had only himself to think of.

Without a word, he led her back the way they had come, using the night shadows that clung to the low places to the best possible advantage, and returning to the horse and then riding away, with Oulay behind him, without the sentry any the wiser. It gave him a certain measure of satisfaction, and a feeling of power, to know that he had held the fate of those four men in his hands.

Less than an hour later, Sergeant Farrow and his White Mountain companions were met by Short Britches. The old scout was coming up behind them, pushing his horse hard. Farrow recalled seeing Short Britches with Barlow at Fort Union, and he wondered what the man was doing way out here.

"You didn't see him," said Short Britches, looking at Farrow and the bronchos with a faint contempt.

"See who?" asked the noncom. "What the hell are you talking about?"

"The Netdahe. I followed his trail all the way to your camp. He was there at daybreak. His sign is fresh. I rode through the night to get closer to him. But when I saw your tracks, I knew that you were cavalry."

"How did you know that?"

"I knew," said Short Britches. "I need your help because he is Netdahe. He is going south. Maybe two hours away now."

"Why are you chasing him?"

"He has taken Barlow's woman."

Farrow's eyes widened. "Cochise's daughter?"

One of the White Mountain bronchos asked Farrow what the old scout was saying, and before Farrow could translate, Short Britches repeated himself in the broncho's tongue. The White Mountain Apaches spoke excitedly among themselves. Short Britches listened to them and a faint smile touched the corner of his mouth.

"Well," said Farrow dryly, for he'd been listening to the bronchos' conversation too, "I guess we'll give you a hand."

At that moment the White Mountain bronchos rode away, steering their galloping horses back in the direction of the camp they had recently vacated. Farrow shouted for them to come back, but to no avail. The sergeant snorted, and shook his head.

"Damn fools," he muttered. "They've got this notion that they owe Barlow. Soon as you mentioned that the Netdahe had his woman, they were sold on being heroes."

"The Netdahe will kill them," said Short Britches calmly. "But maybe they will slow him down long enough for me to get him in my sights."

He patted the Big Fifty, riding in its saddle sheath, and then turned his horse around to follow the path taken by the White Mountain bronchos. Sergeant Farrow fell in alongside.

When the White Mountain bronchos caught him, Kiannatah was just entering Skeleton Canyon. They'd pushed their horses hard to get in front of him, and had just settled into their hiding places when he arrived. One was positioned midway up the steep rocky slope to his left. A second was in some boulders at the base of the sheer rock face that loomed up on his right. And the third was located farther up the canyon.

The first shot killed Kiannatah's horse. Kiannatah jumped clear, rifle in hand, as the animal fell. Oulay tried to do the same, but she wasn't quick enough— her left leg was pinned beneath the carcass from the knee down, and the impact with the ground dazed her, knocking the air out of her lungs. Kiannatah had landed on the run, instinctively making for cover, but when he saw Oulay's plight, he turned back, diving behind the dead horse as more bullets came his way. The carcass gave him some cover from the broncho on the left slope, but the one in the boulders on the right had a clear shot—and took it. The bullet caught Kiannatah in the shoulder. Thinking that his prey was hurt more seriously than was, in fact, the case, the

White Mountain broncho made the mistake of breaking cover, moving out into the open to get a clean
killing shot. Kiannatah blocked the pain from his
mind, fiercely fought to clear his thoughts and his vision, and fired before the White Mountain broncho
could do so. The latter died on his feet, the Netdahe's
bullet entering just above his right eye and blowing
away the back of his skull as it exited.

Kiannatah quickly studied Oulay's situation—and
realized that he wasn't going to be able to pull her
free, or lift the carcass enough for her to crawl out
from under it.

"Lie still," he said. "They won't waste a bullet if
they think you are dead."

He didn't know that the White Mountain bronchos
had come to save Oulay. All he knew was that he had
been a fool. These had to be the bronchos he'd seen
in the camp earlier this morning—the ones he had
refrained from killing because Oulay had asked it of
him. This, he thought angrily, was what came of for-
getting that he was Netdahe. A part of him cried out
to leave her behind; she was no good for one such as
he; she made him weak, willing to betray the silent
vow he had long ago made to the ghosts of his murdered family.

But even as he left her there, pinned beneath the
dead horse in the canyon bottom, he knew that he would
not go far. He would go back for her once the other
two Apaches were dead.

The White Mountain broncho on the left slope saw
him coming, and retreated laterally, dodging with the
agility of a mountain goat between the boulders. Kiannatah fired twice and missed both times. Kiannatah
was worried about the third Apache—who had yet

to show himself—but not worried enough to give up the chase.

His prey squeezed between two slabs of red rock, one canted against the other. Kiannatah knew better than to follow. Instead, he climbed higher. The wound was rapidly sapping his strength; he had to deal with his enemies quickly, before he became vulnerable. As he'd suspected, the broncho had turned to crouch in ambush on the other side of the rock slabs, expecting Kiannatah to come through the crevice between them. He too was possessed of a warrior's extincts; though Kiannatah made no sound, the broncho whirled, realizing his error, and caught a glimpse of the Netdahe— a heartbeat before Kiannatah's rifle spoke. Then his world turned black.

Kiannatah did not spare his second victim even a glance as he moved on, away from the telltale powder smoke, searching for the third White Mountain broncho. He expected the man to be farther up the canyon, and so was startled to see him out in the open at the mouth of the defile, crouching beside Kiannatah's dead horse. He wasn't alone, either. The yellow-leg soldier was there. They were trying to kill Oulay! Or perhaps free her. Either way, they were trying to take her away from him.

For the first time in his memory, Kiannatah was afraid. He feared the possibility of being without her. Of being alone.

Enraged, he leaped to the top of the nearest boulder. "*Yudastin!*" he shouted, bringing the rifle to his shoulder, hoping to draw their attention away from her just long enough for him to get off a shot. If he killed one, maybe the other would forget Oulay and seek cover.

Out of the corner of an eye he saw the flash of sunlight off a rifle barrel, somewhere on the slope to his left. And in that instant, with his mind in turmoil over the possible loss of Oulay, he did not understand what was happening. There had been only four men in the camp this morning and here, now, he could account for all of them. He was slow in accepting the possibility of a fifth adversary—he didn't *want* to accept it, because if there was a fifth man his chances of keeping the woman became much more unlikely. For a heartbeat he hesitated, desperate to kill one of the men down there with Oulay, even though his instincts cried out for him to find cover. For once, he argued with his instincts. And then he felt the impact of the bullet, felt himself being hurled off the boulder, falling, and as he fell, he heard the thunder of a big-caliber rifle, heard it dimly as the day suddenly began to darken . . .

When Short Britches reached the canyon bottom, Farrow and the surviving White Mountain broncho had managed to free the pinned Oulay. Farrow noticed that the old scout looked troubled. Standing there with the Big Fifty cradled in his arms, he was scanning the rim of the canyon.

"Didn't you get him?" asked Farrow.

"Yes, I hit him," said Short Britches.

"Then what's the problem?" Farrow was starting to get nervous. "Is he dead or not?"

"He is gone. There is much blood where he fell. I think he *will* die."

Farrow scanned the slopes. "Maybe we'd better track him down and make sure." He spoke without much enthusiasm.

Short Britches shook his head. "No." Even badly

wounded, the Netdahe was dangerous. He figured they'd have a fifty-fifty chance, at best, of killing the renegade before he killed them. "We got what we came for," he said, looking at Oulay.

Farrow nodded. He didn't need much convincing. "Are you all right?" he asked Oulay. "Can you walk? Our horses are yonder." He nodded in the direction of the canyon's northern entrance.

"Yes," she said.

"We'll take you back to Barlow."

"Yes, thank you."

As they began walking away, Oulay surveyed the canyon slopes and noticed that the one called Short Britches was watching her intently. She could see in his eyes that they were thinking the same thing. She hoped they were both wrong, but Netdahe were hard to kill.

THE PRE-CIVIL WAR SERIES BY
JASON MANNING

THE FIRE-EATERS

0-451-20917-6

The year is 1862, and Lt. Timothy Barlow has taken a
post in President Jackson's War Department. Raising a
civilian army, Barlow quells a rebellion in South
Carolina—but the war has not yet begun.

WAR LOVERS

0-451-21173-1

Retired war hero Colonel Timothy Barlow returns as
right-hand man to President Jackson when there's
trouble brewing on the border—trouble called the
Mexican-American War.

**Available wherever books are sold or at
www.penguin.com**

SIGNET

Charles G. West

EVIL BREED
0-451-21004-2

The U.S. Army doesn't take kindly to civilians
killing their officers—even in self-defense. But
Jim Culver has two things in his favor: the new .73
Winchester he's carrying—and the ability to use it.

"RARELY HAS AN AUTHOR PAINTED THE
GREAT AMERICAN WEST IN STROKES SO
BOLD, VIVID AND TRUE."
—RALPH COMPTON

Available wherever books are sold or at
www.penguin.com